Humberfield

By

Kingsley Pilgrim

Grosvenor House
Publishing Limited

The right of Kingsley Pilgrim to be identified as the author of this
work has been asserted in accordance with Section 78
of the Copyright, Designs and Patents Act 1988

The book cover is copyright to Flora Aranyi

This book is published by
Grosvenor House Publishing Ltd
Link House
140 The Broadway, Tolworth, Surrey, KT6 7HT.
www.grosvenorhousepublishing.co.uk

This book is a work of fiction. Any resemblance to
people or events, past or present, is purely coincidental.

A CIP record for this book
is available from the British Library

ISBN 978-1-80381-546-6
eBook ISBN 978-1-80381-547-3

"I've been trying to chase happiness, but it keeps slipping through my fingers."

Acknowledgements

Writing a book, be it fact or fiction, is hard, and this particular one involved the patience and support of many people along the way who I would like to thank.

My family have always been there for me, and I love every single one dearly.

Dexter 'Rudi' Roberts for his continued tech support and friendship.

My editor, Rachel Rowlands.

Beehive Illustration and Flora Aranyi for the front cover.

And thanks to these lovely people as well. Many have been around long before I started this writing journey and still continue to inspire and amaze me:

Darren Baker, Brendan Maguire, Olivia Pollard, Paul 'Shifty' Lay, Natasha Roye

Steven and Joanne Higham, Mary Pollard, Kay Jones, Darrel Bassant, Jill Sayles, Natalie Idehen, Clare Cooke, Louise McDonald, Tina Field, Ross Carmichael, and the staff at Electrolux in Milton Keynes.

Director Daniel Alexander and all the cast and crew of my short film *Carly*, a slight precursor to this book and available to watch online.

Thank you so much for bringing all these characters to life for the screen.

Cheers to all the people who paid good money to read my books; I really appreciate the support and hope you enjoy.

Guess. Try. Hope.

Also by the author

In the Dominant Species Saga

Paintshark
Glimmerfin
Immortopia

Contents

The Boy with All the Stilts

Alek Kaminski

5 Melody Way

Waughton

Humberfield

"Bang, you're dead," Alek Kaminski said softly.

He held the rifle so steady in his hands; he could allow a tiny bit of movement from them but none at all from his feet. As he lay across a rooftop on a block of flats, his concentration was fixed on the apartments opposite. Dressed from head to toe in black combat attire, he held his finger perfectly close to the trigger.

A bedroom window on the other block was shut, but there was a figure clearly visible, illuminated by the bedroom light behind them. A man was getting dressed, not even bothering to pull his blinds down. Alek heard the laughter from some teenagers walking along the path behind the flats where he lay and crouched lower on the roof. There was no way they could have seen him from their viewpoint, but he wasn't taking any chances and kept his eyes on the man in the room.

"You've been working out, haven't you? Been hitting the gym a lot, I see? Won't be long before that body of yours will be a bloody mess. I pull the trigger, and that buffed-up frame will be gone forever."

Alek shuffled on his front; it was uncomfortable lying on the roof, and his stomach felt uneasy. He put his rifle to one side and gave his stomach a rub, it was stirring, and he knew trouble was brewing inside. He had to get the job done quickly before his stomach gave way. Groaning slowly, Alek picked up the rifle and looked through the sight back to the bedroom.

The man had gone.

"Ah, where did you go?"

His bedroom light was still on, so Alek knew he would be back at some point.

"Carrick Simmons, you were one of the nicest kids at school. You were great at first, you wanted to get to know everyone and were kind, but then you joined the cool kids in that pack, the kids who bullied and laughed at everyone who was different. You just stood there and giggled; you watched as those piss-taking bastards took joy in picking on every kid who was different."

Alek instantly corrected himself. "Not in a racist, homophobic way, just nerds, I guess. I thought we could be friends, but that didn't happen, and then you became just like them, evil inside. You laughed at my stammer, you laughed at my clothes, you laughed at where I lived."

He gave a quiet cough.

"You made things worse for me. I was always conscious of my stutter, but things never got better for me, going on first dates knowing I couldn't get my words out and never ever getting a second date. Have you any idea what that feels like? No, of course not, because nothing went wrong for you since we left school 15 years ago; you were handsome, smart, talented, and everything right just fell into your hands."

A plane flew overhead, and Alek watched its flight path, wondering if any of the passengers onboard led a life sadder than his own.

"University, travelling and seeing the world on holidays, festivals, parties, you had it all, and you never knew I even existed. Some people don't change; they just get better at hiding the filth that they really are. Well, I'm taking all of you down who laughed at me, starting with you, Carrick."

Alek frowned.

"No matter how hard you try to scrub yourself clean, I can see the dirt of being a bastard under your fingernails."

He took another look around to see if anybody had spotted him lying down on a rooftop on a weekday evening.

"Do you remember what they called at me at school? Do you remember my turn at show and tell?"

Alek didn't replace the rifle to his eye; he just focused hard into Carrick's bedroom.

"My parents loved the arts. Every weekend we'd go to the theatre, cinema, a new exhibition at a gallery, one time we went to a circus and it was great, seeing all those cool performers, fire eating, trapeze artists who were all fantastic, but it was the stilt-walkers which interested me the most."

It was starting to get cold, but the wind didn't detract him from talking.

"I asked my parents for a set of stilts for children, and when I got them it was great. I practised outside all the time and was becoming quite good at balancing and walking."

He leaned forward, thinking Carrick had just walked past another window.

"Then the show and tell morning came at school. I thought I'd bring my stilts in with me, to show everybody how good I was at stilt-walking."

Shuffling off the rucksack on his back, Alek unzipped it and took out a bottle of water, sipping it slowly.

"I admit, I was nervous, walking onto the stage in front of everybody on stilts, but I never fell off, but like I said, I was very nervous, so nervous in fact that I couldn't control my bowel movements. I messed myself on stage, Carrick, in front of the whole school; it was like a brown slug, moving slowly down my legs, leaving a trail of crap, and every one of you bastards was laughing at me."

"Shit stain stilts, Rumpelshitskin; they were the names you made up for me. That was when you completely changed, and all these awful names stuck with me throughout my school years, and you were a part of the piss-taking, Carrick. Every day for years, I was the token laughing stock in class; you and the other beautiful people made sure it was hell for me."

The bedroom light was still on, and Alek grew more concerned. Carrick walked back in. He was dressed in a fine suit which fit around him very well and was finishing up his hair in the mirror.

"Going on a date, are you? Dressed up with your chiselled chin, tanned, muscled arms and a six-pack stomach. Well, you won't be getting far, Carrick. Your night is about to end right now with a simple pull of this trigger."

Alek had Carrick firmly in his rifle's sight but hesitated.

4

"Nope, you don't get away with it that easy. I could easily blow you away right now, but there's no satisfaction in that. I want to get right up close to you, introduce myself to you and then witness the horror on your face as I end your life with my gun."

He knew Carrick always had a knack of getting his own way at school, and probably nothing had changed, but he was determined to stop it tonight. Carrick's light was still on, and he quickly made his way down the roof and immediately started to climb up to Carrick's bedroom, it was a long climb but Alek's confidence in getting his kill drove him on.

Having a moment of pure simplicity was great, just having to kill Carrick seemed so easy now; the rifle training he undertook and the ease it took to obtain a rifle in the first place was finally coming into effect. He was still thinking about the look on Carrick's face when he eventually ended his life.

Alek found the climb up to his flat long but easy; there were still no witnesses to his ascent up Carrick's wall, and dressing in black obviously helped.

Carrick's window was ajar.

"Ignorant," Alek murmured.

He moved it open more so he could slink into the bedroom. Perfect silence lay around the room and the home, and Alek pulled out the rifle. He needed to show how brilliant he had become in the months of gun training he had taken.

Alek turned towards the open bedroom door; he was terrifyingly casual in the way he carried the gun. He couldn't hear Carrick and took a gulp for confidence as he looked forward to finding him. He opened his mouth, still whispering.

"Okay, so here we go, you bullying idiot. Your piss-taking days are finally over."

He didn't get an attack of nerves or conscience.

As he walked forward, he noticed a red dot had appeared on the wall to his left.

It looked like a laser pen dot, which cat owners use to tease their pets.

"What the hell?" Alek was still whispering.

Alek turned around and headed back to the window he had just entered to see what was going on. The dot followed him as he looked out of Carrick's bedroom window; it darted from left to right like a dying fly before finally settling on his chest.

A quick moment of terror and realisation hit Alek's face.

"No, wait, no, wait!"

A bullet struck him; no sound, just the horrific impact of being shot.

Alek stumbled backwards. He tried to reach out to grab the window frame for support, held on briefly and then plummeted out of the open window. There was a greenhouse settled many apartments below Carrick's flat. He fell silently towards it, unable to change anything with his descent.

Alek smashed into the greenhouse and shards of glass easily sliced through his skin. The top of the greenhouse fell onto him as he landed, puncturing through many parts of his body. Shattered glass panes were covered in blood as Alek's body finally came to a still.

On the flat opposite Carrick's was another figure dressed entirely in black. The figure had rocked up on the roof moments after Alek had left to tackle Carrick personally. Watching how Alek had fallen from the window, the person in black looked to see if there was any movement below, it was hard to see all the way down towards the shattered greenhouse, but it seemed the job was done.

Removing glasses from their head, the figure stared at the shattered mess and put the glasses aside, squinting heavily. Neighbours' lights around the greenhouse illuminated the night.

Shaun Kunder sighed heavily, and then a smile crept onto his face.

"Well, well, well, Carrick Simmons. How the mighty have fallen, literally."

His voice was loud and clear, taking confidence in every word.

"Not saying much now, are you? Not bullying people with glasses now, eh?"

He spoke slowly, enunciating his words to the window.

"What did you call me at school? Blunder Kunder, because I wore glasses, couldn't see where I was going and constantly bumped into people; you were always laughing at me, making my life hell."

There was a rush of excitement in his voice.

"I'm glad I was the one to finally set you straight and put you right where you belong. Isn't karma a bitch?"

Shaun thought hard, his nostrils flared harder, he wanted to reminisce over the good times of being at school, but there weren't any; Carrick made sure of that. He'd already plucked up the necessary courage to end the life of the perpetrator of his school bullying, and he was sure his work was complete.

Taking one last look at the bedroom with the light still on, Shaun knew it was time to make his exit as people were now coming out of their flats to investigate the sound of glass breaking. He hurried over to the edge of the flats, carefully and slowly making his descent.

His night of obscurity was finished.

* * *

Carrick Simmons sat in the back of a taxi. He smiled, satisfied as his friends were already waiting for him at the new bar in town. He sent another message on his phone to tell them that he was on his way. It was a lovely night, and everything was going to plan.

"Ah bugger," Carrick groaned.

"Pardon me?" The taxi driver turned around and then looked to the road again. "Something wrong?" he asked.

"Not you," Carrick replied. "I've left my bedroom light on."

"Do you want to go back?"

He shook his head quickly and looked straight back to his phone.

"No, it's fine. It can stay on, no big deal."

Blackhoard

Gemma Hopper
15 Daisy Court
Hawkston
Humberfield

The wind wasn't helping Gemma. The rain was bad enough, but the wind was turning her umbrella inside out constantly; hard water on her face caused her to keep her eyes shut as she weaved her way through weary-eyed travellers on the pavement trying to get home from work as well.

She knew having a car would have really helped in this rain-soaked situation, but she was already on her eighth driving test and was advised not to carry on by her nervous and elderly instructor. Everybody in her family could drive, her mum and dad were speed freaks; they loved watching racing programmes like *Top Gear* and *Formula 1*.

Gemma didn't need to drive when she lived in London, she had moved there for work straight after university, and with the tubes and buses for transport, it never was a problem. Only when she moved back to Humberfield after being made redundant did it become an issue not having a car, especially on a day like today.

Her job wasn't the best, and a step down with pay, she was probably overqualified for the position, but it was a job and it would have to do until she could get back into her chosen field. She missed London so much, her friends, bars, shops, galleries, music gigs. The list could go on and did whenever she felt down about having to move back to her home town.

Hawkston, in Humberfield, was a small estate, so people tended to know each other's business, which Gemma completely forgot about after living years away in London. Heads weren't down on the walk to work now, people looked you in the eye, and some even said 'good morning'. She wasn't home yet, just walking on a high street.

It did take some getting used to for her, but hard rain on the face was a pain wherever she moved to. The rain was becoming unbearable; she had to get out of the wet and focused on the nearest pub to duck into.

Many people had the same idea and were running in front of her to get out of the rain. For some reason, she swung a look at the chalkboard situated at the front of the pub. It was a witty and funny message to encourage customers inside. Gemma walked in and shook her hair. A drunken man staggered past her, and she nervously ducked into an alcove as the guy ambled past.

"It's not normally like this; the rain is bringing all sorts in."

Gemma looked up to see a waitress looking down with a smile. "Can I get you a drink?"

Gemma stepped out gingerly. "Oh yes, absolutely. I mean, sorry, yes please."

The woman took out a pen and notepad. "So what can I get you?"

"I just want to find the freedom to be me and not have to worry about the burden of modern-day life."

The waitress put the pen back in her pocket. "I don't think we have that on the menu." She peered at Gemma over her glasses.

Gemma giggled nervously like a schoolgirl and looked fully at the waitress. "Sorry, it's been a long hard day."

The waitress continued. "Well, if you still want a drink or something to eat, give me a shout."

Gemma quickly spotted a recently vacated table and made a beeline for it. The waitress followed her, taking out her pen and pad again. She looked at the menu, checking out the vegetarian options. The table adjacent to her had a large group of men sitting there. Their loud laughter unsettled her, which the waitress picked up on.

"Long hard days usually means a large glass of something at the end."

Gemma instantly perked up. "Yes please. Could I have a large Pinot Grigio, please?"

"No, problem. Would you like anything to eat?"

"Um, yeah, probably. I'll just have a look."

Her phone beeped, and she looked at the screen intensely, leaving the menu. The waitress left her to it.

Looking around at the bar, people having a good time, Gemma tried hard to forget about her problems, the rain was still heavy, and the transport wasn't so great in Humberfield as it was in London, so some time out for herself until the rain stopped seemed like a good idea. Her laptop was now on the table, and she tried hard to keep herself entertained with work until her drink arrived.

She stiffened slightly at the raucous laughter from the lads' table opposite her. Trying hard to ignore them, Gemma focused on her screen. None of the guys was looking over at her, but Gemma had her 'What-the-hell?' glance stored, ready to use if any trouble started.

With her head buried in her laptop screen, she didn't notice one of the loud guys approach her table; she never had time to sort out her glance.

"Hi, excuse me."

Gemma took one look at the man looking directly at her. His eyes were hopeful, and she knew what was coming next, a cheesy chat-up line and some rubbish to make her more uncomfortable than she already was.

She nervously raised her eyebrows. "Yes?"

"Is anybody sitting here?"

Gemma looked at the chair and back up to the man. "Yes, sorry, my friend is meeting me soon. She should be here in a minute."

The guy instantly backed away. "No worries."

Gemma watched him walk away to another table further down the eating area. There were two women at the other table, and she watched as the man interrupted their conversation. She wondered what he was saying to them and wished she was sitting closer. He said some words to them and pointed to a spare chair at their table.

The two women smiled, and the man took the chair and smiled as he brought it back to his own table to give to a friend who had just turned up. Gemma sighed heavily. She wasn't to know that the guy wanted a chair for his friend. She was sitting alone and didn't want any unnecessary attention; she worked bloody hard, day in and day out, and just wanted a little time for herself.

The waitress came back with her wine. "Here you go. Do you want to start a tab?"

"I'm sitting on my own."

"Doesn't matter these days, people come here at 8am with their laptops to get away from working at home, and they don't leave until closing time."

"Really?" Her voice was becoming more softly spoken by the minute.

"You'd be surprised," the waitress answered.

It was only when Gemma looked up at her when she placed the glass down that she saw her overwhelming beauty. She was captivating and gorgeous. The waitress looked around her mid to late twenties, the same as herself but without the forlorn look stuck on her face and the tired brown eyes. Her figure was slim, and Gemma guessed it was toned under her tabard.

Gemma paid for the wine with a card swipe and still held her eyes towards the server. "What's your name?"

The question completely threw the waitress off guard. "Excuse me?"

"I might order some food and stay for a while. I would like to know who's serving me?"

The waitress turned around and looked at Gemma. "Sophie, my name is Sophie."

"Pleased to meet you, Sophie."

"You said you might order some food?"

Gemma looked away from staring at Sophie and picked up the menu. "The chalkboard outside said you had some specials on today; that joke on it was hilarious, by the way."

Sophie smiled. "Not many people get the joke."

"Subtle but funny."

Trying to be subtle herself, Sophie kept looking at the menu, hoping Gemma would soon order.

"What would you recommend?" Gemma asked.

"I would go for the buttermilk chicken."

"I'm a vegetarian."

Sophie stroked her hair and thought for a moment. "Okay, well, we have a Sri Lankan vegetarian lasagne, Italian style salad mix, veggie sausage and cheesy mash, cheesy as in the dairy product and not because it's a fan of ABBA."

Gemma wiped her runny nose on a serviette. "Vegetable lasagne, please, with salad, no chips."

"Okay, anything else?"

"Have you worked here for long?" asked Gemma.

"Not long, a few months. Would you like another drink with it?"

Gemma pointed to her full glass. "Fine for the moment, thanks."

"Your food might be a while, I'll warn you now as we're extremely busy. Best get another wine in."

"I like your sales patter, good job."

Sophie furrowed her eyebrows. "It's not finished."

Gemma nodded. "Yes, I will have another glass of wine, thanks."

Sophie made a note. "Right, that's all done for you."

"Thank you, can I ask you a quick question?"

Sophie checked her watch ever so quickly. "Yep."

"Are you afraid that another woman may steal someone you love away?"

Sophie instantly backed away and held her hands up. "Right, this is getting creepy now. What's with all the questions?"

"Sorry, I know that sounds totally rude, and I apologise."

Sophie's enthusiasm for the order had completely waned. "I'm just going to sort your order out and leave you alone."

"No, please don't leave. I'm just going through a tough time at the moment."

Both women hesitated; Gemma broke the silence first. "I lost my job in London and decided to move back here, couldn't afford the rent so moved back in with my parents, found another job and stayed at home to save for a flat of my own."

"Is this going anywhere? I've got other people to serve."

"My dad is having an affair."

Sophie stood unmoved. "Well, that's sad, but what's that got to do with me?"

"Have you ever been cheated on? Or cheated on somebody?"

Sophie looked hard at her, trying to take it in. "Listen, I'm going to go now and get your order."

"You never answered my question."

"Why should I? It's nothing to do with me what your dad does."

"I didn't say that." Gemma rubbed her eyes after raising her eyebrows. "I never said it was, I just asked.

"Are you insinuating I'm having an affair with your dad?"

"No, it's just this is all new to me."

Sophie's phone buzzed in her pocket. She picked it out and ignored it.

"Aren't you going to answer that?"

"It's not your dad, by the way."

Gemma wanted to thrash her arms wildly as Sophie walked away. If only she had the guts to do it.

***

Gemma was sure that Sophie wasn't going to be bringing her order. She was pretty harsh on her and thought it would definitely affect her getting her food in a decent amount of time. Plus, she wondered if Sophie had asked one of the kitchen staff to tamper with her lasagne; phlegm and mayo didn't sound that appealing. A feeling of uneasiness crept up on her the more she thought about it.

It was still raining heavily. Gemma thought she should have tried to get home straight away; stopping off at this pub didn't seem like a good idea now. She tapped away at her laptop as the pub became more busy. After a while of observing rain-drenched drunks and hopeful couples on a first date, Sophie arrived with her food. There was an awkward silence as she placed the lasagne and wine on the table.

"Enjoy," Sophie said dryly.

"So are we going to talk about the elephant in the room?" Gemma asked.

"I'm not sleeping with the elephant in the room if that's what you mean."

"That's nice, never thought I'd get a bestiality gag with my order."

"Do you want a head count of people I've slept with recently?"

"There's no need for that."

"There's also no need to be accused of having an affair with a complete stranger's dad." The fun in

Sophie's voice from earlier had completely vanished, it was more defiant, and her eyes didn't leave Gemma's at all.

Gemma took a deep breath. "Look, I'm sorry, it's just that I had a great job in London, lost it and my flat and had to move back in with my parents."

"Again, nothing to do with me."

Gemma looked like she was going to cry. "I found my dad's suitcases tucked away in the spare room, they were packed, so it was obvious he was going away, probably with his new mistress."

"Have you spoken to your mum about it?"

Gemma was surprised by the new concern from Sophie. "No, not yet, don't want to worry her about it."

"Have you mentioned it to your friends, other family or people at work?"

"Not yet. Both Mum and Dad were only children, and it's just me as well, no brothers or sisters."

"Any friends you could talk to?"

"Yeah, but always speak to my family first."

"I guess blood can be thicker than water sometimes."

Gemma took a slow sip of her wine. "Both can be easily spilt, though."

Sophie looked around and knew she had spent far too much time on her table. "Well, I really hope you sort things out and talk to somebody; it's obviously bothering you."

Gemma just shrugged. "It is what it is, as people say."

Sophie knew that Gemma was complete in her conversation. She held out her hand for a shake. "No hard feelings."

After shaking Sophie's hand, she watched the server walk to another table.

"No feelings for you at all, you cheating tramp," Gemma whispered.

Taking out her phone, she went to her photo gallery and picked out some pictures.

Gemma was suspicious of her dad for a while. He had cancelled lunch dates with her and her mum, dressing up to the nines just to apparently see old workmates, he never wore the aftershave she bought him over numerous Christmas years, yet now he was splashing it all over himself like it was going out of fashion.

She'd followed him on one occasion and watched at a restaurant as he joined Sophie. Gemma stood from a distance, taking pictures as they sat together, held hands and hugged each other. The meal ended with a tender kiss on the cheek which was enough for her to see. She rubbed her face to take care of her tears and followed Sophie on foot, making sure she wasn't spotted.

Sophie didn't live far away from the restaurant, and Gemma was happy to spy on her day-to-day routines, especially where she worked. It was no coincidence she ended up in this pub. Gemma knew exactly what she was doing; it wasn't the chalkboard that bought her in, it was Sophie.

Time moved on, the lasagne still sat on the plate, she was supposed to eat it at least 40 minutes ago, but Gemma's eyes were focused on following Sophie around the pub. Serving and smiling, Sophie looked to have not a care in the world. Another member of staff came to take the empty glasses from the table next to Gemma; she then moved on to her table with a handful of pint glasses but still had arm space to carry some cheap crockery.

"Everything alright with the food?" she asked.

"I didn't check."

Her fingers itched as she passed the uneaten food to the girl and ordered another wine. The girl judged Gemma's demeanour and hastily left. Rain was still pelting it down; it hadn't stopped at all. Sophie didn't bother Gemma again, but they did share some uneasy glances as she walked past with customers' food and drink. The night continued on, as did the rain. Quite a few empty wine glasses were building up on her table and the pub was starting to empty now; people were either heading home or to another drinking hole.

Sophie was getting ready to leave, she had her coat on, and she was getting big hugs from her colleagues. Gemma strained to see why and then blinked hard with horrified eyes. Sophie was pulling a suitcase behind her.

"Well, well, well," Gemma hissed.

There wasn't any wine left on her table, and she really needed another drink, but Sophie was heading out of the door and she had no time to order another one. Gemma went to stand up and instantly wobbled.

Oh for god's sake, I'm so drunk, she told herself.

She held on to the table. Sophie could wait for a moment as she really needed another drink.

There's no way she'd rock up to my home with a suitcase in hand to take dad away, surely? Gemma thought.

"No way, no fucking way." It was more than a whisper this time.

Gemma stumbled up to the table opposite her. Most of the loud lads were still drinking heavily and had no intention of leaving soon. She sidled up to them and quickly slipped a hand to grab a full pint of beer on the table.

"Hey!" A young man shook his head in disbelief as his pint went easily down her throat.

The whole table of lads watched in bemusement as Gemma downed the whole pint in seconds. She slammed the pint glass down on the table and wiped her mouth.

"Cheers, boys."

As she walked out of the main pub door, the crowded table cheered at her confidence or cheek.

The wind and rain hit Gemma hard as she left, and she made sure her laptop was tucked away safely from the wet. The water hitting her face didn't help. She spun her head to look around the roads, trying to catch sight of Sophie. She took another look at the funny chalkboard before she left. Gemma saw Sophie on the other side of the road. She wasn't too hard to spot dragging a suitcase behind her. She blew out a lucky sigh and headed straight after her.

Where are you going? Not back to my house, surely, to be with my dad. Why would you do that?

An image of Sophie and her dad together quickened her steps towards her. Gemma hurried her steps, trying hard in the rain and in heels.

Don't you dare come to my house.

The streets were still busy, and the many wines she had at her table were beginning to affect her. Sophie quickened her steps, and Gemma had to do the same. She had tried to be incredulous in the past, but it was obvious her dad was having an affair with Sophie, and no matter how drunk she felt, she really had to see where she was going with her suitcase.

You're going to take my dad away.

Gemma made up the steps she needed to catch up with Sophie, she was way out of breath and it showed. They both passed a bar where a gaggle of drunken girls on a hen night left slightly before them. The bride was in a wedding dress with L plates on the front and back, and her friends staggered next to her holding condom balloons and t-shirts with the bride's name on them. Gemma felt in good company as they were all completely drunk, but it was a Friday so nobody cared about the next day. They shrieked loudly as they, too, were feeling the annoying rain. The whole group waited at a pelican crossing to head off to another bar with better cocktails and hotter bar staff.

I won't let you break up my family.

Sophie shuffled up among the hen girls waiting to cross, and Gemma joined the group too. The traffic lights turned red for the vehicles. Some boy racers were out speeding away through the town; it didn't matter what time of the day it was, the louder and faster the car was all they cared about.

One car sped right across the zebra crossing just as the hen girls were about to walk.

The girls screamed at the car as it failed to stop, swearing and waving their fists at the car. Another car sped through the crossing, and a few girls just made it across to the other side and also screamed in anger. The girls yelled louder.

Gemma was tired, drunk and had enough.

She had followed Sophie from the pub and wasn't sure what she was going to do next. Her eyes stirred as she heard another car racing towards the crossing. Sophie and the other girls expected that the car wouldn't stop and they were right. A third car flew over the crossing without a thought of stopping.

"Get a life!" they shouted.

Sophie waited with the other girls until the road was clear and made her way across the road. Gemma stumbled behind them. Sophie and the rest of the hen group were unaware of her. More pedestrians joined them as they reached yet another crossing.

The boy racers had long sped away, and the traffic from the other direction seemed to be moving at a steady pace. The bride pressed the button on the control panel at the side and waited for the traffic lights to change.

A delivery van was speeding up next, hoping to beat the light change. Either it was very late for its next drop-off or just a useless driver, but it didn't seem like stopping. Gemma lifted her head above the others to see what the traffic was like and saw the oncoming vehicle. She squinted as the rain was getting in her eyes. Gemma wiped her face clean and then shoved Sophie into the path of the van.

Sophie's horrifying scream was cut short as she hit the front of the van and her head went through the windscreen; the delivery driver braked hard. Her body was sent flying against the iron railings, and it came to rest with a sickening thud on the side of the road.

Screams carried on from the hen night girls. The driver staggered from his van, his seatbelt had worked, but that wasn't his concern.

The driver knelt beside her bloody body and held it close. "I didn't see her. She just stepped out in front of me!"

The screams continued as Gemma stepped backwards and away from the shocked crowd. Nobody had seen that she had pushed Sophie to her death, and that worked well for her. Her eyes were still fixed on the crying hen night crowd, and she was still focused on them as she made her way to a quieter side street. She breathed heavily and hard, and it wasn't returning to its normal state as she waited until she could take in what was happening.

The sound of sirens could be heard in the distance.

* * *

The bus ride home wasn't long, but it felt like an eternity to Gemma. She constantly looked out of the window to see if any police cars were following. Some did pass the bus at speed but not to dramatically swerve in front of the bus and arrest her. She still thought of horrible things happening if she was stopped by the police, imagining what it would be like to spend the rest of her life in prison.

The bus was heading for her stop, and Gemma stood up and pressed the stop bell, swaying and holding on to the handrail. She got off and ran to her parents' house, not even noticing that the rain had stopped, frantically digging into her bag to pull out her house keys as she reached the front door.

Her mouth dropped when she walked through. There were suitcases lined up along the hallway along with her dad. She frowned and moved a little closer to him.

"Where have you been? I thought you were coming straight home after work."

She instantly dismissed her father's question. "Where's Mum?" Her eyes darted around her dad, her voice filled with trepidation.

"Upstairs."

"Mum knows about this?"

"She helped me pack."

Gemma was just plain furious now; her emotions were all over the place. "Mum is packing to help you leave?"

"It was her idea."

There was a very awkward silence until Gemma broke it. "Where is my mum?"

"I told you, upstairs."

Her dad carried on moving the cases. "Are you sure you're alright?"

Gemma puzzled over that for a moment and shouted upstairs. "Mum!"

There was no answer. "What have you done with her?"

"Nothing. What is wrong with you?"

"Wrong with me? What's wrong with you?" Gemma folded her arms against her chest. "I know what you've done. I saw you with that girl in that restaurant, hugging and kissing her."

Her dad's face fell completely. He rubbed the back of his neck and sat on the foot of the stairs. "You weren't meant to see that."

"But I did, I saw everything. How could you do that to Mum? You disgust me."

"I was going to tell you sooner; you shouldn't have found out like this."

"So, you're just packing up and running away with your tramp and getting Mum to pack for you? You're a pissing coward, Dad."

"Okay, I'll let the swearing at me slide as you're upset, but you've got it wrong."

"Upset? I'm more than upset, you cheating bastard."

Her dad's eyes shot up. "Wait, I think you've got things mixed up."

Gemma shouted for her mum again.

"I think she's in the shower. Look, Gemma, please listen to me; there's something I need to tell you. That girl you saw me with, please sit with me."

He tapped on the bottom of the stair for her to come join him. Gemma hesitated before slowly joining her dad.

"I just want to say that your mum and I love you so much; we always have and always will. You have grown up to be a remarkably talented and kind person, and I am so glad and blessed to be your dad."

"Blessed?"

"Is that too much?"

"Little bit."

"Okay."

He peered down to the ground and reached for her hand. "Your mum and I were meaning to tell you sooner, but we never found the right time."

He clutched Gemma's hand softly. "Your mum and I struggled when she first gave birth, the baby wasn't planned, and we didn't know how to cope. We both thought we could handle it, but that wasn't the case; it was a traumatic experience for her and..."

He offered a nervous smile, but Gemma wasn't having any of it and snatched her hand free. "Giving birth is a hard experience, a painful one." She shoved out a breath. "Mum did it, not you."

"It just wasn't working out. We tried so hard to bond with our baby but just couldn't do it."

"What do you mean?"

"We didn't know how to cope, and there was only one path to take. We gave her up for adoption."

Gemma tried to speak, but the words were stuck in her mouth, giving her dad more time.

"Three years after we gave her away, your mum fell pregnant again, and we were in a better place, a happier place. That baby we had was you. We didn't tell you about her; there was no need. We believed she had a new life, and so did we."

The neighbour's dog started barking frantically, knocking her dad off his stride. "She found us, tracked us down recently and wanted to meet her birth parents."

His frown deepened. "I let her down. We should have been there for her, given her more time, made us a family, so I met up with her in that restaurant. I wanted to see her and explain why your mum and me gave her way; we needed to set things straight between us."

Gemma instantly rose from the stairs and put her hands over her mouth, backing away fearfully. "No, no, no, no, no!"

Her dad stood up and tried to calm Gemma down.

"Look, I know it's a shock, but we planned to all go away together. It was a surprise, it was your mum's idea to go on holiday somewhere different, so we can all get to know everybody. She packed the cases, and we were hoping to tell you before she arrived; she's coming straight from work and her bag is packed as well, so get your bags packed and welcome your sister back to our family. She's now called—"

Gemma was now crying uncontrollably.

"Sophie," her dad said. "Her name is Sophie."

By the time her mum had finally made her way down the stairs, Gemma had already fainted into the packed suitcases, knocking them all over like dominoes.

A Night with Brian

Darren Perkins

11 Regan Place

Oxley

Humberfield

13.25 The Enigma Tavern

"The party has arrived, motherfuckers."

"Will you stop it?" Darren looked disapprovingly at his friend Wayne. "Every bar we come to, you have to say that."

Wayne put an arm around his concerned friend. "Mate, it's our last night on your stag do. You turned down the booze cruise to Amsterdam for a weekend in Southend, so at least you can appreciate it when all we're doing is announcing the Humberfield boys are here to cause some trouble."

Wayne held his hand high, anticipating a 'high five' from Darren; it didn't come. "What the hell is wrong with you?"

Darren looked at his watch forlornly. "Lauren hasn't messaged me in ages, not even a phone call."

Wayne gave a smug smile. "It's your stag do, and she's been calling you all weekend; you had a let-off for five minutes and you're panicking."

Darren seemed to ignore him and study the new bar they had entered. It was quite a wide selection of friends, his two brothers, one older and younger, the younger one enjoying the weekend more than his siblings, plus old and new workmates and lifelong friends had come to Southend for Darren's last days as an official single man.

The group had mixed fairly well since the start of the drinking weekend, awkward silences between them were eased out slowly with the trickle of cheap pale ale. It was the group's last day of drinking before heading back to Humberfield on a late coach.

Darren really didn't want to be here. The whole weekend stag do was organised by his friend Wayne. They had worked together for years in the same office but still went out for drinks even when Wayne moved up the administrative ladder and they didn't see each other as often.

The quiet side of life is all Darren ever wanted, he never really liked a fuss or big events. Whereas Wayne was the complete opposite, he was the life and soul of any party, and he'd talked his way into becoming Darren's best man over his brothers.

They didn't mind. Despite years of living and growing up with Darren, none of them thought they could find anything interesting or funny to say about their own brother and were happy to pass the best man duties on to Wayne.

Plus, his fiancée, Lauren, was happy to get rid of him for a few days. She was having a joint hen party with another girl in Torquay for her own weekend away.

Wayne looked around the bar and waved his hands triumphantly. "Look at this watering hole, it was made for us. It's like the ancient mighty Spartan army having one last drink in Rome before heading out to battle. Bring me my ale, young wench."

Darren held up a questioning finger. "Actually, the Spartans were Greek, and wench is an old middle English term dating back to—"

"Look, no one cares, Sherlock. My only aim is to get you so drunk today that by the end of the night you'll be shaking like a shitting dog."

"I'm not really in the mood."

"Was you in the mood when you put that shirt on this morning?"

Darren looked down at it. "Why?"

"I was just wondering if it came with a dimmer switch?"

"Lauren picked it out for me."

"She's not stupid. No woman would approach you wearing that shirt, fair play to the girl."

A polite smile is all Wayne got from Darren as he undid his scarf.

"Okay, let's get this day of drinking over with, shall we?"

"God, you're miserable. This was planned all for you, and you've done nothing but whine like a stuck pig all weekend."

"Look around, Wayne. Nobody really wants to be here; most of the guys from work backed out."

Wayne stopped talking and leaned in. "What about the rest of the guys from work, why didn't they come?"

"Had better things to do, apparently."

"All of them?"

"Yep."

"What about Jenkins?"

"His mum died," Darren replied numbly.

"Again? I'm sure he used that excuse last year when he was on the sick."

"Perfect, just perfect," he sighed.

"Listen, we don't need him or anybody else who couldn't be bothered."

"You do know that the more people who turned up would have meant the coach cost would have been cheaper."

"Not a problem for my mate."

"You're lying."

"Of course I am." Wayne smiled.

There was levity in his voice, but Darren knew his friend had a point. Everyone knew he didn't want to be here, and from the tired, drunk looks on his mate's faces, neither did they.

It was time to step up.

"So what's the plan for today then?"

Wayne knew Darren was faking it but went along with the façade anyway. "Well, we get drunk up here and then move to different bars all day until we get to the strip club later."

Darren mimed tired horror at Wayne. "There's a strip club?"

Wayne's eyes widened in trepidation. "No stag night would be complete without one."

There was a strained cheer from the group causing the other customers to acknowledge the sad stag party.

"What time is the coach leaving again?"

"Late enough," Wayne replied to the stag.

"Time to go back to drink school, Daz." Wayne turned back to the whole group. "Plus, I am an outstanding teacher."

Darren smiled a little and headed to the bar before Wayne. "You still scare the hell out of me."

Wayne and the group followed him. "The best teachers do."

Nobody but Darren cared about the décor; it was a microbrewery with a steampunk feel which was wasted on everyone else. The group got their drinks and filtered through to a second bar showing a football match. All seats were taken, but the group found some space to stand and watch the TV screens or just stare out the windows to re-evaluate their life.

The bar was packed, and Darren made his way to get the first round in. His friend Mark was his drinks wingman, waiting patiently behind to help carry the drinks over.

Ordering drinks at half-time was always going to be busy and a mistake, but the bar gods were on his side today and his order was quickly taken.

On his left were two stunning-looking girls; they were dressed like they had just walked off a Milan catwalk and stumbled into the bar by mistake. They stood out like a sore thumb in a bar full of middle-aged men watching football, and Darren knew they wouldn't be here for too much longer. On his right side stood a balding older man who was clinging to the bar to stay on his feet. He was wearing a Tottenham Hotspur football top which was also clinging on to his great waist.

Darren could feel the man's eyes reading him. He wished the attention was coming from his other side, but the girls were already drinking up fast, getting ready to leave.

The man manoeuvred towards him and glanced again at Darren. "Hello, mate, I'm Brian Simmons. I'm drunk, an alcoholic, and so are you."

Darren felt his nose twitch. "Why would you say that? Are you sure?"

"Yes, I'm pretty sure my name is Brian Simmons."

"No, I mean, how are you sure that I'm an alcoholic."

"You've just bought eight pints, bit of a giveaway."

"On my stag weekend, mate, these drinks aren't all for me."

Brian shuffled in closer. "They will be as soon as you're married." He snorted hard, trying to keep himself relevant. "My condolences."

This was the part he hated about going to the bar. Darren knew there would always be some drunk idiot waiting to talk to him. This weekend couldn't get any worse in his eyes. He simply nodded to Brian as his drinks turned up.

Mark took three pints in his hands while Darren just took one and had help with the others from the stag guys. As he moved away steadily and calmly, his last view of Brian at the bar was him fumbling with his phone. He dropped it, picked it up and tried to press on the screen, struggling to stay on his feet as both hands were in use and couldn't help his bar support. Brian dropped it again and fumbled on the ground to pick it up.

Darren gave one look back as he delicately made his way from the bar.

"Jesus Christ," he sighed.

17.30 The Shepherds Cross

"Do you like mutts nuts?"

"Is that a trick question?"

Wayne waved a packet of peanuts in front of Darren, who looked perplexed.

"Curry-flavoured peanuts? Best wait for the real thing later. Besides, you know we're eating later, and you had a bacon and egg sandwich with your pint, plus peanuts."

Wayne held a very long shrug. "Yeah, wasn't the best idea. The bacon was underdone, stick some jump leads on it and it'll start breathing again. Anyway, how's your drink?"

Darren pushed a pint glass of very brown liquid to him. "Try it."

Wayne put the glass to his mouth and took a sip, instantly turning away and pulling a face. "What is that? Tastes like witch's piss."

"It's one of their house ales, brewed on site, apparently."

Wayne wiped his mouth clean and snapped his lips. "They should include that on the Bushtucker Trials; no celebrity in their right mind would drink that."

Darren chuckled louder than usual; the drunkenness which he had tried so hard to mask was actually beginning to kick in. Wayne raised an arm to celebrate his friends behind him, who were feeling the effects of drinking all afternoon too. He left to check up on the few who were drink struggling.

Darren attempted to take another sip, but he froze as a familiar voice turned up.

"Well, well, well, look what we have here. It's my man getting married." Brian appeared straight up next to Darren.

He was looking the worse for wear, much more drunk than Darren was. Making a supreme effort to sit on the bar stool, Brian stared down into Darren's eyes, his voice a slurred whisper. "Mate, I barely know you, but you are making a huge mistake."

"A mistake. What do you mean?"

"Google it."

"I know what it means, but you don't even know me, and you're bashing my wedding."

"I'm not bashing you, mate. I just know you're about to sell your soul in a few days' time."

Darren's stomach ached and so did his ears. He tried to look around Brian to see Wayne and glare wildly for leaving him at the bar alone. Wayne was oblivious to Darren's bar problems.

"What exactly is your problem with marriage?" Darren's eyes closed in thought. "Brian," he remembered, which was an achievement, going by how much alcohol he had drunk today. Waiting for a reply, he looked at Brian's bottle of beer, which looked much nicer than his own drink.

"Nothing really matters."

"That's Queen, isn't it?"

Brian was too drunk to get the song reference. "Friends come and go, even family leave after a while, but marriage will always stay with you; even with divorce, it's still a stain."

"Don't you think that's a little harsh on the millions of married people in happy relationships around the world?"

"They're idiots but not arrogant, they don't know any better. People only marry because they get bored in life and have nothing better to do."

Darren didn't want to make conversation but seemed he had no choice with Brian's depressing views on marriage. "Mate, I'm sorry you feel this way about marriage but don't go ruining my stag night."

"Do what I did, just leave and get away, make a brand new start before it's too late."

"Well, you can feel free to leave me at any time."

Brian didn't answer straight away, he just rubbed his face slowly and sighed. That was when Darren could clearly see his tired eyes, his nose bright red from the alcohol.

The bruises on his face were also hard to miss. "What happened to your face?"

Brian rubbed it for a second time. "Sometimes my views on marriage don't just offend you."

"Somebody punched you in the face?"

Brian paused. "No, I mean the pavements can be quite cruel to an old drunkard like myself."

Darren's concern disappeared. "Ah, you fell over."

Brian noticed Darren's eyes straining to concentrate on his drink. He smiled and gestured politely to the barmaid for another bottle. "Yes, what a trying weekend for the pair of us, but your wedding dream is beginning while my wedding nightmare is ended."

Darren tried another sip from his drink and grimaced again. "Do you hate marriage that much?"

Brian mimed a horror face at Darren.

"There's someone out there for everyone else."

Darren's eyes didn't move.

"Marriage for me was like being a musician on the Titanic; you knew something terrible was happening, but yet you stayed and played on."

He looked forlornly at the bar.

"I decided not to go down with the ship. Marriage didn't work for me, and I'm happy and free finally, but that shouldn't mean I should be darkening your day with my woes."

Brian rubbed his poor face. "Do you really love her?"

"With everything I have."

Darren was trying to wipe away the flecks of spittle coming from Brian's mouth without him noticing.

Brian began to clap mockingly.

"Well, being in love is hard, you have to work at it."

"If it's natural and reciprocated, it shouldn't be hard at all."

Brian kept up his slow handclap.

"Don't applaud a fish for swimming," Darren said.

The barmaid came back quickly with his drink. Brian thanked her warmly and slid off his barstool with surprising ease. "Congratulations, young man, on your upcoming nuptials, you seem like a good man, and I hope you and your partner shine like stars."

A sincere smile came from Darren. "Thank you."

A sudden thud caught their attention, followed by glass smashing. They both turned around to see what the sound was and saw a man slowly raise himself from the floor with broken glass around him. "Looks like someone has had one too many, like me."

Darren studied the guy as he apologised to the bar staff. "He's with us, that's Piss-take."

"Bloody right it's a piss-take; that's a lot of glass on the floor for the bar staff to clean up."

"No, that's his name, well nickname."

"I don't get it?" Brian's eyes were still glazed but he tried to focus on Darren.

"Piss-take? Why is he called that?"

"He used to steal people's beers in nightclubs until somebody caught him out and replaced a pint of beer with a pint of urine; he tried it and never stole another pint again. Hence the name Piss-take."

"A pint of pee?"

"Was a long night, I guess." Darren smiled. "Do you have any positive memories of dating and marriage?"

"In life, your direction is more important than your speed."

"Speed was always difficult for me."

Brian looked at Darren in his wheelchair. It was the first time all night that he had bought it up. "I'm sorry, man. I didn't mean to offend."

"You didn't. People usually ask me about my chair all the time when they first meet me. You didn't, you looked past that and thank you."

"Futon."

"I'm sorry?" Darren asked.

"The only date which stood out for me, I met a girl at a bar, we got on, and she came back to my place. She was very drunk and claimed she couldn't remember her address, so I literally made her coffee and gave her my futon to sleep off the booze for the night. When I woke up the next morning, both her and my futon were gone; she left my wallet and car keys, just took the futon."

"Must have been one hell of a comfy futon."

"Got a wife from it, though."

Darren was shocked, his eyebrows raised. "How did you—?"

Brian cut him off. "It's a long story, and this is a short night."

He pointed to Brian's Tottenham Hotspur football top. "Shame about the result earlier."

Brian was confused briefly, a sip from his bottle helped. "Oh, my top? I'll let you into a little secret. Do you know what aposematism is?"

Darren shook his head.

"It's a warning from some animals that they aren't worth attacking. Some frogs have colourful markings on their skin as a warning to predators that they're poisonous and to stay away."

Darren was suitably impressed that even in Brian's drunkenness, he could still hold a conversation.

"That's why I wear this top."

"I don't get it."

"Tottenham supporters are the most miserable football fans on the planet. When I wear this top at a bar, nobody comes up to me; it's kind of like my own animal warning."

"That is pretty harsh, dude."

"Works every time. Enjoy your stag night, Darren."

"You going to be okay?"

"I'm shitting roses, my good man. Never been happier."

With his hands tucked into his coat pockets, Brian left the bar. As Brian left, Wayne came over from drinking with the others and sat on the now vacant seat next to Darren.

"Didn't want to disturb you and your new boyfriend."

"Good one."

"Who was he anyway? Looked absolutely hammered."

"You are the master of understatement, Wayne."

Darren sipped his drink and just gave up, leaving it behind a pillar on the bar. He slapped and then rubbed his hands together like a market trader dealing with their first customer of the day. "Right, are we ready to go? I need a curry and a lap dance."

"I'll check to see who needs to drink up and then we'll leave." Wayne had a grin on his face. "You've changed your tune. You couldn't wait to get back home before."

"Well, in a few days' time, I'm going to be spending the rest of my life with the woman I love so much, someone who I love so dearly and is the first person I want to be with when times are hard and times are great, so I think I can handle a few hours eating dodgy curries and watching almost naked girls slip and slide up a pole."

Wayne began to laugh.

"Expertly done, I have to add."

"Thanks, mate, that's just how I feel."

"No, I meant the pole dancers, experts at their craft."

He smiled as Wayne had a slightly smug look on his face.

"I take it that the chat with your new friend is the reason for the change of mood?"

Darren beckoned to the others to finish up and turned to the exit.

"You have no idea," he mumbled.

00.30 Sweet Angels Gentleman's Club

"Unbelievable."

Everyone turned around or bent their head to the side to see what had caught Wayne's attention. The group had just left the gentleman's club and were heading back to the hotel and their coach, they'd already checked out, and it was the long drive home left.

The club came highly recommended and had good wheelchair accessibility. They had earlier eaten there, and the food and service didn't disappoint. Darren was tired now; it had been a long day and an even longer weekend. It started raining in the afternoon and hadn't stopped. He was glad the pub-hopping throughout the day had ended and just wanted to get back on the coach and get home.

Even the girls dancing didn't prove to be a distraction. However, Wayne's voice was doing the opposite.

"What?" Darren asked.

"That bloke over there. Isn't that the same guy we've been seeing all day in every boozer we've been in?"

Darren went to open his mouth and was cut off by Wayne.

"He's absolutely battered; he must have been drinking all day."

"So have we, to be fair."

"Not as bad as that, though."

Darren actually didn't speak next. He was shocked into silence at how drunk Brian really was. Brian was clinging onto a lamp post, bent over as the rain soaked through his Tottenham shirt. On the ground was a box from a fast-food shop. Brian struggled to pick it up, then stayed on his knees to eat the soggy kebab.

Before anyone could speak, Darren was already over the street to help him. "Hello," he said faintly to Brian. "Are you okay?"

Brian's eyes glazed over, struggling to focus.

"Do you remember me? It's Darren. We met earlier."

There was still no reply from Brian, and he reached for his food box again. Darren called over to Wayne as Brian chewed on the wet kebab mumbling incoherently.

Wayne stared over at him for a moment; he was having trouble with Brian. "Bloody hell," Wayne groaned. "Wait here," he said to the others and followed Darren.

As Wayne reached the other side of the road, he realised how drunk Brian was.

"This guy is absolutely wasted."

"Tell me something I don't know," Darren said impatiently.

"A Smurf is three apples high."

"It was a rhetorical question."

"I know, just didn't think I'd be watching a drunkard eating a soaked kebab in the pouring rain."

Brian was still mumbling to himself as he took another bite from his kebab.

Wayne helped him to eat it.

Darren leaned over and slapped Wayne's arm. "What are you doing?"

"Bloke wanted the kebab, so I gave it to him."

"The guy is still drunk. Don't give him any more food; it's after midnight."

"He's not a Gremlin. The more food he eats, the less he talks."

Darren's concern for Brian continued. "He's eating late, his body might keep calories as fat and he'll put on weight."

"I don't care how fat he could get. This isn't how I had planned your stag night to end."

Darren rolled his eyes. "He's drunk and needs our help, we have to get him home."

"Leave him. We need to get back home."

Wayne's words were said too loudly as Brian gave him a drifting stern look.

"Look at him, he's wet all over, his trousers are soaking."

"It's raining, Wayne. Of course they would be wet."

Wayne took a sniff and pulled a face. "That's not rain."

Darren rubbed his nose, aware of the smell coming from Brian's trousers. He stared hard at him. "Brian, I'm going to look in your pockets for a wallet. Is that okay with you?"

"Good idea. I could do with a kebab myself," Wayne said hastily.

Darren ignored him and waited for a response from Brian. It didn't come, so he looked through all the pockets in Brian's coat and found a wallet. "Result, I've got something."

Wayne snatched it from Darren and rummaged through it. "Well, this is interesting."

"What?" Darren asked quickly.

"He's from Humberfield. He literally lives just a stone's throw away from you."

"Really? Where does he live?"

"Queensbrook."

Darren looked upwards in thought. "Yeah, there is space on the coach."

"It's a minibus. Let's get it right, you don't have that many friends."

"Well, whatever, let's bring him back with us."

All Wayne could do was nod, and he waved the rest of the group over. "Are you sure this is a good idea?"

Darren gave a look to Wayne, whose eyes were flicking back and forth from Brian to the rest of their oncoming friends.

"Wayne, the guy can't even walk. We can't leave him here, he's coming back with us. It's the right thing to do."

Wayne's eyes softened. "Okay, let's get him on his feet and home then, slack nuts."

* * *

Darren's older brother didn't drink; he was on the stag night to support him and nothing else. It was him who offered to hire and drive the minibus to Southend and back to Humberfield. The weekend of booze was fine, but the faster he drove, the quicker he would be away from all of his brother's mates.

"Your brother is flooring it a bit."

"He just wants to get home," Darren replied to Wayne, who had left his seat to check up on him and Brian.

"So do you, I can tell. You really haven't enjoyed this trip, have you?"

"What makes you say that?"

"You've moaned at every moment during this stag, and the only thing that got you moving was that drunk bloke who doesn't even know what day it is."

Darren stared at Wayne, and then his face slowly softened. "All day long, that bloke, Brian, has been badmouthing the idea of marriage to me, and soon I'll be making the biggest decision of my life. What he said got to me a bit."

Wayne put his hands to his face and then dropped them, letting out a sigh. "Everyone here on this coach."

"Bus."

"Yeah, well, we're your real friends. We'll be here no matter what happens with your marriage, but if something bad was to happen, then you and the missus will talk and sort it out like adults, don't listen to him."

Darren shook his head. "He was so down on marriage, though."

"Doesn't mean you have to be. Look, this guy obviously has issues, and in all honesty, you should have left him on the street and made him someone else's problem."

Darren gave a slow sigh. "I couldn't leave him alone. It just wouldn't be right."

Wayne turned away and headed back to his seat. "Fair play to you, Daz, trying to help this drunk out, but you're wasting your time."

Both Darren and Wayne looked at the sleeping Brian.

"Nice guys always finish last," Wayne said as he returned to his seat.

Darren watched him leave and then eventually sat back down.

"At least we can sleep at night," he mumbled beneath his breath.

* * *

The bus ride from Southend back to Humberfield took just over three hours, including a rest stop at an all-night café for food and toilet breaks. The sleeping stag group members stirred as the familiar sights made them sit up in their seats and long for home. It then made a slight diversion up a street which nobody recognised.

"What was the house number again?" Darren's brother asked as he drove up into a cul-de-sac.

"Fifteen," Darren replied.

"Okay, I'm just parking up now. I can't see the numbers."

Wayne looked at his watch as the bus pulled up to the kerb. "It's well late. Shut that engine off before the neighbours start kicking off."

Darren's brother switched off the running motor. "Well, at least he wasn't sick on the bus; I'd lose my deposit," he grumbled.

Wayne replied, "I'm surprised you made it here when you did. You work from home and still can't get to work on time."

"I hope you are not going to make a habit of this, dropping off a strange bloke home at the end of your stag night."

Darren checked on Brian, who was still fast asleep. He lent in to lift him up gently.

"Actually, bruv, I only plan on getting married just the once, so probably not."

"Good for you." Wayne smiled.

Even though it was very late, Wayne was bubbling with energy and helped to carry Brian off the bus. None of the others offered to help but just moved their legs inwards as the groom and best man made their way down a different aisle. The bus door opened, and Wayne carefully led Brian off.

Wayne's heart was racing in his chest as Darren made his way out with his chair. "You sure about this?"

"Too late now." Darren was just as nervous, which he thought was odd as Wayne always came across as so confident, but it had been a long weekend, he guessed. Many outdoor security lights came on as the trio made their way closer to Brian's address on a winding footpath.

Number 15 was in front of them; the outside light flicked for a moment and then came on. Darren stopped chewing his lip and made his way forward to the front door. He prayed the doorbell worked, as it didn't seem right to be knocking at this time of night. The bell worked and played a nursery rhyme tune.

"That would get on my nerves in a heartbeat."

Darren knew nothing about Wayne's words, the hall light came on, and a silhouette came to the door. Slowly opening it was a woman who pulled a blue dressing robe tightly around her slight frame. Her face was pale, with inquisitive eyes and prominent freckles on each cheek, and long dark hair, which she placed behind her ear carefully.

She stared forward past Wayne and Darren. "Brian? Oh my god!"

Wayne moved closer with Brian as the woman stepped outside. "What happened to him?" Her voice and whole body were shivering.

Momentarily distracted by her question and concern, Darren hesitated to allow Wayne to answer instead.

"He's a little worse for wear, had a bit too much drink, so we thought we'd bring him back home, found his address in his wallet, don't worry, there wasn't any sand in it."

The woman took Brian from Wayne, but Darren still held his other side. Brian was now puffing heavily, but his eyes remained closed.

"Sand? Where was he?" Her voice relaxed a little.

"Southend, at my stag do, but he wasn't invited. Well, I mean he could have come if I knew him, which I don't, but he seems nice and—"

Wayne had to cut in. "What my mate is trying to say is that we saw Brian, who is your, um?" Wayne rolled his forefinger in fake forgetfulness, trying to get a reaction from her or at least an answer.

"He's my husband."

"Okay, well, getting him home safely seemed like the only decent thing to do in his condition."

She acknowledged Wayne's words and hugged Brian, and it was an age before she let go. Darren's mouth dropped open and a smile emerged. Brian's wife was genuinely concerned for her husband, and it lifted Darren's spirit, ending his weekend well. The love she showed him was in stark contrast to the conversations they had about marriage in Southend.

The woman finally pulled away and looked deep into Brian's eyes. "What am I going to do with you? You silly sausage." She took hold of his shirt again and pulled him closer to her. "I love you, Brian."

Those words stirred something inside Brian, and he replied with a slow whisper. "Where?"

She looked up at the two guys. "Thank you for bringing him back to me."

Simple, polite head nods came from the two.

"You've come all this way. Can I offer you something to drink?"

Wayne looked at Darren, and they both shook their heads. "No, it's fine. We live a few miles down the road, so just doing the decent thing."

Her eyes were now focused on Wayne's lips. "You're good men, thank you again. I don't know what I would do without him, he's my Anthony, and I'm his Cleopatra."

"Just like Ozzy and Sharon Osbourne," Wayne added.

"Or Romeo and Juliet," Darren piped up.

"That didn't work out quite so well for them, mate."

Darren squinted while pulling a joke face. He caught the woman lifting her lips with a smile and took it as his cue to take Wayne and go home.

Brian didn't look back as he entered his home with his wife. She did turn around, though. "Goodnight, guys."

Brushing the hair away from Brian's neck, the woman kissed it tenderly and closed the door quietly behind them.

Darren's brother tooted the bus horn, causing an irate shout from Wayne. "Hey! It's late, stop that."

Darren nudged him. "You shouting is just as loud."

The front door was shut, and there was nothing left for the two guys to do except head back to their impatient driver.

Inside the house, the woman helped Brian to the kitchen. She punched him hard in the face, almost rendering him unconscious. He fell against the fridge and onto the floor.

His wife began to kick at his sides and head. "You abandoned me! You thought you could leave me!"

Brian didn't move. He couldn't any more.

"You made me look stupid. You embarrassed me!"

He couldn't answer. His jaw was broken.

"Look what you made me do!"

The kicking continued; it never stopped.

Southend was nice. He liked it there but didn't have time to tell anyone how fun it was.

The darkness and pain were coming back, he didn't miss them, but they swept over him and covered his whole body.

The pain left first, but the darkness stayed.

* * *

Wayne and Darren took their respective seats back on the bus.

"Is that it? Can we go now?" Darren's brother asked.

Darren waved him on. "Yes, bruv, thanks for the concern, by the way."

They drove on in silence.

Wayne spoke first. "I know I was taking the piss earlier, but that was a pretty good thing you did, taking that poor drunken slob from Southend back home. A lot of people would have left him, but not you."

Wayne reached into a carrier on the floor and pulled out two cans of beer, handing one to Darren. They touched them together with a smile between them.

"Have a good wedding, man. You're the best guy ever."

Darren winked at his best man.

"So I keep telling people."

Red A

Bennett Kiss
40 Carlton Street
Tuppence Park
Humberfield

Bennett's stomach leapt like a dolphin at a Sea Life centre, whether it wanted to be free or knew its worth in entertainment. She rubbed it again, but her little hands weren't working.

"See? I said you shouldn't have eaten them."

The voice from her best friend was annoying, like an irritating new ringtone, one where she couldn't lower the volume.

"Oh my god, what's happening?" Bennett grimaced.

"I'll give it 10 seconds before you—"

The contents of her stomach beat her friend's sentence.

Libby looked at her watch. "Three seconds, a new record."

She had to turn away as it sounded like a bucket of water being thrown out onto the pavement, plus the smell had just hit. Bennett took a deep breath; her mouth tasted awful.

"They may not let us back in."

She tried to take stock of her friend's words. She was too sick to go back in there anyway, which was a shame.

It was at the opening of a brand-new exclusive building in the club district of Humberfield. The whole place was made to entertain, a multi-storey structure filled with nightclubs and restaurants littered through top to bottom with a spectacular view of all the other luxury buildings in the district if you caught the sun right.

Throughout the building, gorgeous girls in the tightest and shortest of black dresses were handing out drinks to businessmen and rich city kids, many of the men would have given anything to have the opportunity to sleep with the girls, and they tried, but the girls refused. Times were changing, thankfully, and this was just a hostess job for the evening and nothing else.

Libby grabbed Bennett by the arm and pulled her to an alleyway around the corner. "You have got to sort yourself out quickly."

Bennett's eyes were glazed over, and she giggled after wiping the sick from her mouth. "Better out than in."

"Why do you have to drink so much?"

"I'm not too keen on this job, but it pays for my booze, and I need the booze because, between you and me, I'm not too keen on this job."

Libby's eyes shortened with a glare. "You had better not ruin this night for me."

Bennett looked at her friend, not sure what she was supposed to add, so Libby continued.

"I've got a big audition tomorrow. I just wanted to work tonight and then chill out before the afternoon."

"I have no idea why you keep going for this acting stuff; you haven't had a proper acting job in ages. I would just leave it if I were you."

"So what do I do then? Stay being a hostess forever?"

"No, you get yourself online with a channel on social media and make funny stuff, you get loads of followers, and then people pay you to advertise their shit, and you make more money."

Libby groaned.

"Yeah, everyone knows how popular you are; we've seen your figures."

"True, but I also like doing this; it's where I started out, and it's fun."

"That guy you got off with and then was sick all over was the son of the billionaire owner of this new building."

"Oh, I remember now. He was quite hot, wasn't he?"

"He was 17."

"Well, it gives him something to remember me by when his fine little arse comes knocking in five years' time."

"Oh for god's sake." Libby shook her head in disbelief; she wriggled her fingers in front of Bennett. "Why do you have to ruin things for me? I was having a really good time in there tonight."

As drunk as she was, Bennett was having none of it. "He's a wannabe drug dealer and a rich, spoilt little brat. I was doing him a favour being sick on his built-up shoes, gave him a taste of the real life. Plus, there was an army of *Love Island* wannabes in the queue to get in his mum-bought boxers, need a magnifying glass when they get there, though."

Libby was crouched down behind the alley wall and watched the bouncers from the club look up and around like meerkats on steroids. "Well, whatever he did, we have to get back in there."

Bennett replied without even raising her head from her knees. "We're outside. Why do we have to go back in?"

Irritated, Libby pointed to the identical black midi dresses they were wearing, which fit every curve of their bodies. "Because we work there as hostesses."

"Do you think they'll sack us?" Bennett asked in a sarcastic voice.

Libby tried to smile, but inside she was fuming at her friend. "They paid us to do a job tonight, just hand out champagne and make the guests feel comfortable, and you went past that with the rich lad."

"I didn't do anything that bad to that little idiot. Well, nothing he will be checking up on Google later for anyway." Bennett started laughing through drips of puke.

"You sound as serious as a reality TV star giving their 'most honest interview' on a daytime talk show. You do know as soon as the cameras have stopped rolling, they start snorting the finest of the white stuff up their noses. Stop being so hypocritical."

This time, Bennett's head rose from the pavement and stared out Libby. "This place you love working at so much is a drugs den and full of rude, sexist, racist, city boy idiots, and if you want to go back in there, feel free, but I'm not. Sod that lot of bigoted dicks."

Libby didn't answer straight away but raised her top lip to show her teeth. "Our clothes, handbags, phones, our keys to get inside our flat are still in the locker room."

Bennett's drunk eyebrows rose.

"You had to ruin it."

"Look, the only way back in is through the front, and they have security guards there. It looks like we're not going home tonight."

Bennett's sick mood had gone, but she was still unsteady on her feet as she yanked her skirt up and stooped down to pee. "So what do we do?"

Libby waited for the stream of urine to finish from her friend before answering. "Well, I think we have to bin this night off and come back in the morning. Hopefully, all parties involved will have sobered up by then and be more understanding. We can go to my parent's house; they're away for a few days in Bournemouth, you can stay in the spare bed."

Bennett pulled her skirt back up, rubbing and patting it down so it fitted perfectly again. "Isn't Bournemouth full of old people?"

"Parents had me late."

"Fair enough. We ready?"

Libby nodded and they began to walk to the town centre. "We can't book an Uber, no phones, so just have to catch a cab, and I'll pay them when we get back to Mum's."

"For god's sake," Bennett moaned.

"You don't have the right to get annoyed; this was your fault from—"

Before Libby could get her rant out, a loud booming noise came up from behind her, it was a car engine which sounded a little too close for her liking. The revs were deafening as a black car rose gracefully onto the pavement and towards them. Libby's body went rigid, and her face froze in terror.

Bennett screamed as the car bore down on her in a perfect line, crashing all the outside tables out the way laid out nicely for the bar diners. The car wasn't driving aimlessly, it was heading straight for her and Libby; it accelerated hard as customers nimbly dived out of the way like Olympic gymnasts.

"Libby!"

Bennett got past the shock of what she was seeing and launched herself towards her friend, and pushed her out of the way. The girls landed in a tangled heap on the road, and Bennett tried to roll them further away from the car, which roared past them, still on the pavement and smashing its way down the avenue.

Bennett got to her feet quickly and wiped her now bloody mouth due to it meeting the road so heavily. "You stupid dick!"

Her knees matched her mouth as she yelled again. "What's your problem?!"

Libby made her own way up; the scorching pain on her arm was from it being scraped across the road. "Oh my god," she gasped. "Jesus Christ."

Bennett calmed her friend as they hugged, both tearful.

"What the hell was he thinking?" Libby sobbed.

"I think that was a terrorist attack."

The pain in her arm was already becoming unbearable, and she could barely comprehend what Bennett was saying. "What?"

"It's what you see all over the news, nut jobs driving cars into people on the streets."

Libby wanted to touch her arm but instead eyed up Bennett curiously.

"I don't think that's the case; it's just a stupid drunk driver."

"Really? What, are you mental? He tried to run us over! Drunks send odd body pics and chat shit at bars; they don't drive cars on pavements trying to get your number."

Libby finally rubbed her arm. "I'm not sure."

Bennett looked disappointed about Libby's lack of support for her theory. "What aren't you sure about? It's definitely a terrorist. I'm calling the police."

"You can't," Libby sighed.

"Why not?"

"Our phones are still in the nightclub."

"Shit," Bennett hissed.

"What about a pay phone?"

Libby managed a choked chuckle through her pained grimace. "It's the 21st century. When's the last time you saw a working phone box?"

"Ridiculous," Bennett muttered as she rubbed her face. "My ear hurts. Can you hear that buzzing noise?"

A shake of the head from her friend confirmed it for Bennett.

She looked at the car's devastation on the pavement and was concerned, not just for the mess but the reaction of the pedestrians. "Why isn't anybody doing anything? Why isn't anybody saying anything?"

Libby scanned the vicinity. People were just picking up tables and chairs from the road and carrying on as if nothing had happened. Even the pub managers didn't seem alarmed at all; they just helped to pick up their debris.

"That's odd. Why aren't they contacting the police?"

Bennett played with her ear again and shifted her attention back to her now concerned friend. "Because they are in shock, some lunatic tried to run them over, the police should be here now, and there's no emergency services, they come minutes after an attack or accident, but not now."

Libby looked at the calm customers and tried to stay calm herself. "No, something isn't right, it's not—"

Libby shuddered as she stopped mid-sentence, reaching her hand out to Bennett. "We have to go."

"What about the police?"

"We have to go now!"

Bennett turned around, her face filled with terror as the black car circled around the street and was about to come at them again. "God, no," Bennett whispered.

"Run!" Libby screamed.

The girls ran off as fast as they could. The management in the club made it clear that the girls had to wear high heels for hosting duties, so the two girls flipped theirs off and ran with bare feet down towards the next block.

The car moved and twisted easily down the road, like a shark sensing a change in movement from its prey.

"Where are we going?" Bennett panted.

"I don't know, anywhere!"

The girls fled past more bars, not daring to enter as the car was almost on them.

Libby grabbed Bennett's arm and almost tore it off as she swung her friend behind some big refuse bins at the back of a pub. The car raced past them. Whoever was driving failed to notice the girls duck out of sight.

As they both tried hard to catch their breath, Libby noticed a trail of blood leading from the street up to the bins where Bennett and herself were now hiding. Bennett had stepped on some glass on their escape from the car, and her foot was bleeding heavily.

"You've cut yourself," Libby said.

Tears began to form in Bennett's eyes before she could speak. "Why's he doing this?"

She was crying fully now as Libby poked her head above the bin. "Libby! Why is he—?"

"Be quiet!" Libby shushed.

The car was approaching quickly, and Libby just about got down before it roared past.

Bennett's breathing had become more frantic, and it took a slow back rub from Libby, who was also taking deep breaths, to calm her down.

"Breathe, just breathe."

Bennett slowed her breathing rate down and remembered her antenatal classes, she was never pregnant, but she did go to support her sister. She took one more breath and then spoke. "Where do we go? To the police?"

"No," Libby said, her eyes squinted as she thought. "We stick to the original plan. We go back to my parents."

Bennett was focused on every car that went past but nodded her approval and slowly and painfully stood up. "Let's go then."

"Don't put weight on it." Libby pointed out the bloody foot of her friend.

"I'm okay."

The pair left their hiding place and walked up the road and then into the main high street. The traffic was still flowing, and the streets were busy. There wasn't a police car or ambulance in sight as the chaos caused by the black car only in the last street seemed to have been forgotten by the general public, nothing had changed. People were still walking along the street, enjoying their night.

"This is so messed up," Bennett observed.

Libby looked around, eyes wide, staring at the whole set up of streets. "Does look kind of strange," she replied.

Libby scanned the area and noticed a bar with a long queue of people like a snake's tail wrapped around the building. "We can try to get into that club and call for help or at least stay there for as long as possible."

"Do you think they'll helps us?"

"Helps us? Why are you talking like Gollum?"

Bennett's eyes tried to reason past the mistake, and she shook her head. "Help us, I mean, sorry, don't know where that came from."

"You okay?"

"I'm okay, just afraid for you and me."

Libby eased her closer and gave her an arm rub. "Let's go."

The girls walked towards the queue, crossing the road with caution, looking out for all cars, not just the one chasing them. It was a popular club, made famous by footballers and their glamour model girlfriends, plus people on reality TV shows. They sidestepped the crowd and made their way to the front, and the door security men eyed them up. They looked stunning in their hostess uniforms, and the doormen pulled away the velvet rope to let them in until they noticed Bennett's bleeding foot.

"Sorry, can't let you in tonight, girls."

"Why?" Bennett sounded like a child.

"Health and safety. You're bleeding; you should get that looked at."

"I will, babes. I'll get it checked out later; we just need to get inside."

The other doorman stepped forward. He too looked at the girls and noticed Bennett clutching her high heels close to her chest. He whispered to his colleague.

"Can you put your shoes on, please, miss."

Bennett hesitated and looked to Libby, who spoke up as the other man started letting others in from the queue. "Please, is this necessary?"

"It is if you want to get in this club."

"Listen, you—"

Bennett calmed her friend down. "No, it's fine, babes. Hold on."

Bennett leaned on Libby and tried to put her shoe on her bloody foot. It slid onto her heel with the glass still inside; it was only on for a matter of seconds until Bennett wailed in pain, which was all the doormen needed to make their minds up.

"Like we said before, you can't come in tonight, girls."

Bennett collapsed to the ground and burst out in tears.

"That's another reason why she's not coming in; she's drunk."

Libby put her hands together in a praying motion. "Please! You have to let us in."

"I don't have to do anything, miss."

"Listen, this sounds crazy, but there is a guy in a black car who has been chasing us all night. We don't know what he wants or who he is, but he has tried to run us over twice already, and we don't know what to do. He's already smashed through Keene Street driving on the pavement."

The first doorman radioed through to his control and waited for a response as Libby's nervous eyes never left him. His head shifted left to right as he listened to what his supervisors were saying. "Apparently, there was a minor incident earlier on that street. A car mounted the kerb in front of a bar and then drove off, nothing big."

"Nothing big? He tried to kill us!" Bennett screamed from the ground.

People in the queue started to get their phones out, anticipating some drunk girl humour that they could film and show their mates at work.

"We don't have any proof, but it's true," Libby continued. "All we're asking is that you let us in for a few minutes, and then we can call the police and get ourselves straight. We have no phone, so please?"

The huge mountain of a man consulted his partner on the door while keeping a check on the girls. There was a lot of head nodding until the big second doorman turned back to the girls and shrugged his shoulders.

"OK, girls, this is what's going to happen."

Before he could finish, Bennett struggled on her foot. "Unbutton your trousers."

"What did you say?" The bouncer's frown increased.

Libby instantly forgot about the night's events and grabbed her friend. "She didn't mean it."

"I did, you let us in now, and I will give you the best night you've had in those cheap trousers."

The bouncer sighed and rubbed his bald head. "I was going to say that you could come in and wait until the police turn up, but the situation has changed now."

Bennett went for the bouncer, and he moved back with caution. "No, nothing's changed. I'm sorry I said that, I didn't mean to." The panic in her voice continued. "Please let us in. I didn't mean to say those things. Please, I'm begging you, he's going to kill us!"

As the bouncer spoke, he looked at the restless crowd and back to a nervous Bennett. "If you're being chased by a madman in a car—" He began to get the crowd moving through the club doors. "Why not unbutton his trousers too?"

"No, please, I'm begging you, please, let us in!"

"Sorry, girls, not tonight."

The bouncer switched attention back to the crowd, and the girls were left on the street.

Bennett looked at him, eyes filling with tears. "Please!"

The bouncer cracked one last look at her. "Goodnight, ladies."

Libby looked him up sharply and then dragged Bennett away. "What did you do?"

"I don't know!"

"We had one chance of getting away from that bastard in the car and you blew it."

"I'm sorry!" Bennett cried.

"You're sorry? What do we do now, eh? We are screwed now, thanks to you."

"I'm sorry!"

Libby scoffed. "Stop saying that; it won't help."

"What do we do now?"

Libby scanned the buildings on either side of where they stood, looking at possible entries from where a car could appear between the gaps in the alleyways. "One thing is for sure is that we can't stay here. Maybe try another club, and this time keep your mouth shut."

Bennett simply nodded, grabbed Libby's hand and followed her friend back into the street.

Libby bit at her nails and turned behind her. "Who did you piss off?"

"What?"

Libby glared at Bennett and broke off the hand chain. "I said, who did you piss off online? There must have been some freak who you annoyed on your countless social media accounts, all your photos of you on so many holidays, or just playing around with that useless dog of yours in loads of new outfits. What insane idiot fell for your crap and thought they had a chance of being with you? What guy did you upset?"

Bennett's eyes were confused. "I thought you liked my dog Dizzie? I gave you his brother."

"Hate dogs. Why do you think I gave it to my mum? Stupid shit machine."

"Why are you saying this?"

"Because for some strange reason, that stupid dog only responds to cheesy 90s dance music. Mum has to play that Timmy Mallet song 'Itsy Bitsy Teeny Weeny Yellow Polka Dot Bikini' every time she wants to take it for a walk."

"This is not my fault," Bennett cried, but Libby wasn't in the mood to be sympathetic.

"Because I'm sick of covering up for you, at work, when we were at college, nothing's changed; I'm still having to clean up your shit everywhere we go. People are laughing at you, they think you're a dick."

Bennett's expression darkened. "Who says that?"

"All the other girls at work, you bring it on yourself. The other day when we were talking about what was your earliest childhood memory?"

Bennett's eyes closed in thinking. "I said I remembered being breast fed."

"Bennett!"

"It's true."

"Stop lying!" Libby said with gritted teeth before speaking again. "What was the other stupid thing you said? How you can never watch Paul Mckenna on TV."

"Don't look in his eyes."

"Oh, for god's sake!"

Bennett handed Libby a savage look and bit her lip slowly. "I get your point, we have to go now."

For once Libby listened to her friend and tried to retain some dignity. "Yeah, let's go."

Bennett wiped some tears away and followed her best friend, wiping snot away from her nose and checking on her bleeding foot. "No one is going to help us now, are they?"

Libby took her friend's hand again. "It's just us two."

The girls continued their walk back into the street. They both looked at each and every person who walked past them, wondering if they were the driver of the car, trust was fading.

"Am I a laughing stock then? Is that how the girls at work see me?"

Libby pointed to a side alley. "We can hide down there."

"You didn't answer my question," Bennett demanded.

Libby silently swore and answered. "What do you want me to say? The things you do to people are questionable."

"What things?"

"Now isn't the time, Bennett."

"I want to know."

Looking around to see if they were really safe, Libby focused back on Bennett and let go of her hand. "You want the truth? Shall I tell you how the girls feel? They don't get you. Sometimes you are so great, kind and thoughtful, and at other times you're withdrawn and angry and want to fight everybody, plus you live in your own world, this bubble where nothing outside it exists. I'm constantly lending you money and never get it back, like for those concert tickets."

"That wasn't long ago."

"They were for Prince."

Bennett grimaced. "Isn't everybody like that in life?"

"Not like you; you're so secretive and deceptive. Look what you did to poor Connor."

"He knew what he was getting into; he didn't mind the setup."

Libby tried to save her anger as the whole night was worse than Bennett's attitude.

"You meet some guy in a bar, you chat him up, and he falls for you, but you fail to mention to him that you've already got a boyfriend, so you start dating him but only see him at weekends and the odd evening and never let your family meet him, while telling your proper bloke that you were working on weekends. What kind of person does that? You dated Connor for two years, and he didn't know anything about your life."

"Jesus Christ," Bennett sighed. "I didn't hear you complaining when he sent us gift bags filled with chocolate and wine. You kept your mouth shut then, didn't you? OK, yeah, so I had two guys on the go at the same time, so what, who gives a shit? I'm not the only person who does that, people do it all the time."

"Then be better than them," Libby snapped. "When you really put your mind to it, you can accomplish anything, just don't be like one of those two timing people in life."

Libby's eyes went back to realising where they were. "We have a madman in a car trying to kill us, I don't have time to babysit your crap. If you want to be a cheating tramp then fine, but all I want to do is survive this night."

Libby walked further down the alley, looking behind her as Bennett failed to move.

"You really don't care about anything, do you?"

Bennett failed to answer, her face cold and impassive as she listened to Libby shout again.

"Fine, stay here then, but I'm leaving."

Bennett watched her friend walk away and then raised her arm, shouting out at the same time. "Wait, slow down, I'm coming too."

Libby stopped and turned in the alley as Bennett opened her mouth again.

"We can't all be angels like you."

"Guess not."

Libby stopped and beckoned her friend to join her. "This car is like the shark in *Jaws*. It won't stop until we're both run over and dead."

Bennett clutched her shoes and limped towards Libby. "I would rather sink with you in an ocean of sharks than drown alone."

Libby managed to chew up a smile. "That's so not your saying. Where did you get it from?"

"Instagram, Melyssa's page."

"Oh, forgot about her. Is she still going to that hen night thing in—" Before she could finish, Libby was already up in the air, spinning like a firework that had just exploded.

Bennett's body stiffened, and she was unable to scream. She never saw the car lurking around the corner and neither did Libby.

Libby came crashing down onto the pavement. She moaned and laid her head on the kerb; she couldn't speak, just gurgled blood. The car had sped past Bennett and just waited, its engine still purring.

Bennett looked around, there was nobody in the side street, but she still tried. "Oh my god, somebody help me!" she screamed.

All the streets were packed with people out for their pre-weekend drinks, chatting and laughing, but this side alley was empty; nobody was coming down there. The engine revs from the car began to grow. Bennett found her legs and ran straight towards Libby, ignoring the blacked-out windows as the revs increased.

She cradled Libby's broken body in her arms. With no phone and nobody around to help, all she could do was scream again. "Please, somebody help us!"

Bennett turned her attention to the car. "Leave us alone, you bastard!"

Libby's eyes flickered briefly as she saw Bennett, her body was broken, and her face was leaking so much blood, Bennett held her friend tight. "It's going to be fine. I'll get you out of here."

Libby looked past Bennett at the black car whose increase in revs was unbearable now with a dreadful screeching of its tyres. "Move."

"What do you mean?"

Libby's eyes were fading as she coughed up more blood. "Quickly."

The car reversed over Libby before Bennett could move, crushing her against the pavement.

Bennett's scream echoed around the alley. "Libby!"

Bennett watched transfixed as the car drove forward and then reversed back over Libby's broken body. The driver's rear tyre rested on Libby's head, blood oozed slowly from her mouth as the engines revved again, and her eyes remained open, unable to move with the car on top of her.

"Please? Why are you doing this!?" Bennett screamed again and collapsed in a heap on the floor, crying hysterically.

With her eyes locked on the car, Bennett's face twisted in pure terror as the realisation dawned on her what was about to happen. She shook her head frantically in between sobs.

"Please don't," she whimpered. Bennett saw the final scared look in Libby's eyes.

The night was filled with loud partygoers and people out for a long relaxing drink after work. None of them heard the car wheelspin over Libby's head. A spray of blood hit Bennett square in her screaming face. The wheel bore deep into Libby's head, grinding out bone and brain all over Bennett. Blood poured over her face as she screamed for the car to stop.

Finally it did. There was nothing left of Libby's head; it was like a broken boiled egg with the insides hollowed out.

Panicking, Bennett wiped off the bloody hair from her face. Some was her own, most of it was Libby's. She screamed louder with every strand she swept from her eyes. She backed away from the car, still looking at the hole where Libby's face used to be. There was nothing she could do, and she only took the time to throw up before taking off in the opposite direction.

* * *

Sebastian Vorshie was tired, and it wasn't due to work. The start of the weekend, Fridays were usually the busiest time of the week. His little burger bar door was always swinging open with customers wanting a late-night coffee to sober them up or a greasy burger to end the booze night on a high.

A little competition was good, and the coffee shops were friendly, exchanging ideas along with friendly banter and bags of 50ps of change with one another. Then the bigger companies came in, the popular fast-food chains, McDonald's, KFC, Burger King, Subway; they were built within months and completely wiped out his trade. One by one, the high street cafés closed down, and it was just one cafe left. He had quite a variety of foods, Polish and Romanian specialities, which was probably why he was still open, plus he could just about afford the tremendous rent he had to pay for the spot.

Even for a Friday night, it was quiet, and Sebastian came from behind his kitchen and sat out front; there were a few diners there eating a full English breakfast and some drinking coffee to sober them up.

He sat with his own cup of tea and finally began to read today's copy of the *Sun*, not his preferred reading material, but he bought it for his customers to browse through as they were eating, that and the *i Paper*. It was a steady night and nothing out of the ordinary, that was until Bennett walked in and sat by the window.

"Good god," Sebastian said in English.

He dropped his paper and immediately went to the girl. Her clothes were completely soaked in blood; she picked up the menu and scanned through it, still shaking.

"Are you okay? Do you need some help?" he asked.

"Yes, can I have a quarter pounder with chips, please, and a Diet Coke."

"Miss, your clothes, what's happened?"

Bennett's eyes rose with surprise. "Yes, you're right, I need help. Could you leave out the onions and gherkins and maybe just a water instead of the Coke, please?"

Her voice began to get shaky, but Sebastian just listened, calmly waving away his concerned waitress.

"Is there anybody I can call for you? Family, a friend maybe?"

Bennett glanced at him through scared eyes. "Not sure if onions are good for you, I need to watch what I eat. I need—" Bennett choked on her last word and then broke down. "I need my friend! It killed my friend!"

Tears instantly began to flow and she became hysterical. "They killed her, they killed her."

Sebastian immediately called back his waitress. "Anca, can you take this woman upstairs, she needs help."

Sebastian helped Bennett to her feet and tried to wipe some blood off her front.

He tried to shield her away from the other customers as Anca took Bennett upstairs to his flat. He took out his phone, ready to call the police but hesitated as he watched Anca lead the girl away.

Looking at his shocked customers, Sebastian followed Anca upstairs, hoping he wouldn't be long.

He heard a thump on the landing as Bennett collapsed at the top of the stairs. It was to be a longer night than Sebastian had hoped for.

* * *

Moonlight streamed in through the kitchen window of the flat. Bennett awoke on a sofa in a small room directly opposite. She blinked and covered her eyes from the light, which prompted her to raise her head when she heard somebody else in the room.

The fact that her clothes were missing was a concern, she had only a blanket and her underwear on her. Anca, a woman roughly in her mid-twenties with bright, inquisitive eyes, looked at her; she stood absolutely still like she was playing the game 'Statues'.

"Where are my clothes?" Bennett demanded.

"They are being washed and dried because they were covered in blood," Anca spoke, determined not to be walked over by a complete stranger.

"I have just moved out, so I don't have any clothes here and the rest I sent to a..." She paused, her English was very good but one word was difficult to say. "Charity shop? But you can take this."

Anca simply bent down and picked up a pink nightgown off the floor. "This is all that I have left here. You can cover yourself until your clothes are clean and dry."

She handed the very flimsy robe to Bennett, who held it up in the moonlight.

"How long have I been here?"

"You passed out and have been asleep for..." She paused. "One hour, you can change in the toilet."

Anca was very softly spoken; each word came out like a little whisper.

Bennett tried to smile as she took the nightgown and headed to the bathroom.

By the time she had changed, Sebastian had returned, Anca had made some tea, and after a brief conversation in Romanian, she left the two to walk downstairs.

"Thank you for the gown," Bennett said. She played with the long belt.

"You're welcome," was the reply from Anca. "Oh wait." She quickly turned back. "You have no shoes, one second." Anca looked over Bennett's shoulder. "I get something for you."

Anca then ran back upstairs and past Bennett in the lounge. She picked up some old, tattered trainers lying at the side of the couch and offered them to Bennett. She had a delicate smile on her face. "These were going to the charity shop as well." Anca laid the trainers on the ground and went back downstairs.

Bennett sat down and shifted uncomfortably on the couch, pulling the gown tightly across her chest and staring at Sebastian.

Her foot was still bleeding; he looked at the red on the end of the couch.

Bennett followed his eyeline, and the bloodstain her foot had left. "Oh, I'm sorry about that."

"It is fine. That cut needs a bandage." He went to examine it, and Bennett pulled away instantly. "I'm not going to hurt you."

She clutched her forehead; it was pounding. "Why didn't you call an ambulance for me? The girl said I was out for an hour."

He hesitated.

"Is that girl coming back?" Bennett slowly growled; she trusted no one now.

"She had to go back to work, only her and my chef, Rafa, are in the café now; we still have to work. Please, my name is Sebastian, and this is my home. Are you hungry? If I can't tempt you with anything on the menu, then I'll be expecting a visit from Gordon Ramsey at some stage to slap my wrist."

Bennett was unconvinced as Sebastian took a seat in his own kitchen, speaking louder as she was still on the couch.

"You came into my café, blood-soaked and bruised, I offer you help, and you refuse? What more can I do? Please, your foot needs looking at."

"Are you some sort of doctor?" Bennett's voice softened to sarcastic.

"I used to be back home in Iasi." The confused look came again from Bennett. "Romania," Sebastian added.

"So everybody in your country hated that Brexit thing. Is that what your people are called?"

Sebastian thought really hard about what she had just said and struggled to get his words across. "People from Romania are Romanians, not remainers. I think that is what you mean?"

Bennett pushed her tired eyes open with her fingers and held them for a while.

"Please let me see to your foot."

Bennett nodded, left the couch, and sat at the kitchen table, looking around the room. Sebastian left his chair and rooted around one of the top cupboards in the kitchen. He pulled out an old tattered first aid kit and laid it on the table. "How did you do this?"

Bennett didn't answer.

"I'm sorry. I didn't mean to pry."

Sebastian held her foot in his hand and softened his touch as Bennett grimaced. "It looks like you have some glass stuck in there, I can get it out, but it will hurt, I'm afraid."

"Great bedside manner you have there."

"Sorry, it's been a while since I was a doctor. Please wait for a minute." He stood back, went to another cupboard, and reached for a bottle of white wine. Sebastian set it on the table, took a glass from the sink top, washed it out again, and poured some of the wine into it. "This may help."

Through gritted teeth, Bennett spoke again after taking a swig from the glass. "Can I ask you a question?"

"Only if it's personal; that seems to come up next when somebody asks that." Sebastian replied, not even looking up.

"If you are a doctor, why are you working in a café on a Friday night?"

"It's an honest living. People come in, order their food and gaze out the window as it slowly gets cold, while others like to make small talk with Anca, but most of the time I'm left alone."

"Why? I thought being a doctor was an honest living."

"I thought you were only asking one question?"

"It's been a shit night." Bennett squirmed in her seat in pain as Sebastian removed a sliver of glass from her foot; he smiled beneath his glasses.

"I was a doctor for many years, a good one, worked hard, listened, studied well, but working hard became working long and then longer."

"Isn't that what doctors do? Work hard all the time? Everyone knows that; you should count yourself lucky after the night I've had."

Before Sebastian could speak, Anca re-entered with two cups of tea and placed them on the table. She noticed the only glass of wine which Bennett was drinking.

"How is it downstairs?" Sebastian asked.

Anca just made a 'so-so' movement with her hand and left.

"What's the deal with her? You banging her?"

"I don't understand what you said."

Bennett sighed. "Are you two in a relationship?"

Sebastian got her words, and replied with a sigh of his own. "I don't think my brother would approve if I laid with his daughter."

Bennett thought for a moment. "Oh shit, she's your niece."

"Yes, she is, and please refrain from using such language in my home."

Bennett felt an unease in the room, knowing she had clearly crossed a line and stared out the window, the moon still bright. "I'm sorry."

"Shall we start again?"

"Yes please."

Sebastian carried on nursing her foot, and this time she looked down at him, dark eyes with thick eyebrows above; he pushed his glasses back up onto his face as he delicately wrapped a bandage over the cut.

"You were talking about working long hours back home."

Sebastian's dark eyes lifted slightly. "So you were listening then."

"Yes, I thought you may come on to me or try to kill me, so best pay attention to what you were saying."

"I was thinking the same thing. I was hoping you wouldn't get any funny ideas of jumping on me as I'm married."

Bennett actually chuckled. A sudden gust of wind blew in from the kitchen window, making her wince slightly. "Like I said, it's—"

"Been a shit night." Sebastian finished her sentence.

Bennett threw him a look.

"Excuse my language. When are you going to tell me what happened to you?"

Sebastian got up and took another glass from the sink top, and poured himself some wine. "Anca doesn't like me drinking, but it's not often I have guests here."

The early fear in Bennett's eyes had gone, and she relaxed a little, waiting for Sebastian to continue.

Taking a moment to get his words right, he continued. "Like I said, I was good at my job as I was exceptionally great at university. Medical school was a walk in the park, and I was so talented that I not only worked in hospitals but also treated the finest and richest people of my district; a private doctor if you like. And while I was that confident in my work, I was also becoming addicted to alcohol. At first, it was just a social drink with what little time I spent with friends, and then it became more frequent, a glass before work in the morning became a bottle and then when I finished at night, another bottle or two."

"Did you drive to work?" Bennett asked, her eyes wider than normal.

"Yes, it became quite normal to do so. I wasn't proud but it was easy to mask."

Sebastian ran his forefinger on the rim of his glass, contemplating what to say next.

"Well, drinking and not getting caught was a gift for me, not one I'd care to repeat now, but I was an expert at turning up at work and keeping up appearances, as you say. Even on the drink, I could work so many hours and not get tired; no one suspected a thing. I guess I was a functioning alcoholic."

"Did you drink at work?"

"That would have been a step too far for some, but easy for me."

"So what happened?" Bennett asked, sitting up straight.

"There was this patient of mine, nice man going through a rough patch with his wife, going through a messy divorce, as I remember. He was showing early signs of depression, lack of sleep, feeling tired all the time, withdrawn and moody, he just said he kept falling asleep at inappropriate times. I thought nothing of it and failed to give him a thorough examination as I was low on alcohol and wanted more, so I prescribed him some tablets. His condition improved slightly, and things were fine for a while, plus I think he and his wife had reconciled, but that wasn't to last and things took a bad turn."

"Not sidetracking from what you're talking about, but your English is very good, by the way."

"As is yours," Sebastian added.

Bennett pressed her bandaged foot.

"Does that hurt?" he asked.

"Still waiting to know what you did," came Bennett's reply.

Sebastian regarded the intense look in Bennett's eyes. "My patient's bad turn came when he went back to work behind the steering wheel of a coach. He was on the motorway driving some people out on a day trip, and everything was fine until someone on the coach collapsed. Do you know what narcolepsy is?"

Bennett squinted hard with both eyes. "It's when someone keeps falling asleep, right?"

Sebastian drew his head back in a sweet surprise. "Yes, how did you know?"

"My uncle has it. We didn't know what it was at first, just thought it was his idea of getting out of doing the washing up at Christmas."

"Unfortunately, there wasn't a doctor on board, and my patient managed to pull into a layby, according to witnesses."

"Did the person get treatment?" Bennett asked, her eyes focused sharply on Sebastian.

"Yes, they did, but only after the coach had ploughed into a parked car also on the hard shoulder."

"I don't understand?"

"It was the driver, my patient, who collapsed; the coach hit a stationary car that had broken down."

"What happened?"

Sebastian took a swig from the glass of wine. "Do you want something to eat?"

"What?"

"I live and work in a café. Are you hungry?"

"I'm fine, thanks." Bennett spoke softly.

Sebastian went to the fridge and pulled out a plate wrapped in foil. "You British love your Sunday roasts; that was what I found most intriguing when I moved here. No matter how bad things get in your life, you always have time for a roast, get the family ready and invite friends around; all problems seem to go away with meat and gravy. Even though I'm surrounded by food every day, I too got caught up in adopted tradition and do the same every week."

Pulling off the foil, Sebastian looked at the plate. It was filled with roast potatoes, some vegetables, plus roast chicken and Yorkshire puddings.

"I've watched so many cookery shows over the years, from Jamie Oliver, Gordon Ramsey and countless guest chefs on daytime television shows to cook the perfect Sunday roast, and no matter how hard you prepare or try—"

Bennett waited for him to finish.

"Five, six if you included the pet dog."

"I don't get it, I—"

Bennett was genuinely confused as Sebastian quickly closed her down. "A family were waiting in the car for a breakdown truck to pick them up, they were completely wiped out as the coach crashed into them, all of them in the car died."

Sebastian took a knife and fork from the drawer and neatly cut into the chicken.

"The thing with alcohol is it makes you think you can take on the world or lead you down a dark and lonely path. Either way, it numbs you; things or routines you've done for years, you've known for years, with drink involved, they all disappear." He took a bite out of the chicken.

"I'm sorry," Bennett said.

"Don't be sorry."

Bennett became nervous and tested the dressing on her foot by standing up.

"I drove to work drunk, I consulted my patients drunk, and I misdiagnosed the coach driver's heart condition because I was drunk."

"Wait? I thought you said he had narcolepsy."

"He did, but also had a bad heart which I failed to notice. He didn't fall asleep at the wheel, he had a heart attack. He was jailed for manslaughter because, in a tragic twist of fate, he was drinking too, and it all came out about my own drink problem."

Bennett folded her arms, waiting.

"I lost my medical licence, and I was jailed for gross negligence, suspended for two years. But the anger from my community was understandable, they didn't want a doctor with blood on his hands living near them, so I came to England some years ago to stay with my brother and his family. They took me in, and so did the town of Humberfield. I work at my brother's café now with my niece and nephew."

"When I said sorry, I meant for the family, not you."

"Not a day goes by when I don't think of those children in the car."

"My heart bleeds for you," she hissed.

"I really wished mine did at first, so I could be free from all the guilt and suffering I had caused. I was to blame for the death of that family."

Bennett pointed at the wine bottle. "Didn't stop you drinking though, did it."

"When things are hard or on top of me, I like to pour myself a drink. When Anca sees it, she probably tells my brother, but I just like to watch the drink in the glass."

"Why? I thought being involved in killing a family would make you give up."

"Because—" He stopped. "I'm sorry, I don't know your name."

"Bennett."

"I'm Sebastian. Pleased to meet you."

Bennett was unmoved and still staring at the glass.

"Because, Bennett, I'm an alcoholic. I need a drink every day and every night. There is not one hour that goes by when I don't want a drink, but I've been given a second chance here in England, and this struggle to stay sober is a long hard battle but I cannot give up."

Sebastian took the glass of wine and poured it down the sink. "I will not give up, thanks to you."

"Me? What did I do?"

"Because before you came in, I was heading back upstairs from the kitchen to finish this bottle, your distress was a distraction."

"Happy to oblige," Bennett mumbled.

Sebastian moved slowly forward from the sink. "It does help working here with the drinking, Anca keeps an eye on me, and the customers keep my mind off it, but she is moving out now, and I'll be on my own."

"Yeah, I know, she said."

"It wasn't fair to burden someone so young, my niece, with all my troubles, constantly looking out to see if I was still drinking. It never goes away, and you should always avoid temptation, but sometimes bottles look…" He paused. "Nice."

"You're an alcoholic, Sebastian."

He smiled at Bennett and stretched his fingers, made two fists and then opened them again. "We don't always get what we need."

Sebastian suddenly reclaimed his thoughts. "Oh my God, you said when you first came in that your friend had—"

"My best friend has just been killed," Bennett said stone-faced.

Sebastian hesitated.

"She was run over by a maniac in a car. Wonder if he was drunk too?"

Bennett was satisfied she could put weight on her foot and headed for the stairs. "Thank you for dressing my foot, my clothes please?"

"Ah, I think Anca has washed them and they are probably in the dryer now; it shouldn't be too long."

"I've nothing to wear apart from this nightdress."

"Just a second." Sebastian tilted his head towards the bottom of the stairway and then shouted to Anca in Romanian.

Within moments his niece poked her little head around the stair corner and shouted back; there was frustration in her voice which Bennett could sense in any language.

The look on Anca's face told Sebastian all he needed to know.

"I'm needed downstairs in the café, forgive me."

Bennett gave him a longing look.

"Yes, your clothes are in the washer drying machine. Let me check for you." Sebastian went back into the kitchen and switched off the dual washer dryer, checking Bennett's hostess clothes. "Not dry yet, just a few minutes more."

She took the trainers that Anca had given her before they were destined for the charity shop; it was a completely different look for her now from when the night had started.

A pink nightgown, hair pulled back and trainers that looked too small for her, and she was ready to leave.

"Wait, don't you want to call the police? Your friend has lost their life."

"I bloody know that, Sebastian!" Bennett struggled with trying on the shoes. "Sorry, I have to go."

"Wait, let me call the police for you. I should have done it sooner, I'm sorry."

"Sorry won't bring Libby back to me, will it? Sorry won't bring that family back."

Sebastian wasn't surprised by her tone and sat back down at the table. "You must call the police and report this."

"What good will it do? That car was targeting us, it hit Libby and killed her. What am I going to do? What am I going to do?"

Sebastian looked at his watch.

"I'm sorry. Am I keeping you from something?" Bennett's face twisted.

His eyes focused on Bennett. "When I knew what I had done and the enormity of causing the deaths of that family, I deserved everything that happened to me. And the most horrific thing about it was that when it came on the news, I was in a drunken state, saw the broadcast out of the corner of my eye, went back to sleep, dismissed it. Nothing newsworthy as far as I was concerned. Then the police came, and that was that. I remember after the trial, I sat at a table not too dissimilar to this one at my house and contemplated my future. I thought about what I had done and what to do; I went to a cupboard where I kept my tablets for pain relief."

Bennett was interested and turned from the stairs.

"I took out two tablets from separate bottles, one was coloured red and the other blue. I put them in a separate cup and shook it, then with my eyes closed, put each tablet behind my back and after another shuffle held my fists over the table."

"Pills to kill yourself?"

"No," Sebastian said quickly.

"Two pills, red means you stand up to face your problems head-on, you stay and fight for everything you believe in, and blue just means you run away and keep running."

"What one came up?"

Sebastian eased a smile. "I'm in England with its fish and chips, stiff upper lip; that's what running away does." Sebastian left Bennett at the stairs, went back into the medicine cabinet, pulled out a small freezer plastic bag, and handed it to her.

"What's this?"

"It has two tablets inside, the red and blue. Whatever you want to do, just take a moment to look at them and see how it goes; it's up to you where your life goes from here."

Bennett clutched the bag without a word.

"So can we please call the police now?"

This man was calm and pleasant enough, and apart from the odd hiccup, he was genuinely trying to be nice to her. Bennett spoke, going back to being nervous as something was finally going to be resolved about tonight.

"Yes please."

"Then let's go downstairs and wait for them. I'll bring your clothes down when they are dry."

"I can't sit in a café with just a nightgown on."

"This is Humberfield on a Friday night. Believe me, we've seen worse." Sebastian's voice was tired but sincere.

As they headed downstairs, Bennett heard her host on the phone to the police behind her, and it slightly calmed her nerves as they reached the bottom. The café was still quiet for a Friday, and Anca was in the back of the kitchen talking to her brother, the chef. She watched as her uncle and guest headed into the front of the café. Sebastian turned back and went towards the till, he opened it and pulled out a single £20 note and walked back to Bennett, waving it in her face.

"The police are on their way. It's a busy Friday night, so not too sure when they will arrive, but they will come. This is for you."

"I can't take it, you've done enough."

"Please, I insist." He took Bennett's hand, placed the money in her palm and closed it.

Sebastian's words seemed more comforting now, still not many people in the café, but Bennett knew it was safer here than outside. She opened her mouth and nothing came out, but tears began to flow down her face. Her arms became open to an embrace and Sebastian dutifully obliged.

"Thank you so much, Sebastian."

He responded by just holding Bennett tight. She was reluctant to let him go.

"The police will come, and you can hopefully put this horrible night behind you and get justice for your friend. Now, would you still like that burger while you wait?"

"Yes please, but no chips," she whispered.

Sebastian opened his eyes and saw Anca's own eyes bulge in terror as she pointed to the window. "Unchi!" she yelled.

"What's wrong?" he asked.

Bennett's eyes flicked open and looked towards the café window. She didn't even know what the café was called, the writing was back to front, it didn't matter as a car was about to drive right through it. She never heard its approach; it was silent and wanted to be.

"You bastard."

The whispered words from Bennett's mouth confused Sebastian.

"Why would you say—"

Sebastian didn't finish his sentence as the black car crashed through the café window and shattered glass flew everywhere, showering his customers, who tried to duck for cover. Bennett made a jump to the ground, and her dive was accelerated because Sebastian had helped her down with a push. By the time she looked up, the car had sent his body spiralling into the coffee machine. He was dead already as the start mechanism kicked in and a flat white began to pour onto his head.

"No!" Anca went to her uncle and cradled his lifeless body in her arms.

The customers fled through the door and open window. Bennett looked over to Anca. "Is he dead?"

Anca didn't look up.

"I said, is he dead?"

"Yes, he's dead! You killed him. You shouldn't have come here."

Bennett knew she couldn't reply and gave a long look at the crushed body of Sebastian. Holding the money and bag of tablets tight, she turned to try and run away with her injured foot in tight-fitting trainers.

That was until under the cover of smashed glass, the black car driver's door opened, and a figure stepped out. It was a man dressed in a magnificent black suit, his face was white as clay and his head was square like an old 80s computer game pixel. As his legs left the car, he stretched to his full height; it was a strange sight and unbelievable how someone so big could fit into such a small space. He surveyed the damage his car had caused and noticed Anca holding her uncle.

"That was not meant to happen." He spoke with a deep voice, as expected with a man that size, but each word carried a long, drawn-out rasp. He had trouble breathing, but his supreme confidence overrode that. He looked firmly at Anca. "I heard that he was dead. You are quite loud for such a little person."

Anca laid Sebastian's body down and shifted her body away in fear.

"Shame, I was looking forward to a full English breakfast."

Anca let rip a cry of anger. Grabbing a knife from the table, she ran towards the figure by the car, screaming. The man in black picked her up with ease by the throat and held her aloft as she feebly kicked her legs against him; he increased the pressure on his hand as she began to gurgle.

"Stop! You're killing her," Bennett screamed.

His head spun at an incredibly strange angle and looked behind at Bennett.

"Have you not seen this night at all? That was the general idea."

The chef cowered in the kitchen, not even attempting to help his sister.

As the girl slowly stopped kicking, the man dropped her to the ground, and Anca started coughing. His eyes shot her a glance. "Actually, it's not your turn yet, girl, you aren't ready."

The driver was still looking at Anca and then his eyes switched back to Bennett. "Guess I'll just have to do with you."

Even after everything she had seen tonight, Bennett's stomach flipped over. She turned and ran through the still working front door and back out on to the street, every step was pure agony due to her injured foot.

The driver hesitated as Bennett fled the scene, his whole head twisted again at a weird angle as his eyes hit the chef. "Don't suppose I could have a breakfast takeaway?"

* * *

Bennett was feeling easy running again; her foot was easing with every step, Anca's trainers were way too tight, but she couldn't risk injuring her foot again. Looking behind her with every step to see if that man was following her, she knew he would be eventually; her pursuer had a face now, and it was awful.

He had attacked her three times tonight. She stopped to catch her breath. She had nowhere to go and no one to turn to. Libby was the clever one, she had the ideas, she had the brains, and now she was gone forever.

With her head bent down over the street drains, Bennett retched as she thought about Sebastian's death; she rubbed her stomach and looked around her. A car had just driven through the window of a café, and apart from the shattered glass falling on drunk customers, nobody really seemed bothered. Releasing a cry of pure anger, she lowered herself down onto the pavement, sat on the concrete and began to sob.

A few people passed by and rubbernecked at the crash scene, but that wasn't Bennett's concern: she kept on crying as nobody seemed to notice her. The crash site was quite a way behind her, and there was still no sign of any emergency services, no sirens to be heard anywhere despite the thick smoke leaving the hole in the café window, but the important thing was that there was nobody chasing her at the moment.

A middle-aged woman walked by with two small dogs; they barked at Bennett and scared her to her feet. "Sorry!" the lady said. "They're not normally like that."

Bennett put up a hand apologetically even though the dogs were still yapping away at her. "It's fine."

The woman carried on walking, and Bennett looked past her; it was obvious that the police weren't coming. Bennett didn't know why this man was after her, but he was willing to do anything to get her, the car had already killed two people tonight, and she was damn sure that she wasn't going to be the third. She had to find a more crowded place than the café to hide, the more people around the better. In horror movies, all the teenage kids played by actors in their thirties who were being chased by demons just had to make it through to the morning. That was what she tried to convince herself anyway.

A queue was forming at another nightclub ahead of her. Bennett took another look behind her and then limped on towards the club. She wasn't dressed for a nightclub with just a pink nightgown and cheap trainers, but she had to get inside, her life depended on it. The last time she was in a queue, she panicked, which resulted in Libby getting killed; that wasn't going to happen again. Bennett mingled in with the queue and took the dirty looks from the other impeccably dressed clubgoers. Her palms were sweating, and she wiped them vigorously on her now dirty gown and moved towards the door, constantly looking over her shoulder and shaking.

After straining her neck behind her for ages, Bennett checked her face in the club window, wiping away the tears as she reached the front of the queue.

The doormen checked out her stained attire. They looked her up and down and noticed how she limped to the door, one of them stopped Bennett from entering.

"It helps to make an effort when you dress to come out."

Bennett remained calm and breathed in slowly. "It's been a rough day. Can I please come in?"

"*Can I please come in?*" The smaller doorman of the two mimicked her words, and then both of them started laughing at her. They weren't as professional as the ones Libby and her encountered before, and it showed. The taller man spoke next, built like a wardrobe with the arms of a blacksmith, Bennett was momentarily trapped in his gorgeous eyes, but she wasn't going to jump him tonight.

"Listen, love, no offence, but there is no way you're coming in this club tonight dressed like that."

The moment was ruined, but she still had to get in. "Please? I need to get inside." She felt the tears trying to make an entrance along her face again and shut her eyes tight.

For just a few minutes, she had to stop playing the victim. She wiped away a single tear, arched her back straight and put her hands in her nightgown pockets, feeling the bag of tablets Sebastian had given her. The queue of clubbers was growing uneasy at the hold-up; this was her last chance.

"Listen, love, you're holding up the queue. You aren't coming in because you look like crap."

Bennett thought fast. "Yet your missus still prefers me on her than you."

"Oooooohhhh!" The crowd behind her threw their hands up in glee, knowing she had just completely done the doorman.

Bennett didn't even look back at the sounds of the queue, she just concentrated her eyes deep into the rude guy on the door. Everybody behind Bennett was still laughing and wailing in hysterics at her quip.

The smaller doorman's face fell as even his colleague was struggling to keep a straight face. "Like I said, you can't come in. Your shoes look like a tramp has tried them on first."

Bennett was getting a stomach of steel just at the right time, she glared at the man.

"If my auntie had balls, she'd be my uncle."

"What?"

"You're stating the obvious, dipshit, telling me something I already know? The shoes are rank, but I'm so hot, men and women will buy me drinks all night; more cash for the club so they can keep you in job. So are you going to let me in or not?"

The people in the queue who heard the conversation were totally enjoying the putdowns to the doorman from Bennett. They laughed at her every word but wanted to get inside themselves. There was a group of lads standing directly behind Bennett, one stood closer to the bouncer, he had a polite grin on his face and perfect skin that hadn't seen a spot in years, and his bright blonde hair distracted Bennett briefly.

"Listen, mate. As far as I know, trainers, smart or not, were still a part of the dress code; we just want to get in, just let her inside, come on, man."

The two doormen spoke quickly as they heard more frustrated groans from the back of the queue.

"Come on, mate."

The smaller doorman frowned and checked the restlessness of the crowd before nodding and removing the velvet rope. She paid her entrance fee with Sebastian's money and hurried inside. The wall of music hit her straight away as she eased past the other clubbers, she would usually head for the bar on a standard night out with Libby, even when they were working as hostesses. That was never going to happen and she had to focus, Bennett looked behind her but it was impossible to pick out anybody she knew in the club. She just wanted to escape and stay safe, just making her way deeper into the club was the best she could do for now. A tap on her shoulder made her swing round with her hand in a fist.

"Hey! Whoa! Take it easy." Bennett's eyes focused in the dark and recognised the man from the queue who stood directly behind her, his hands raised in mock surrender.

"What is your problem?" Bennett snapped. "Sneaking up on me like that."

"Look, I didn't mean to frighten you, just wanted to check to see if you were alright."

Bennett looked at him, unblinking through hollow tired eyes. "I'm fine. Just go away, go back to your mates and leave me alone."

The man wasn't convinced as he studied her pale face and dirty clothes. "Are you sure? You look a mess."

"You don't know me. What's your problem? Is this how you get your kicks? Stalking girls in nightclubs?"

Bennett's raised words were gaining interest from others who weren't dancing, making the guy nervous, but he continued. "Listen, I'm not a creep. You seemed upset outside, that's all, but if you want me to leave you alone, I'll walk away right now."

She gave a condescending smile. "That's the smartest thing you've said all night."

"Fine," he said with purpose. Knowing he was wasting his time, the man turned to walk away.

"Wait!" Bennett suddenly remembered something which could easily save her life, making him face her again.

"What now?"

"I need your phone."

"Wait, so you have a go at me, and then you want to use my phone? You are some kind of special."

Bennett's front was slipping slightly. "Please, I just have to make one call, just one."

The guy eased off as Bennett was shaking in front of him; he reached into his pocket and handed her his phone. "Here you go."

Bennett snatched it from him, dialled three numbers frantically and held it to her ear, only to hear nothing.

She tried again with the same result, so she shoved it back to him. "It's not working."

He looked at the phone and saw who she was trying to call. "You won't get a signal in here. Listen, are you sure you're okay? Are you in some sort of trouble?"

Bennett shot him a look.

"I'm not trying to judge or pry, I'm just honestly trying to help, no tricks or cheesy chat-up lines, it's just me. I'm Milo."

The music was pounding, she just about heard his name but remained silent.

"Listen, let me get you a drink and then if you want to talk about it."

She pointed to her eyes. "I need to use the…"

Milo got it. "Ah, the ladies? Yeah, just down that corridor and turn left."

"Thank you."

Milo just smiled and headed to the bar.

"It's Bennett," she whispered as he walked away out of earshot.

Milo's reassurance helped a bit as she watched him join the others waiting to get served, her sad expression lifted slightly as she headed to the loo. The nightclub was heaving, it wasn't an upmarket club like the venue she worked at. It was a dirty, hard, hellhole with the music cranked up to a 10, but it was packed and that was all Bennett needed to be safe. She made her way to the restroom and splashed some water on her face; it wasn't long ago that she had done the same thing at Sebastian's flat.

When she lifted her head from the sink, her gaze stayed on the mirror in front of her. The pretty face that had started the evening was long gone, girls to either side of her were laughing and giggling about their fun night out as they applied more mascara, talking about who was having an affair and sleeping with their boss. It was too much for Bennett, and she headed into a cubicle and locked the door.

She sat hunched up on the toilet and just listened to the other clubbers come and go.

Closing her eyes, she rested for a little bit. She was due that.

A banging on the door awoke Bennett, and a voice outside was growing louder by the second. "Hello? Are you okay in there? You've been inside for ages."

Her eyes flicked open, shocked that she could have fallen asleep. Bennett was on her feet in an instant as the knocks continued outside. She burst through the toilet door and grabbed the girl by the neck, pinning her against the sink. "What time is it? What time is it?"

The girl shook her head in fear as she struggled to breathe.

"What time is it?" Bennett yelled again.

Struggling in Bennett's grip, the girl slid slowly down to the floor, and her friend came to try and intervene. "Get off her, you crazy bitch!"

Bennett back-slapped her easily and watched as the girl's friend crumpled to the ground. She turned her attention back to the original girl, who was struggling in her grasp. "I'm guessing buses leave every 10 minutes from outside this place. If you don't want to be under the next one, just tell me what is the time?"

"It's 12.30! It's 12.30 in the morning, you psycho!"

"Oh no!" Bennett released the girl and dashed out of the toilets.

Still uneasy on her feet from the sleep, and the music blasts weren't helping, she made her way through the corridor and back to the bar. If she had stayed awake, then she could have been more aware of her surroundings.

Milo was nowhere to be seen, but that was expected and not a concern for her. Anybody would have left by now, even without the hint of hooking up, with the amount of time she had spent in the cubicle. Detaching him from her thoughts, she scanned part of the club for the man in the black car, but there was no sign of him.

She was beginning to think like him. She knew that he wasn't going to let her go or rest tonight, and he was probably in the club now.

Bennett couldn't concentrate. The sounds of the nightclub were getting louder and becoming more of a distraction than she'd thought; she just had to get outside and take her chances on the street again. Even though she had left him at the bar for ages, she could have really done with that drink from Milo. Whatever it was, she would have downed it in an instant. A giant screen above her was showing the entire clubbing night, including the DJ, a beautiful Japanese girl, Hikari, enjoying herself behind her decks, twisting and wriggling in time to her beats set up by a computer, the days of turntables and vinyl were long gone.

She looked at the screen again and just stared at the DJ in her element, turning knobs and waving to the crowd. Bennett wished this would have happened just the day before, and then she could have stayed, could have had fun, but she knew having fun was long gone now, so she pushed further through the clubbers.

She passed another smaller bar and took a quick glance to her left; forcing her eyes open she spotted

Milo chatting to another girl, both holding drinks. His mouth was moving in a happier way than she had ever seen. Bennett stood nonplussed for a moment and walked on.

Milo noticed her over the shoulder of the new girl. "Hold this." He handed the drink to the girl.

"Hey wait!" she called out.

Milo was already upon Bennett; he swung around her front, blocking her way. "Look, I thought you had left, you didn't come back."

Bennett looked at the faint scoffing from the girl holding two drinks at the bar and directed her eyes straight at Milo. "It's fine, we weren't dating or anything. Glad I fell asleep, in all honesty."

Milo grabbed her arms and Bennett instantly shook them off.

"Hey, you left me alone at the bar. What was I supposed to do?"

Bennett was clearly uncomfortable. "I don't care about you, I'm glad you found a new skank to keep you company for the night."

Milo protested. "I waited for you, and you didn't come back. I did nothing wrong. I wasn't going into the toilets to find you. What did you expect me to do?"

She slapped his shoulder with fake approval. "You're full of crap, and I get that, really I do, but here's the thing, like I said, I don't care."

She turned to walk away, and Milo spoke up louder. "I did nothing wrong. You can't blame me for leaving." Bennett gave a hint of curiosity as Milo ranted on. "You know what? I was just trying to be nice."

She didn't notice the figure move slowly behind Milo. It wasn't until he loomed over him that Bennett saw a knife. She stood completely still as the tall man placed the knife firmly into Milo's back. He moaned softly, then collapsed onto the floor. Bennett didn't move as everybody just thought it was just another drunk clubber and carried on dancing. The tall man stepped over Milo's body, and Bennett took a fearful step backwards.

She kept an eye on the tall man as he looked her up with a cracked smile. The girl at the bar grew tired of waiting and holding a pint and a glass of wine. She took a sip from her pint and walked towards Milo lying on the ground, almost tripping on her six-inch heels as she almost forgot to see a step below, shaking her head in disappointment.

"Oh, for god's sake, can't you handle your drink?" The girl placed the drinks on the ground and shook Milo. "If you don't get up, I'm leaving in five minutes."

Bennett was still walking backwards, her eyes not leaving the tall man who now bumped into the girl.

"Excuse me," she said politely, barely heard.

The tall man tenderly placed his hands on her face and rubbed her cheek before twisting her head, snapping her neck instantly and turning to Bennett. "That was a shame; she was a real head-turner."

Bennett wasn't shocked anymore at seeing two dead bodies but unlike the people in the café, the clubbers didn't share her sentiment. Screams now echoed through the club walls louder than the music.

"Now this is a party," the tall man said under his breath.

His knife stayed away now, and he targeted specific people; some he allowed past him, others he broke down in an instant, using his fists and huge feet. Bennett stood still as others scrambled past her.

"Call security!" someone yelled.

The panic grew worse, and it was harder to keep tabs on the tall man, so Bennett turned and ran back into the club, there was a stampede towards the front door, and she knew she would have gotten trampled. Two security guards ran over to the scene and were easily dispatched by the tall man; he wasted no time in splitting one's head open like a grape while the other tried to put his elbow back in place as it was twisted at an unnatural angle by the tall man.

He was flinging the clubbers around as if they were all in a giant wrestling ring. Nobody could stop him.

Bennett noticed a door which led to another dance floor upstairs and made a break for it. Hordes of people were screaming and coming in the opposite direction, desperate to get out as hysteria spread. Reaching the doors, Bennett tugged at them frantically, but they were locked; it was then she saw the sign stating it was closed for refurbishment. "Shit," she cursed.

Looking back at the bar, she saw a door with a 'staff only' sign. With an ability she never knew she had, probably due to adrenaline, Bennett vaulted over the bar top, landing heavily on her injured foot, she yelled in anger more than pain. Two women sat hunched behind it, shaking and now fearful of Bennett. "Where does this go?" Bennett assumed they were both barmaids.

One girl went to open her mouth but covered it immediately with her hand as a bottle smashed above her head; the other girl quickly answered Bennett's question. "It leads to the kitchen."

"Is there a way out through it?"

The girl nodded. "Yeah, out to the streets."

"Then why are you still down here?"

The first girl felt through her hair for glass splinters and whispered angrily, "Because he might see us and kill us."

Bennett looked at her and saw a serious blankness looking back. "If we crouch down, he won't see us," Bennett said.

"He might do."

"I'm not dying behind a bar tonight." Bennett moved on all fours, a relief for her aching foot and gently pushed the door open. The two girls followed her through.

All three girls stood up as they crawled through the doorway.

"Okay, where next?"

Bennett let the girls take over and waited as they ran past her.

"Over here." The redhead shouted. Bennett didn't notice her hair in the dark. She took a few cautious steps forward and then followed them. Running through a maze of ovens and shelves, the trio made it to the kitchen back door. The red-haired girl crashed through it and onto the street; the other barmaid and Bennett were soon behind her.

All three girls ran up the side street, the two barmaids screaming for help. Bennett lagged behind, running on her heel instead. "Wait for me!" she shouted.

The other girls were already far ahead at the top end of the street. She saw a flash of car lights in front of them and stopped dead. A black car stood in their direction, and the girls ran straight towards it. Its engine began to rev as they ran closer, waving their arms in the air for its attention. Bennett's eyes hardened in the dark as she heard the engine grow louder.

"Oh no."

The two barmaids were right in its path, and Bennett knew what was about to follow. "Run!" she screamed to them.

The girls paid no attention to Bennett's cry as they reached the car. They banged on the bonnet and windows, trying to get the driver's attention.

"Move out the way!" Bennett continued to try to get the girls' attention, waving her hand frantically while hopping slowly behind. She lowered her hand to grasp at her side as even limping was now too much for her; she breathed out just simply to catch a little breath.

"Please leave them alone!" Bennett looked at the car flatly, tired and expecting the worst. The car was up to its full revs, and the girls were still banging on its exterior until the engine suddenly died and the car remained still.

"Open the door, please, please help us!" the red-haired girl yelled.

"Don't open the door, you bastard," Bennett said through gritted teeth.

"Come on, let us in!" the other girl implored.

The car didn't move, and Bennett just waited, her mouth tensed as the car was quiet.

"What are you doing, you prick?" she muttered.

The driver released the handbrake, and the car rolled silently past the two squealing barmaids.

"Hey, where are you going?" The girls' arms were raised in annoyance.

The black car continued to gain momentum. The headlights suddenly came on and the engine started.

"Bloody typical." Bennett sighed.

Bennett backed away in her usual position; she had done it all night and was becoming tired more than frightened. Instead of running back into the street, she simply returned to the nightclub kitchen door. There was no handle from the outside; it was a fire door which could only be opened from the inside. "Come on!"

She glanced over her shoulder, and her eyes hardened again. The car was still on its way as she expected, and Bennett turned and limped further down the street; thunder rumbled overhead, making her swear. Looking up before the inevitable rain, Bennett saw a building in the distance and wiped her hand down the back of her neck.

"Follow me then, you bastard," she whispered.

The pain of the tight trainers was beginning to strain on every step, but she made it to the new building, flinging open the doors and looking around. The multi-storey car park should have been closed at this time of night, but the car barriers were open, and no doors were locked. Bennett wasn't sure what she was thinking of by seeking sanctuary in a car park while being chased by a car, but she was running out of ideas and the thought of staying on her feet all night was fast becoming a reality. As Bennett struggled with the stairs, she heard the ominous screech of car tyres racing around the car park; she was already up to level 7 when she heard the car move up ahead of her.

She stopped at the doorway leading on to the next level and waited, just seeing if the car would keep going, it did until even the hard revs became distant. Sitting on the cold concrete steps, Bennett removed the shoe on her injured foot; the dressing was soaked through with blood. Both shoes were doing more harm than good. Prising the other shoe off, she left them off her feet and wriggled her toes; something so simple felt so good after the punishment she had inflicted on them all night.

Glancing at the door, Bennett considered staying in the same spot until the morning.

She had some sleep at Sebastian's flat and in the nightclub toilets, but that wasn't enough. She wanted her own bed, her beautiful king-size bed and Idris Elba to bring her breakfast while she watched *Love Island* on a lazy Sunday morning, but if Idris couldn't get her poached eggs right, he was gone, the perfect poached egg meant more than a man with the sexiest eyes.

Bennett shook her head, she was drifting away, and this was the time to focus. Clenching her teeth, she pressed hard on her foot wound; it made her moan with pain and bang on the concrete floor with her hand, muffling her mouth with the other hand.

The pain was incredible but enough to keep her awake. She hadn't heard the car for a while, not knowing if that was a good thing or not, fighting tiredness was becoming more difficult and she curled herself up into a tighter ball against the wall. Suddenly a door slammed open from one of the lower levels.

"Hello?" Bennett asked and immediately regretted it, obviously giving away her location.

Heavy footsteps followed the door shut and Bennett rose to her bare feet. A male voice quickly followed. "Police!"

As soon as she heard a voice from the emergency services, Bennett's head rolled back in relief; not the tall man but a new stranger. "Hello?"

"Police, we had a call about some disturbances at this address." The voice was young, it had authority but was unthreatening.

"Hello, I'm up here." The wave of relief was still with Bennett as she quickly got to her tired feet. "Please come," she called.

"Are you hurt?" the voice asked.

"I've hurt my foot. I can't walk." Bennett looked over the bannister of the stairwell and saw a beam of light from a torch making its way towards her.

"The paramedics are on their way. Is there anybody else with you?"

"Just me. I'm on my own," Bennett shouted back.

"Would you repeat that, please?"

"I said I'm on my own."

There was a silence which made Bennett's stomach clench. It was like the same silence she encountered a few years ago at Christmas dinner at her uncle's house. The whole family was watching *Top of the Pops* year review when her 13-year-old cousin announced that she was pregnant. Her uncle never said another word for the rest of the day, just sat in his chair, his eyes twitching, while his wife berated their daughter. They never did find out who was the Christmas number 1.

"Hello?" she called again.

The silence stopped. "Ok, stay where you are. I'll be right with you." The voice was concerned.

Bennett looked over the stair balcony. The torch was still zig-zagging its way towards her. She kept her eyes on the light and the heavy footsteps which followed. The steps became faster as they came nearer to her. Bennett cautiously made her way higher up the stairs, the dirt from the floors soon covered her one bare foot and the bandaged one, trying to make an effort not to step in glass again. She trod on something hard and winced with the pain as she pulled out a small stone from her remaining good heel. She was limping now on her last good foot.

The light shone directly in her eyes and blinded her slightly. "Oh." She cleared her throat; there were more nerves in her voice now. "Hello?"

"Almost with you now. Everything is going to be fine."

"Thank you." Bennett's voice tried to sound bright.

"One more thing, miss," the policeman called out.

Bennett swallowed a hard lump in her throat. "Yes?"

"How would you like to die?"

The voice was dirty and firm. It was the tall man at the nightclub. Obviously, he could now add mimicking the voice of policemen to his CV.

"Shit," she spat out.

Running up the stairs, Bennett moved around the edge of the bannisters on each floor, eyes locked on the torch. The light was more steady, the tall man knew where she was and wasn't letting her out of his shining sight.

"What the hell is wrong with you?!" she screamed.

"Just your time. You lasted longer than I'd expected, unlike your friend."

She didn't reply.

"Are you listening to me? You are going to die tonight."

Bennett felt the hairs on her neck rise even more. She continued to run up the stairs and to the next level; before she went to the door leading outside to the car park, Bennett tracked back and looked over the railings. She finally caught his gaze, lifting her eyebrows; there was nothing behind his eyes, just an emptiness. He held his glare and smiled.

The saliva in her mouth would never have reached him, so she just spat it out on the ground and ran back to the final door leading to the car park roof. She ran to the edge and looked over, cars were still driving by, and people were walking past. It was no use shouting for help; she was too high up for anybody to help her, and the only person who tried to ended up dead.

Bennett expected the tall man to come flying through the door that she forgot to shut after her, but there was nothing. Coughing and wheezing with complete tiredness, she took a step back from the edge. The door swung slightly, but there was no sign of the tall man. She pulled her long nightgown cord tight around her waist. There was still a chill in the air, but getting to bed wasn't on her list of priorities at the moment.

Despite the pain from both feet, Bennett made her way around the edge. The only way down was the door and the driveway that the cars would use to enter and exit the levels, and were right next to each other.

There was quite a distance between the top and the next floor down; the door was still open, but if she attempted to go through, she would end up in the arms of the killer. She thought about the drop and leaned forward to take another deep look; it was at least 100 feet down to the bottom. She stood motionless, gazing at the ground as the night wind whipped around her. The nightgown became loose again, and Bennett took both ends to tighten around her waist before a noise behind her made her look. Driving at a snail's pace was a car. Bennett knew it wasn't someone in one of the many cars spread out all around her; she had heard that engine sound all night.

Bennett slowly turned her head to the sound of the motor and then towards the sky.

The moon was still bright as it was from Sebastian's kitchen. She fiddled with her gown again, not even looking behind her. This time, she simply untied her robe and let it hang open, the long belt dropped to the floor, and Bennett picked it up, contemplating what to do next. The car came to a standstill, and the driver's door opened, and the tall man stepped out.

"It's been a long night for both of us," he said. "I just want to get this over with. I trust you can understand that."

"Not really." Her voice was rising. She didn't stray far from the edge but turned around to face him. "You're not going to let me through, are you?"

"You've lasted longer than I'd expected, but yes, I only want you."

"Why me?"

He ignored her question. "Excuse me for just a second." The man held up his finger for Bennett to wait and walked backwards to the car. Keeping his eye on her, he leaned into the driver's side and switched off the engine. "I'm sorry, I was struggling to hear you."

"Why are you doing this to me?"

"If you just accept it, I'll make it as painless as possible."

Bennett couldn't see a different way, feeling the barrier behind her. "I'll jump off right now."

"We both know that's not going to happen. You would have done so earlier in the evening if that was the case; you are strong and resilient." The man's voice was emotionless even though he was praising her. It was as empty as one of the many wine glasses Bennett and

Libby drank at the start of the evening, even if they were meant to be working.

His look was cold and dark; the moon which had illuminated Sebastian's kitchen was still full and gave some light to his features. "You have to die tonight, there are no alternative options, I'm afraid."

Bennett looked over the edge and then back to the man, she started to tremble.

The man saw her fear and inched forward. "You are making this night more difficult, please just accept your fate."

"Drop dead," she said.

"That isn't going to happen to me, I'm afraid. I don't expect you to understand why you have to die."

"Is someone putting you up to this? Are they paying you? I can double it on payday." Bennett felt her head was going to explode with pure rage at the audacity of this man, thinking that she was going to let him kill her, he had tried all night and failed, and she wasn't going to let him finish his task now.

"I'm sorry life started too late for you to enjoy it."

"God, you're annoying. You're like that pubic hair I found in my burger at a fast-food restaurant last week."

They stood in the cold wind, not taking their eyes off each other. The man shook his head slowly, disappointed more than anything. "This is turning into a playground slanging match. We don't have time for these proceedings."

"Proceedings? What, are we in court now, dipshit?" Bennett was looking frustrated. Her words had no effect on the oncoming man who was about to kill her.

"You're stalling, Bennett. This is totally understandable in your current situation, but you'll be gone soon, and by tomorrow, nobody will remember you or this night. But thank you, this has been a most intriguing hunt, and just to make things clear, you should have died before Libby."

Bennett stared at him in silence. "What was that you said?"

The man checked his watch. "English."

Bennett tried to hide her oncoming tears and pulled her nightgown straight in one forceful jerk. "Bastard," she sobbed.

"Life is a bastard, we just have to deal with it, but not for long in your case."

The man continued walking towards Bennett. She looked beyond the railings and back to him as her heart hammered against her flimsy nightgown; barefoot and broken, she wiped her face clean and called out to him.

"You've been chasing me all night in a car, and that's now how you want to finish it? Up close with a knife in my gut? Kind of easy if you ask me. Why not get in your car and run me over like you did with Libby and Sebastian? That's what you do, isn't it? Just kill people for no reason."

"There is always a reason. Are you ready now?"

Bennett answered quickly. "You coming to kill me with a dirty little knife, that's very big of you, dick. Do you get your killer kicks by getting really close to a stunning piece of slice like me? Why won't you get into your little toy car and run me over, you too scared to get up close and personal?" Bennett was finding her flow. "Stabbing people? You stupid prick, that's very manly of you. Knife crime is on the up and you think it's cool to go around shanking people up and—"

Stooping down on the floor, Bennett hoisted the night gown up. "Do you mind? Didn't get the chance to go in the nightclub, fell asleep right away."

Surprisingly, the tall man turned away.

Bennett's eyes relaxed for once as she began to pee on the ground. The stream of urine flowed out of her and made a little zig-zag path through the small weeds on the concrete, she shook her leg as some pee rolled on her foot. "Sorry about that, chuckles. You know you should really smile more, babe." The fear and trembling were slowly beginning to fade. If she was going to die, it was to be with a little more confidence and an empty bladder.

The man slowly nodded and gave a half smile. "This is good, Bennett, you have conquered your fear."

Bennett suddenly got excited and began snapping her fingers above her head. "Wait, I know this one, my brother is the world's biggest nerd, and I know that quote. He made me watch that film every time it was on TV."

She calmed down and breathed in. "It's what Darth Vader said to Luke Skywalker in *The Empire Strikes Back*."

His smile grew. "You have a lonely existence, Bennett, one which will end now."

Bennett went silent for a moment. "Screw you. I'm safe."

The man sneered. "You are not."

The man started walking towards her again. Bennett bent down and collected some stones from the ground, and she threw them at the tall man hoping at least one would slow him down; it was frantic now as none of her throws were having an effect. One finally aimed right and struck him on his right cheek. The man stopped just to wipe the blood from his face. Bennett grabbed some more stones and scrambled to her feet; she had hurt him and wanted to see more blood from the bastard.

"Come on!"

She threw more stones, and the man just smiled as they sailed effortlessly past him. Bennett looked frustrated as her new stones were completely missing the target.

"I'm getting bored of this now, Bennett. You were an unusual case, but I doubt at this point there is not too much to discuss about your upcoming demise."

"You've taken my best friend from me tonight and some nice bloke who just wanted to help me." Gesturing with more stones in her hand, Bennett stepped back and let her back rest on the metal railings.

Her eyes wore an expression of tired confidence.

"Haven't you been listening to me? I'm done with running, done with the hiding, done with being scared."

"What are you saying? Why are you ready for death?" he asked suspiciously, wondering what her game was.

"I'm ready for you now, but not with your knife. You want me? You want to kill me? Then use what you did when you started this pathetic night, run me over like the bastard you are, get in your silly car and finish what you started." Her bravado couldn't stop her fingers from trembling.

The man shook his head in disappointment. "All that determination to stay alive all night, and you throw it away on a whim, you deserve to die quickly."

Bennett looked at him in horrified silence as he continued his forward steps. "Why aren't you getting in your car? I said run me over."

The only interest in his eyes now was to kill Bennett, nothing more. "I drove all night to kill you, only deviated once with my blade in the nightclub. I believe if

I was to step back in my car and drive you down, you'd probably try to run out of the way for cover."

"No." Bennett wiped away a drizzle of tears quickly. "I won't, I swear. I'm just standing here."

"Your obstinance will come to no avail."

"You could run me over in less time than it takes a drunken, recently dumped middle-aged skank to swipe left on your dating app. Just go with it."

"By blade," he said with no smile.

"By car!" Bennett screamed.

He carried on walking, taking a moment to look at the still bright moon.

"Get in your car, just finish it!" Bennett's cries were falling on deaf ears.

The man regarded her with his dark eyes, his pace quickened. Bennett gripped the top of the railings from behind, and before she could close her eyes, he was standing opposite, knife aloft.

"I'm sorry, Bennett."

"I'm not."

She moved her arms down around his waist, tightened her grip on him like an anaconda with its prey, and much like the snake, she twisted her entire body over the building's edge, taking the man with her. Her head went back and crashed against the side of the building as a violent tug on her left leg made her body jolt back.

Gravity detached the man from her grasp, and as he began to plummet, his last view on earth would have been the sight of Bennett swinging slightly in the moonlight; one end of her dressing gown cord was attached to her leg, the other tied to one of the grills on the railing.

She watched as he fell, limbs flailing wildly. The man looked like the bad guy who fell out of the building at the end of the movie *Die Hard*, another one her film-obsessed brother made her watch.

Bennett didn't hear his body land but didn't have time for relief. She just knew that he had probably died on impact, much as she was about to do. Her weight on the cord was making it loosen from her leg. Coughing and still gasping for breath, Bennett looked away from the moon. She could just about make it out over her robe but had seen it through many stages throughout the night, and in all honesty, it was boring her shitless.

The bag of tablets was poking out from her nightgown pocket, ready to fall as well.

It fell before Bennett could catch it, and she watched it follow the man down the side of the car park; she groaned and rolled her eyes, finding it hard to keep them open.

She slowly tried again and realised for the first time tonight that she was alone and nobody was paying attention to her. Despite the pain and hanging upside down, it was a nice feeling knowing that in a few seconds she would disappear out of sight for good.

If only people would stop shouting at her.

"That's great. I think that's a wrap, everybody."

Bennett opened her eyes and saw a team of people looking down at her from the rooftop, holding phones aimed towards her; their bright lights caused more confusion to her. The voice that she heard spoke again, and it was familiar.

"Get every shot you can, people, record and remember."

Bennett's eyes struggled to stay open. She caught a glimpse of a woman looking over the edge past her, their eyes didn't meet, but Bennett felt more frightened than dying at this moment. Libby calmly looked over the edge and spoke into a small radio. "Can we check on the man, please?"

A voice crackled back on her radio. "Yes, he's fine. The drop was a 100 per cent success, zero harm to himself or others."

The tall man in black who had been chasing Bennett all night was lying on a bed of broken cardboard boxes painted black. They were placed all around the car park, so whatever side the tall man toppled from, he would have had boxes breaking the fall; someone had anticipated every outcome. Bennett didn't even notice them when she hobbled into the building earlier.

He was helped to his feet by a group of people holding clipboards, phones and big cameras. One of them, a girl in thick-rimmed glasses and wearing a massive black coat, gave him a drink in a Starbucks cup, still recording his every move. He looked up at Bennett, ballooned out his cheeks, and gave a thumbs up to her. This man had driven into her best friend, crashed into a café and killed people in a nightclub, yet here he was drinking a latte and laughing with what seemed to be a film crew.

What the hell is happening? Bennett thought.

Bennett finally clocked Libby and her dying eyes attempted to rise.

Libby held her position over the edge and made sure Bennett caught her eye.

"Hey, babes, how's it hanging?"

Bennett remained silent; the dressing gown cord was still doing its job.

"Sorry, babes, that line sounded so 90s and cheesy but just had to use it." Libby leaned further over the ledge as she could.

"I'm not going to bullshit you, babes. This is going to take a lot of explaining."

Tears rolled up Bennett's face, and she wiped them off her eyebrows. A streak of lightning shot across the sky, it illuminated Libby's face, and Bennett was still struggling to comprehend what she was seeing. Libby spoke into the radio, and there was movement from the people below, she then gave her full attention to Bennett.

"You love being the queen of social media, always making silly little videos and seeing how many of your followers like them. To be fair, they were funny at first, just you dancing around like an idiot to popular songs, they were cool, but you got more followers, and you had to be more edgy to keep them, so that's when the prank videos started, embarrassing members of the general public and friends who weren't in the know."

Bennett called out to her friend. "Please, Libby, I'm slipping."

"Oh, sorry, I'll crack on. Yeah, so you are very famous online, only that travel writer girl, Molly Holiday, is the most popular blogger in Humberfield, but you are a close second."

"Please, Libby," Bennett begged.

"Hold your horses, I'm getting there. So that secret boyfriend you were seeing for two years, Connor, wasn't it? You kept him away from your family and didn't introduce him to any of your friends, just had Connor as a weekend thing. Hey, that's your decision, and you can do whatever you like. When I asked to see his picture, you told me he wasn't online and didn't like having his picture taken, and I just went with it until you pulled that horrible prank on him. You filmed it and put it online, you embarrassed that poor kid just to get more followers, and it worked; you got the most 'likes' ever in your history by pulling that disgusting trick on him. Good for you."

Libby coughed and cleared her throat.

"Pardon me, where was I? Oh yeah, the online prank video. When I saw it, I was absolutely speechless, left shellshocked because Connor was my cousin."

Libby couldn't quite see if there was a reaction from Bennett.

"By the way, his name is Harvey, not Connor, don't know if that was your idea or his, but that's why I didn't question it. I'm not even sure how you two met, must have been when he came up for a visit to see me, not sure how I didn't notice. Harvey was a jittery little thing, always was, but he was a conspiracy theorist, so you were right about him not having an online profile, he thought the government was out to get him, so he kept himself away from the internet until that video."

Another streak of lighting stopped her for a moment. Libby looked to the sky and carried on.

"For a person who's not on social media, he became quite famous or infamous, people pointing at him and laughing at him on the streets, coming up to him and showing him their phones with the prank. That's what my uncle told me before his funeral. Yeah, he took his own life, he had issues, big life issues, but he was still my cousin and that video you filmed drove him over the edge."

There was still no response from Bennett.

"When I said my parents were in Bournemouth, they were there to support the family as they laid Harvey to rest. I left early to sort this night out. My whole family turned their back on me as they all knew I was your best friend, they thought I should have stopped it, but I never even knew."

Bennett finally broke her silence. "I'm so sorry! I'm so sorry, I didn't know."

"Of course you didn't. It's all about the views, you don't care. So I thought, how could I punish the queen of social media for driving my cousin to take his own life, so this whole night of pain, horror and torment was all down to me."

Bennett tried to gesture. "I saw you die; the car hit you!"

"Did it really? Are you sure you saw what you saw, babes? You forgot that I'm an actor, struggling but still an actor."

"I don't understand."

"You never did really understand this whole night."

Bennett had stopped swaying, so Libby stepped up her explanation. "I gave my family an idea to get you back, something that will try to avenge Harvey. They were all in favour, every single one."

Both women went silent. Libby beckoned to all the people behind her, a wall of phones and cameras were aimed at Bennett, Libby was unfazed and didn't move.

"It took ages to set this up, to hire the locations, the actors."

"Actors?"

Libby heard Bennett whimper again and waved the other people away, talking again into her radio. "Can everybody please shut off their cameras?"

Even though Libby had called time earlier on filming, some others were still capturing events on their phones, this was about to end.

"Thank you, plus you guys were great tonight. I couldn't have done this without you, really appreciate what you gave in this whole night of filming."

"Filming?"

"Yes, babes, this whole night was a film. From the moment we left work to this time now was completely fabricated. The guy chasing us, who was absolutely amazing by the way, the people in the café, which was my favourite bit, waffling on about drugs and shit, the fake café owner, Sebastian, that is his real name, spent ages rehearsing that speech."

"He's not a real doctor?" Bennett moaned.

"Just a tremendous actor, a stunt actor as well, took that crash very well."

"No."

"Yes, that's what actors do, babes, they act, and the nightclub was all part of this special little project, by the way. Do you know how much it costs to hire an entire nightclub and fill it with extras? Everybody involved in this entire night was an actor in a film, I hired streets, supporting artists, so many actors to shit up your night."

"No, there were car crashes, people died, stabbed and throat slits." Bennett's voice was failing.

"You're not grasping the concept of 'acting', are you, babes?"

"I saw you die."

"You've said that already."

"But—"

"Nobody died tonight, not yet. The stabbings, crashes, were all an act; the nightclub, guys and girls, café, none of it was real, and they are all safe and sound; it cost a bloody arm and a leg, but they are safe, unlike you."

Bennett winced at the information. "You are a crazy bitch, Libby."

Libby wasn't pleased, and her confident mood changed. "Shut up! You shut up right now. You don't get to say anything."

"Truth is a bastard when you're obviously insane."

"Do you know that London has the most CCTV cameras in England? Well over 942,500 and growing, I'm sure cities like Birmingham and Manchester are pretty close. We in Humberfield have nowhere in that capacity, but we have enough to be manageable and manipulated, which my team have done, and pretty well, in all honesty."

Bennett's whole body was growing numb, so she spoke quickly. "I don't know what you mean."

"Every camera in the high street played out an image that we wanted you to see, we changed them, fixed them. It cost a lot of money, but the family wanted justice and put up the money for this elaborate stunt. A lot of tech was involved; the cameras have been showing you what we wanted them to show you."

Libby blew out a long breath and looked to one of her assistants in the corner before gathering her thoughts and returning to Bennett.

"Sorry, not a big orator. You saw a very expensive stunt, not sure how you missed it, but I'm wearing a flesh-coloured protective suit under my dress. The car hit me as we rehearsed many times, and we had one shot to get it right, plus the car didn't wheel spin over my head, obviously. We put up a screen after that with the camera, and it was a pig's head and copious amounts of fake blood. Not sure how you didn't see the switch, too busy crying, I guess, and you turned away."

"Why? Yes, I was crying through this whole night. I thought you were dead; that man chased us, chased me. I thought he was going to kill me. Did you know how scared I was? You're sick, Libby!"

"I thought this was what you wanted, to be a big star on social media? You will be after this video goes virile, for all the wrong reasons, crying like a baby, being scared witless and finally, being a complete embarrassment. You said those words when you filmed my cousin and pretty much killed him. Not nice when the shoe is on the other foot."

The dressing gown cord was only just holding. Bennett was silent and looked around her and then made the same approach. "Libby! Please help me up. I'm sorry."

Libby looked out further to the night sky, anticipating another lighting strike and went quiet for a moment.

"The one thing we didn't account for was you flinging that guy off the roof, that was absolutely brutal, and I have to give you credit for that. The thing is, he was meant to rush at you, and then you both fall off the top of the car park and land on strategically placed boxes on the ground. You're alive, put on social media, and the joke's on you, but then you pulled out that amazing nightgown cord trick; nobody saw that coming, that was amazing."

Even hanging upside down from a multi-storey car park, Bennett could tell that Libby's eyes weren't interested in her and thinking of something else. She slowly pulled at her ear and then took time to look back at her.

"However, if you were to die during filming, imagine how popular you'd be in death. You would be an internet sensation."

"You'll be going to prison for my murder."

"Actually, no. All the actors and make-up artists signed non-disclosure agreement contracts, and my research team and location scouts made sure every CCTV camera was out of action. All people will see is you being chased by a man who has now disappeared; you've got nothing on me."

"Please! I don't want to die. Help me, Libby, we're friends."

"Blood is thicker than water, babes."

"Don't do this, Libby. Please help me."

An idea took Libby completely by surprise. "There's a lorry down below. It's got a flat-bed trailer filled with cardboard boxes which would save you. It's pulled away now but I can easily radio down below to my team and get it back in place."

Libby pulled out her radio and threw it over the edge, it whistled past Bennett.

"If I can make it down from the top of this multi-storey car park before you fall, I'll get the lorry put under you, and you'll be alive."

Bennett's eyes locked hard onto Libby's. "I don't want to die!"

"You'd be famous."

"Please, Libby."

The dressing gown cord was giving way. Libby suppressed a smile.

"I'm on my way."

"God, please, hurry up. I can't hold on for much longer."

Libby simply listened, nodding her head and shivering slightly in the night cold.

"Goodbye, Bennett."

Bennett changed. If she was to die, it was in complete defiance to her former friend.

"Go to hell, Libby."

"Oh, after what I did tonight, I know I'm going. I'll save you a seat when I get there."

She left Bennett hanging and left the top of the car park, heading towards the lifts to take her to the ground level.

The lift door opened, and an elderly couple walked out, looking for their car.

"Are you getting in?" the gentleman asked Libby.

Watching a rat scurry past one of the exit doors, she took out a cigarette and put it to her lighter, watching the flame burn through it. Looking behind her, she turned back and gave a pleasant smile to the couple.

"No thank you, I'll take the stairs."

Targets

Robert Duncan

11 Douglas Drive

Hoffstead

Humberfield

"For Christ's sake!"

Pulling out the Lego piece embedded in his bare foot, Robert Duncan held the toy up and shook it in front of his daughter. "How many times have I told you not to leave your pissing toys out on the floor!"

"Don't swear at her!" his wife shouted from the kitchen as she prepared breakfast.

"She doesn't listen to anything I say. I've told her a million times about leaving her toys everywhere."

A blonde head popped itself around the corner of the kitchen. "I told you about using that language in front of our daughter."

The tone of his wife's voice would have been enough for him to stop soon, but he caught her glare, and that pretty much silenced him straight away.

"Look, I know this case at work is getting you down, but there's no way you should be taking it out on her."

His daughter, Thea, looked up from watching videos on her tablet, and her brother sat on the sofa next to her, engrossed with his own tablet.

"It's not my Lego, it's Jake's."

Her brother immediately took offence. "No it's not!"

"Yes it is."

Robert's scowl returned. "I don't care whose it is, I don't want to see it on the floor. Do I make myself clear?"

"It wasn't me," Thea protested.

"That's enough!" her dad barked.

His wife appeared again through the doorway. "Can I speak with you for a moment?"

For a split second, Robert hesitated; both his kids stared at him until he finally left for the kitchen.

He walked in, concentrating on the illusion that everything was still fine with his wife, but she was at him straight away.

"Why can't you just leave her alone for five minutes."

"It's called parenting. You should try it sometime."

Beth stopped preparing the kid's lunches, this was something she didn't want to attempt to multi-task at. "Don't you dare go there. Do you know what I do every day for the children?"

"No, but I'm sure you're going to make me late by telling me."

"Thea is growing up fast and very sensitive."

"So I can't tell her off because I might hurt her feelings? What kind of shit is that?"

"I told you about the language."

"What, you think making a few sandwiches and taking the kids out after school makes you a good mum? I'm busting a gut at work and trying to bring bread home for this family, and you're making me out to be the bad guy? Take a look at yourself, Beth, you're no saint."

Another woman came into the room. She was much younger and prettier than Beth, who knew it from day one the girl began working as an au pair. She wore the tightest grey jeans, which looked like they had been spray painted on her body, and a white t-shirt which had never touched a speck of dirt.

"Jesus," Beth muttered under her breath.

"I can help with the breakfast if you like?" Her voice was quiet but extremely cute.

"Thank you, but I can handle this, Daniela."

Beth squeezed her eyes at her beautiful au pair. The doorbell rang, and Daniela went to answer it.

"You can get the kids from trampoline world later, though," Beth said as Daniela gripped the handle.

As soon as Daniela opened the front door, she was dead. The bullet struck her forehead at point-blank range before she had time to react. The killer was dressed as a refuse collector, head to toe in a bright orange hi-visibility outfit.

Putting the pistol back in one of the huge pockets in his side, he picked up a package from the front door mat, stepped over the body and pulled Daniela further inside out of sight, closing the door behind him. It was rubbish collection day on the street, and the killer blended in with the other refuse collectors.

Another man picked up the rubbish bags placed by the family's front gate and threw them with perfect aim into the back of the bin lorry which was reversing up the street.

He walked away from the driveway, unaware of what was happening inside, the loud reversing beeps of the lorry made sure he didn't hear what was to follow in the house.

"Who is it, Daniela? Was it my parcel? Glad they knocked this time instead of leaving it outside."

The man walked through the hall and stood in the living room. The children looked at him and slowly put down their tablets, both looking at the kitchen for their dad to come out.

"Daniela!" Robert called again and came back out from the kitchen only to face the man in his house.

"I believe this package is yours." The man threw the parcel at Robert.

"Also, I'm afraid that Daniela isn't around anymore. I would keep the children and your wife…"

The man's voice trailed off, and he stared hard at Beth. "My goodness, I have seen you in so many photos, but it is intriguing to see you in the flesh."

He walked forward to approach Beth. "My father wasn't the best when it came to raising me. I mean, when he has you as a lookout when he robs a jewellery store at eight years old, you pretty much know a normal childhood isn't really going to plan. However, with all his faults, the one thing he did say, which I always remembered and took on board as a good thing, was—"

Before he finished his sentence, the man took out a handkerchief, spun Beth around and placed it over her nose and mouth, chloroform was on the material, and Beth's eyes rolled back into their sockets before she collapsed on the ground unconscious.

"Mum!" both the kids screamed.

"To never strike a woman. Drugging, robbing and killing, however, are a different kettle of fish."

Robert stared at the man, swallowing hard. He patted his thighs slowly and then looked to the kids, trying to remain calm. "Go to your rooms."

The man took the gun out of his pocket and waved it in front of everyone.

"Robert, you don't mind if I call you that? Normally I would refer to you as Detective Inspector McCabe, as you know, but I think we have enough shared history for us to be on first-name terms."

"I said go to your rooms now!" Robert repeated.

"Stay exactly where you are," the man said firmly.

The children only moved their eyes to Robert and nothing else.

"Good, I'm not going to repeat that order again."

"What do you want from us?"

"From them, your kids? Nothing, I believe they've seen what I'm capable of."

Robert looked at Beth on the floor, his eyes glistened slightly, but then he turned slowly and clenched them tight, knowing a single tear shown would frighten the children. The movement from the gun in the man's hand still had the children's attention.

"What we are going to do is remain right here while I explain exactly what is going to happen."

"What can I do about Beth?" Robert asked.

"What was on that handkerchief would knock a horse out for hours; she isn't going anywhere."

"Please, just let my kids go."

The man pointed the gun at Robert. "I have no quarrel with your children, Robert, but they must stay exactly where they are to watch how the stringent rigours of life can affect the minds of the young."

"What do you want?" Robert's tone was heading downwards.

"I expect you think I've finally gone insane after all these years, it's obvious you and I have a unique connection, but it's time to draw an end, a conclusion, to our long-standing association."

Robert kept an eye on his children. "Not sure about our connection, but you were spot on about you being insane."

The man didn't look convinced. "I must have missed that diagnosis, being behind bars at Her Majesty's pleasure due to your evanescent evidence."

The man stopped and rolled his neck around, trying to make it click. "I do like those guns you have mounted on the wall in the hallway, odd location, though. I would have put them in the living room, a more prominent spot." The man turned back to Robert.

"What do you think you did wrong in our long-standing relationship, Robert?"

"I tried to save you, Cameron."

"That was your mistake, my old friend, people like me are beyond help, beyond redemption."

Cameron looked at the frightened children. "I apologise for what I did to your children's future. It's tainted now and off on a different track, thanks to me, that is the biggest misfortune due to my actions."

Robert swung a look at his kids, Beth, then kept his eyes focused on Cameron. "Whatever you're planning, don't. I have a family."

"Everyone does; that excuse doesn't work anymore." Cameron rubbed his throat and pulled at his neck. "Do you mind if I have a glass of water?"

"Are you sure you don't want tea?"

"Tea?"

"Yeah, leaf-based drink often served with milk."

"Water will suffice, easier to prepare so I can keep an eye on your moves, cumbersome at most."

Robert's nerves were on edge, but he nodded his approval as Cameron headed to the kitchen.

"You're probably wondering how I found your address. Well, I managed to obtain the information from one of your corrupt former colleagues from our stay in prison. He was initially reluctant to give me any information on your whereabouts, but garden secateurs always come in handy to jog someone's memory."

Robert handed a glass of water to Cameron cautiously.

"So to cut a long story short, or a long finger, I'm here on your doorstep."

Robert stared at Cameron, head half-cocked.

"I heard you are standing down from your policing duties, early retirement, I hear."

"You heard right."

"I'm afraid I cannot allow you to do that. The fact that everything we've been through, every decision we were working for, which made us the men who stand in these spots, you are willing to throw away just so you can spend the rest of your well-paid days with your feet up watching daytime quiz shows, I can't allow it."

"What are you talking about? You're a criminal, a murderer, a complete bastard."

Cameron sipped at his water slowly.

"Yes, you were there on every step of my descent to the creature I am today. You were the detective, the one who wanted to make the world a better place without me."

Robert was beginning to grow more agitated; the children huddled closer together.

"So I cannot allow you to step down with your duties; much like Batman and the Joker, one can't exist without the other. While I'm out from prison, I need you to put me back, that's the game we've played for so many years. I need you as much as you need me."

Robert opened his mouth slowly in shock to respond. "You're insane."

"I know."

"You're going back to prison."

"I know."

Cameron put his glass of water down and wiped his mouth tidily. "We only have so many heartbeats – make the most of them."

"What? We have over three billion heartbeats in life, so what are you talking about?"

"Ah, yes, sorry, saw a post on a popular social media site from a girl called Melyssa, seemed interesting at the time."

He shrugged.

"That's how we've run this race for many years. I commit a crime, you catch me, and I go to prison. I escape, commit another crime, and you catch me again; that is how our wheels of connection roll, but put a brick beneath it, and the wheels come off."

Cameron paused, Robert waved his hand eagerly for him to continue.

"It hasn't been easy, constantly being trailed by your good self, time and time again, but it has been worth it. Since I have taken a step back from my usual misdemeanours, you have grown bored, hence why you leaving is the brick in our relationship. That is something I cannot allow."

"What the hell are you talking about?" He moved closer to Cameron, knowing his kids were out of earshot. "You've killed Daniela, knocked my wife out, come into my house and threatened my kids. What makes you think I shouldn't break you where you stand."

Cameron pulled out a phone. He took a look at the children before checking the phone's contents, then whispered towards Robert. "Well, it seems, looking at these pictures, you and Daniela were closer than just au pair and employer, and the fact that your wife was packing to stay with her sister, whom she hates, confirms that."

Robert wasn't going to ask how Cameron knew about his affair with Daniela; he obviously had found his address with ease.

Cameron fooled around with his gun in front of the children, like a birthday clown with balloons. Beth was still out cold.

"I know that she knew, that you knew, that she knew you were having an affair."

Robert's hate and fear rolled into one.

"You can charm the birds off the trees, Robert. Your teeth look like they have been knocked out and put back in the wrong way but you always had a way with words, and I'm assuming adding confidence with this is how you got Daniela to sleep with you. It's apparently what women want. I do hope you didn't threaten her about her job?"

"What does it matter? You've killed her."

Cameron puffed lazily. "I think I was a little premature in doing so. She may have been a victim as well, another target for you, unfortunately."

"You won't get away with this."

"I don't intend to. What we went through was outstanding as predator and prey. Which one was I? Who knows? Either way, I cannot let you retire."

"This is dangerous talk, Cameron."

"I'm not joking."

Cameron eyed up the two shotguns hanging on the wall, which grabbed his attention.

"Billions of people in the world, and we trundle through life just trying to find one soulmate. You obviously thought you had found yours with Beth, but your entanglements with the late Daniela suggest otherwise."

Curiosity got the best of Cameron, and he walked towards the shotguns and gently lifted one down with one hand, turning his back on Robert and the children.

"Please don't try any heroics, Robert, and please listen. To try and find someone who is your complete partner in the time we have is hard; it's like looking for a needle in a haystack when you don't know what a needle looks like."

"Get out of my house now, Cameron."

"Not until I have said what I came here to say."

Robert shook his head in anger and disgust. "I think you've said and done enough, Cameron."

Cameron turned around. He had placed his handgun on the floor and was now pointing Robert's own gun at him. "I bet you hunt with these rifles, Robert. I bet you take one down, jump into your SUV and head up to a forest somewhere and find something to track, your target, a defenceless animal much like Daniela. She literally was like a deer caught in your headlights, the headlights being a tired, middle-aged lothario."

"Have you finished, Cameron?"

"Soon. So I'm assuming when you made your kill in the forest, you enjoyed the experience of being in command of the hunt, you came home, put the gun back on the wall, waited, and then with pure arrogance, took it down a few weeks later to hunt again because you became a circle. And that's why we are so alike."

"I'm nothing like you," Robert said with a dry throat.

"No, I'm afraid you are, my friend. Beth was planning to leave, but your plan was to still take the gun down and go hunting at some stage; it's in your nature to find new targets."

Robert had no response for once.

"We both wear the smile of the devil, Robert, and I could be more horrible to you if I spoke about how Daniela wasn't your only target throughout your pretence of a marriage, but your children will have to listen and deal with your lies in their own time and not mine.

"You travelled the length and breadth of the UK and the world to bring me back to prison on so many occasions, and on my every escape from incarceration, you doubled your efforts to bring me back. I know you and I have not always seen eye to eye, but you know I have always admired your tenacity and dedication to the job even though it was a cost to me."

Cameron's gun arm didn't quiver and held firm.

"I need you to keep playing our game, Robert. You are my soulmate, not Beth or Daniela. We are connected in pain and misery, we need each other to enjoy our pity and patience. In life, your direction is more important than your speed."

Robert knew he had to keep Cameron talking if he was ever going to get his family to safety.

"What? You want me to keep working because you're bored? Go to hell, Cameron. Listen, you're free to rob, murder and do whatever you want, but I'm out, I'm done, I'm happy not chasing you anymore."

"Bit of a cop-out, my old friend. You weren't happy with Beth, but the satisfaction you got in life, the thrill of the chase wasn't with Daniela, it was tracking me, and if you end that, then I will end you."

He cocked the trigger of the gun, and Robert pulled his children closer; they were whimpering and stayed close to their dad.

"I hope your family understand the ramifications of your actions, Robert. But if you won't continue working with me, then it's time to end our association once and for all. I wasn't born a liar or a cheat, but I learned those skills in life from you."

Cameron steadied his arm and moved the gun closer to the family to aim.

"I'm sorry, children, but your father bought this on himself."

He cocked his head. The family screamed as Cameron pulled the trigger, Robert's eyes shut in failure. The loud bang was expected, but Robert was surprised that he was still alive as his eyes opened.

On the floor was Cameron's body, part of his head was burnt, his eyes were now black but wide open. Robert cautiously walked over, ignoring his children's protests. He stooped down over Cameron's body. He was dead, but Robert wanted to know how. Robert's lips twitched as he inspected the still smoking shotgun.

Thea left her brother and walked up to her dad. "Please can we go now, Daddy?"

"Not yet." He glanced at his daughter holding her brother and shook his head. "Stay there."

Robert picked up the gun and checked the muzzle and then the barrel. He gasped out loud when he saw what was inside, taking a step back in shock.

Swinging the gun back to Thea, he pointed to the barrel. "What is this?"

The barrel was filled with broken bits of Lego. Robert held the broken pieces in his hand and waved them in front of Thea. "Did you do this?"

Thea kept hold of her brother, and they both ran to Beth.

Kneeling down over their mum, they rubbed and shook her to get up.

Robert paused and leaned forward.

"I said—"

Thea stopped him immediately.

"It was meant for you."

The Lemonade Parrot

Soma Tilby
14 Blissworth Avenue
Robinsview
Humberfield

"You're wasting my time."

"I'm sorry?"

"This clearly isn't working."

The man stood up from the pub garden table and was about to leave before turning back to the woman sitting opposite.

"Oh yeah, there was just one more thing you should know."

The woman was genuinely shocked but spoke a soft reply. "What?"

"I'll let your next failed date tell you."

He tucked his chair in and tried to get the attention of the waitress who had taken their orders throughout the evening. She caught his agitated smile before his intense arm-waving and walked over.

"Is everything okay with your food?" she asked.

He pointed to the empty plates, and she took his sarcasm easily.

"Good sign. Is there anything else I could get for you?" she asked but already knew the answer.

"No thank you. I just remembered there's somewhere else I want to be."

Quickly pulling out his wallet, he laid a handful of bank notes on the table.

"Thanks for the food, and keep the change."

The well-dressed man turned to his seated companion. "Have a splendid life."

He walked away without even taking a glance behind him.

Soma Tilby didn't even bother to look up as he left. She simply poured some wine into her large glass.

The waitress took the money from Soma's date and checked on her, still doing her job but genuinely concerned. "How you doing?"

Soma took a quick swig. "It was never going to work out anyway, he likes marmite on his chips and I prefer a bit of salt and vinegar."

"That's pretty gross but not a deal breaker."

"He also thinks that *Game Of Thrones* is based on a true story."

"Don't they have dragons in it?"

"Dinosaurs, he thinks."

"Ah, okay." The waitress politely smiled as she collected the plates, not knowing exactly what to say next.

Soma carried on instead, enjoying her wine more than her previous company. "Still, you know what they say, combine wine and dinner, and what is the new word?"

The waitress thought hard, looking at the plates as her tongue eased out and stayed by the side of her mouth to help her think. She shrugged. "Is it winner?"

Soma drank some more.

"Every time."

* * *

Tasane Graham took a bite out of her chicken and avocado sandwich. It was shop-bought and the chicken was dry. For once it was a nice day with a bit of sun, so sitting outside a pub was a good option. She took the meat out of the sandwich and dipped a piece in her glass of Pinot Grigio. Covering the whole chicken with wine, she placed the piece into her mouth and chewed it slowly, her eyes rolled in delight. She would have dipped the whole sandwich in the wine, but the look of disgust from her best friend, Soma, made her question her action.

"You didn't buy that sandwich from here; you aren't meant to bring your own food."

Tasane completely ignored her. "Did you really feel like you wanted to kill yourself after this last date?"

Soma paused as Tasane finished her chicken. "He just wasn't for me."

Tasane picked some chicken from her teeth. "Why not? I saw his dating profile on your phone, young, hot and definitely one to take home."

"Just wasn't my type."

"You've had quite a few of these recently. Not happening for you, is it."

"You're doing it again."

A shrug came from Tasane. "No idea what you mean, babes."

"That tone of voice, you use it all the time when I have a bad date."

"This is how I always speak. How many bad dates have you had then? Lost count."

"It's like you are rolling your eyes at me all the time."

Excusing herself, Tasane reached over to the opposite empty table and grabbed a sachet of tomato sauce from the condiments tray. She shook it gently and tore it open, spreading it on her avocado sandwich.

"I always treat my dates right, I don't take the piss, I respect them and listen to whatever they have to say. I dress well and look gorgeous anyway and make them think that when they're on this one date night with me, they are my number one priority."

The avocado was covered in ketchup, and Tasane took delight in putting it into her mouth. "I've got the perfect man for you. He's my hairdresser's cousin, Nicolas."

"You've already set us up."

Tasane was intrigued. "Did I?"

"Yes, he's the one who brought his own crisps to the restaurant."

"What's wrong with that?"

"He ate them with a spoon."

Tasane giggled.

"Okay, what about that guy, Harrison, I think?"

"No, he kept talking about the history of roundabouts."

"Dull, but not a deal breaker."

"In his sleep."

"Oh."

"Nothing even happened with us. As soon as he mentioned the Magic Roundabout in Swindon and wouldn't shut up, I slept on the couch."

"You are hard work sometimes."

Soma could feel her eyes widening as Tasane carried on.

"Listen, if I'm on a date and they start stuttering with nerves, then they are out the door. Don't get me wrong, I'll be polite on social media if I remember you, but you will never see me again unless I want some furniture moved. That's the only reason I've got over a thousand friends on social media; most of them are failed dates. However, if they're confident on our date, then it's obvious I'm going to sleep with them, but if they mess up or cheat on me, they will never see my sweet goods again. I enjoy sex and for the people who like that, it's cool."

Embarrassed, Soma looked around for imaginary support from other tables as Tasane continued. "You are gorgeous and clever, you'll find the one you're looking for, plus you have hair to die for."

"Is that a big thing?"

"You'll be surprised about people who like that colour."

Soma's glass was now empty, as was the bottle on the table. Tasane didn't offer to get another bottle, so it was down to Soma to wave down one of the bar staff to get another.

"You've got this whole dating thing worked out, haven't you?"

Tasane grinned at her friend.

"I know what I want, babes. Life is too short for an avocado sandwich without ketchup."

* * *

"So Desdemona was the wife of Othello, and Esmerelda was the girl from *The Hunchback of Notre Dame*, is that right?"

"Yes, do keep up."

Soma's eyes narrowed at her new date. If she knew he would have been so condescending, then there was no way she would have agreed to go out with him. She nibbled on a piece of grilled chicken breast and watched with revulsion as he slurped on his soup starter.

"Do you know his name?"

She stopped chewing. "The hunchback?"

"Yep."

Soma surreptitiously looked at the passers-by walking past outside the restaurant, wishing that at least one of them would swap places with her or at least her date.

"Quasimodo?"

He clapped sarcastically. "Well done. Did you read the book by Victor Hugo?"

"No, watched the film by Disney."

Soma sipped her gin and tonic, silently waiting for a response. She tried to clear her head instantly and fell back into her usual first-date checklist.

"So what's your keep fit routine then? Would love to know."

The guy looked at his watch, ignoring her completely. "Listen, let's bin this food. I've got my car around the corner. We'll drive away, park somewhere secluded and then you can do me."

The tension wasn't defused. Soma put her glass down. "Excuse me?"

"Look, I haven't got long in this window. We're both adults, let's just get this over with, shall we?"

"Are you for real?" Soma's voice rose.

"It's obvious we won't see each other again. We don't get on, we have nothing in common, at least we can get something from this."

She rolled her eyes in dismay. "Oh, for god's sake."

"What did you think was going to happen? After the first five minutes you knew this date was going to be rubbish and dull, but you stayed, why? I'll give you credit for not having one of your mates ring to get you out of it. I'm not the date you wanted, I'm not a knight in shining armour, I'm just a guy who doesn't want to waste time and knows when things aren't going anyway, so we both may as well get at least something from this horror show."

"You're unbelievable," Soma said.

He slurped again on his soup. "But you know I'm right."

An uncomfortable silence grew between them. Soma quickly finished her gin and tonic and stood up abruptly.

"Where are you parked?"

* * *

Tasane thanked the waiter for taking their food orders. It was yet another new restaurant Soma had found on her app. She had trouble finding the right one with dating but had no problem finding somewhere new to eat. This current place so far had her seal of approval.

"This is becoming a bad habit, babes."

"Does it bother you? Listening to my dating dilemmas."

Tasane yawned, not intentionally, it just happened as soon as Soma spoke.

"Not you, babe, just tired. I was with my main man this morning, and my new girl did her job in the afternoon."

Soma hesitated and bit her lip. "Is that why you were late?"

Tasane just gave a baby smile.

Soma gave a usual eye roll, so Tasane topped up their glasses with wine. She took a long drink and carefully wiped her mouth and stared at Soma.

"What are you looking at? You always make me nervous when you look at me like that."

"You know what? You are like a lemonade parrot."

"I beg your pardon?"

Tasane swivelled round to check out one of the bar staff she'd had her eye on and back to Soma. "Your dating life, it's like a lemonade parrot."

Soma rushed her on. "You said that, but what do you mean?"

"Lemonade has been around for years. It's always been a drink which isn't fancy or in your face like Pepsi or Cola; it's bland, will always be there, but ultimately is boring and forgettable."

Soma shook her head. "Not sure if I like where this is going."

"Parrots repeat any sounds they hear. It's called mimicry, I think?"

Soma looked surprised.

"I have a nature programme on in the background while I'm with my Sunday man."

Tasane was loving her wine and drank more. "Anyway, parrots, they imitate things and repeat whatever they hear, again and again, and again."

"Is this going somewhere?"

"Well, that's you, with every date you go on. Listen, I love you, but maybe when it comes to dating, maybe you are lemonade, stand out and be a Coke or Pepsi and stop repeating the same conversations you have on every date. Don't go through the motions and repeat the same stuff all the time, you're better than that, babes. Be a challenge, don't agree with everything they say, and then you'll find the right one."

Tasane gestured at a girl who was carrying a bucket of white wine from the bar, she assumed it was for her table and made space.

Soma gave an earnest look to her friend. "You are so wrong."

Tasane thanked the girl from the bar as she carefully placed the wine bucket on the table. "I'm so fucking right."

* * *

"So my earliest memory was my dad taking me to his girlfriend's house while my mum was working nights."

Soma gave a nervous laugh as her new date looked anywhere but into her eyes.

"Sorry, not a great start for a first date."

She looked at him and nodded with a smile between her teeth. "I've actually heard worse."

"Really? On a first date?"

Soma just nodded.

"Okay, gives me some reassurance."

"Can I ask what?"

She shook her head. "Best not."

The conversation went silent, and for once, Soma was struggling. She realised her date was really thinking hard for something to say. She sipped on her wine and waited as her date still shook his head in disappointment. He quickly shot in with a question which she had heard before, countless times.

"So what are you looking for in life?"

"To be more shallow maybe?"

The date didn't know how to react.

Music playing from inside the restaurant made Soma leave her seat outside, it was very lucky to have a mild evening at this time of the year, but the temperature was starting to dip. Not forgetting her wine, she headed through the front door and drifted nimbly between the seats of the diners inside.

The music was perfect and so was her chance. Controlling her nervous breathing, Soma slowly started to move to the rhythm of the beat. She felt the eyes of everyone at the tables bearing down on her, which made her sway even more. Soma's confidence grew, and she began to sing the lyrics of the song.

Her date had gingerly followed her inside, and she caught him with a grin on his face watching her sing and dance. She beckoned to him while wriggling her hips, making him laugh and not the nervous laughter from earlier, Soma was genuinely making him more relaxed.

He exhaled heavily and surprised her and himself by joining in on the singing. Not knowing the words completely, his voice wasn't as loud as Soma's, but the effort was appreciated by her. His confidence grew as Soma continued to sing and took his hand, swinging it like they were already a happy couple. The song finished, and a few of the diners clapped happily at them while others were glad the show-offs had finished.

Soma kept hold of her date's hand.

"Come home," she said.

He went.

* * *

The next morning, Soma woke up and immediately reached for her phone on her bedside table. There were messages from Tasane asking how last night's date went.

Soma replied quickly. *Think I've found the one.*

She put the phone back on the side and turned over. Her date lay next to her. Soma leaned over and kissed his bare shoulder. She was happy again, she could feel it this time; things could only get better from here.

Peering over him, Soma noticed the vomit stains on the pillow and on the floor. That wasn't a problem; sick was easier to clean up than blood.

Her date was shivering, and his body was full of sweat. "Help me," he mumbled.

"Of course I will. You're the one."

Soma kissed his back tenderly; the sweat didn't bother her. The drugs she put in his nightcap drink of wine last night had done their job.

"I'm so glad I finally found you, I've been trying to chase happiness, but it keeps slipping through my fingers."

"Please get help." Her date was terrified.

"Don't be silly. I've been looking for you for ages."

Soma turned her date over and straddled him, looking deep into his frightened eyes.

"It's obvious we were meant to find each other. You have no idea how long I was trying to find you."

Her date projectile vomited all over her; she didn't even try to avoid it.

"That's okay, it's fine. I don't mind now that I've found you. You're the one."

She reached into her pillowcase and pulled out a plastic bag, flipping it open.

His eyes froze in fear, and he shook his head in absolute terror. He cried out for God to help.

Soma calmly slipped the bag over her date's head and tightened her grip. He thrashed around wildly, but Soma kept her hold firm.

Her date found it strange the night before that she had kept so many newspaper clippings about a spate of murders in the area, but he kept quiet as he didn't want to spoil the evening.

It was too late for her date anyway.

Nobody was coming to help him. Nobody would ever hear him sing again.

Silent Treatment

Melyssa Woodman
36 Harriet Drive
Greywood
Humberfield

"Why would you think I started taking sugar?"

Kiya stared at the girl sitting cross-legged on her couch. She was still fixated with the view, beautiful hair and ivory skin, almost as white as her blouse covered by a black jacket, which was only spoilt by the grimace on her face as she removed a cup of tea from her lips.

"Sorry, I could have sworn you—" Kiya stopped. "You sure you don't?"

The girl scrunched her mouth up and simply nodded.

Kiya went to take the cup from her, and she shooed her away. "It's fine, don't worry."

The girl strained another sip and placed the cup on a table beside her chair.

Kiya sat opposite the girl on the couch who was looking nervous at everything around her. Watching as the girl played with her long hair and crossed one leg over the other – she didn't remove her high heels, so

Kiya knew she wouldn't be staying for long – she tried to get over the awkward silence quickly.

"Your nails look lovely."

"Thank you." Her reply was quick and polite.

The girl was never comfortable with compliments from Kiya, so that part of her hadn't changed, but she was still so lovely even when she deliberately failed to make eye contact. She was falling for the girl again; her lips and hips were pulling her in.

Kiya breathed hard and mirrored her look to the floor, allowing the girl, Melyssa, her love, to speak next.

"How's work?"

Her eyes flicked back up at Melyssa.

"Yeah, all good, thanks."

"Anything interesting on the horizon?"

"Um, yeah, got some good projects coming up. It's looking really promising."

"Coolio."

Melyssa's brick path of a voice softened, and jerked a smile. "Sorry, I know how you hate me saying that."

"We're not together anymore, so you can say what you want." Kiya's voice had a slight sting.

"I'm just being polite," Melyssa sighed.

"Well, don't. You never cared about my work when we were together so why start now?"

Melyssa tried another attempt at the tea and waited for Kiya to calm down.

"What do you want?" Kiya needed to focus on her ex as she asked the question.

"We have to talk about the rest of my stuff."

"You want to talk about it, you mean."

"I just wanted to ask you when was the best time I could come and collect them?"

Kiya remained absolutely still as now her ex-girlfriend showed signs of uneasiness.

"You could have just messaged me. Why did you come here?"

"I came to see if you were alright."

She studied Kiya fully this time, looking at her messy black hair and the *Jurassic Park* T-shirt she had bought her for Christmas a few years ago. Kiya was so difficult to buy for, but anything film or nerd-related, Melyssa knew she would like, with the condition that Kiya could only wear it inside the flat and not out when they were together.

The flat was a mess, Kiya never was one for keeping anything tidy, but she was hoarding so much rubbish, pizza boxes and wine bottles littered their once lovely flat, plus she stunk. Melyssa used to love having lazy Sundays together in bed with her love, snuggling up watching *Friends* box sets, but now she didn't want Kiya anywhere near her.

"Ease your guilty conscience, you mean."

Melyssa rose from her chair and pulled at her skirt, brushing crumbs off the back. "Fine, I've still got a key, I'll just come when you're not in."

Kiya waved her down. "No, please, sorry, head's all over the place at the moment."

"Yeah, I know and I'm sorry." Melyssa looked around at the place she used to call home. "This place is a mess now, Kiya."

"Move back in then; nobody cleans a kitchen like you."

"Nobody cleans the kitchen except me, bit of a difference."

She couldn't help but give Melyssa her first smile of the visit.

"It's obvious you aren't eating right, Kiya."

"I put stuff in my mouth and chew, not hard to get wrong, but then again the thought of you sleeping with your boss did make me want to throw up a few times."

Melyssa grabbed her bag in anger. "Forget it, just forget it."

"Well, what did you want me to say? You're sleeping with your boss and living with him. Can't you see how that is unprofessional and just plain creepy? He's about 50."

"He's 40."

"Well, that makes it so much better."

"You're a real arsehole, Kiya."

"Me? You have an affair and I'm the bad guy?"

"It wasn't like that."

"No? Tell me, I'm curious."

Melyssa stared at the lounge windows, the ground-in dirt had really caught her attention until she remembered Kiya's question. "We just kind of, sort of, fell in love."

"Was that before you kind of, sort of, fell on top of him?" Kiya could see her edging slowly towards the front door. "No, wait, don't go. It's just so hard seeing you again."

"Please don't."

"Well, what do you want me to say? I still love you, Melyssa."

"I said don't, Kiya."

She stood up and stretched, a sombre expression on her face. "Why him? Why him and not me?"

"I love you, Kiya, but..."

"I know my name. Why do you keep saying it?"

"Stop it."

"Can you at least give me a proper answer? Was I boring you?"

"To put it bluntly, yes, you always were."

Kiya's look for the first time was serious. Melyssa's eyes darted from left to right.

"I didn't mean that."

"You said it, though."

She watched as Melyssa put her bag over her shoulder; whatever she was going to say wouldn't be long.

"Not at first, it was fun for a while, a long while. We went out clubbing, holidays together, new restaurants, moved in together; it was fun trying new stuff out with you."

"So what changed?"

"Nothing changed, that's the problem. After we did all of that, you didn't want to do anything anymore, you just wanted to stay in and watch box sets."

"I thought you liked doing that."

"Not every day, Kiya. You're great, and I won't ever forget the good times we spent together, but somewhere along the line you just stopped being fun."

"So moving in with a guy more than twice your age is?"

Melyssa sighed heavily and headed for the front door. "I knew this was a bad idea, I'm sorry for coming."

Just as she was about to leave, Kiya gave an irritated body shrug. She hesitated, and the expression on her face turned grim. "You can come and collect your stuff this weekend if you want. I'm away with work."

Melyssa shook her head. "No, can't come this weekend, it's Zara's hen do. A whole bunch of us are heading to Torquay, the coast, for a get-together, big celebrations, hired a boat for the massive party, we'll have fireworks and everything."

Kiya gave a chuckled sigh. "Zara? Yeah, so she's still engaged to Luke, was it? Shame, I liked him. Wonder if he knows he's about to marry a cheating tramp; she is still seeing other guys right? Poor guy doesn't even know he's being cheated on."

Kiya suddenly realised her words. "Then again, neither did I."

Melyssa shifted her shoulders, trying not to register what Kiya had said. "I didn't come here to cause any trouble. I just wanted to know when I could collect my things."

"Then what are you worried about? You came to get your stuff, stuff we bought for our home together to make a future for us, but that means nothing to you now. Why are you doing this? Tell you what, take it now, I don't care. I'll make myself scarce for a few hours, and you can take all your stuff to that old degenerate."

Melyssa caught Kiya's dig at her and eased a reply. "Just let me know when I can get my stuff." She headed for the door. "Goodbye, Kiya."

"Wait, stop."

Her ex-girlfriend waited as Kiya flapped her arms.

"What's he got, eh? What's he got that I haven't?"

"My interest," Melyssa said without hesitating and left.

* * *

Fireworks were shooting everywhere in the sky before exploding like a planet in a science fiction film. A girl stumbled on to the top deck from a room blasting music almost as loud as the fireworks and looked at the illuminated sky, and shrieked excitedly as another bang went off. She shielded her eyes from the light, then placed an oversized pair of sunglasses on with one hand, her other held a glass of Prosecco.

Another girl followed from the lower deck, wearing toy bunny ears over her blonde hair, she had amazing brown eyes and her skin was smooth and tanned.

The first girl turned around, she was dressed up in very tight jodhpurs and black boots. She removed a black riding helmet from her head, tossing it on the ship floor to allow her long brown hair to sway tidily in the wind.

"Whose idea was that?"

"Was what?"

"To have that firework display thingy for Zara."

The other girl took off her bunny ears. "I don't think it's for us; it's for an Indian festival, Diwali."

Sasha took a swig of Prosecco and spoke earnestly to Jess. "Babes, you are so clever, knowing all sorts of cultural stuff, that is just so knowing."

Jess gave a look of bemusement to Sasha. "Knowing? Is that some sort of new word?"

"No, babes, it's in the dictionary."

"So how long does Diwali last?"

Jess chewed her lip. "Not sure. I think it might be five days."

Sasha took another swig from her glass. "So why have fireworks in the daytime? How can you see them?"

Pulling a fake expression of doubt, Jess replied, "Not actually sure."

Jess turned and looked to the shore. "What time did you get here?"

"Got down earlier this afternoon to do some shopping."

"Isn't Torquay great?"

"I don't know, maybe when it's finished."

Sasha was unaware of Jess's confused headshake.

"What time are we eating again? I'm starving," Jess said.

"I organised this on the cheap, there isn't a meal."

"What? There's no food?"

"It was the best option."

Jess stared back at Sasha, who was unflinching.

"Best option for your wallet, more like."

Sasha was still unmoved.

"We could have had a buffet or sit-down meal, and you opted for nothing? Thanks, by the way, why couldn't you have told me earlier? I could have got something back at the hotel."

"It's fine. We can get a kebab afterwards."

"Do the girls know?"

Sasha grinned. "Not yet."

Jess looked skywards, hoping the fireworks would take her mind away from her empty stomach then smiled idiotically.

"Dinner would have been around 7.30pm but not for us."

Sasha put her shades back on and snaked her arm through Jess's. "This is nice, but fireworks and pigging out are best left for new years, babe." She held on to Jess with an excited smile.

"We'll dance first and tell the girls later."

"We're going to need a big kebab shop."

The two girls went back below deck, hit by the intense sound of dance music from the DJ. She pressed a few keys on her laptop and went back to playing a game on her phone; the music change had the desired effect on the people in the room. The room was huge, tables were laid out but with no plates on them. It was a hen party in full swing.

Countless girls were dancing and weaving their way around the tables. Skin-tight micro shorts, bikinis, and crop tops filled the party, along with high heels, Ugg boots and trainers for the girls who wisely knew it would be a long night of dancing. Some wore a variety of costumes, fancy dress, exotic, burlesque, but it was plain that each and every girl had made an effort for this gathering.

As the music changed, one girl clambered onto a table and started dancing away, shouting the words wrong to the song and waving her hands wildly in the air. She stumbled in too high heels and fell backwards, crashing into a chair and breaking it instantly. She lay on the ground, winded as if someone had just dropped a huge dumbbell on her chest. She still held on to her phone.

Her friends gasped and then cheered as the girl turned on her side to slowly get up. A few had their own phones out filming her so it was bound to be on social media in seconds. Sasha and Jess moved through the crowd, their eyes scanning the room.

"Where is she?" Jess asked.

There was no answer from Sasha. She was looking as the girl finally made it to her feet, wondering what all the fuss was about until she saw the broken chair.

"Did you fall off the table, Haley?" she shouted.

Haley rubbed her back and nodded with a grimace.

"Oh, babes." Sasha snorted and then gave up trying not to laugh.

Jess pulled her friend to her side. "I haven't seen Zara for ages. Where could she be?"

Sasha was more concerned about her empty glass. "Babes, we're on a boat. Where is she going to go?"

Jess pulled a face, Sasha could be ditzy, but she was spot on this time.

"Look, you know Zara, she's probably raiding the bar or something, which is where we should be."

Sasha's eyes widened as she spotted another girl walking towards her. "Melyssa, babes, you made it!"

Melyssa spotted Jess and Sasha and went for a hug with a happy squeal. Sasha scrutinised Melyssa's outfit. "Did you come here straight from work or something?"

Melyssa did a twirl and laughed. "No, it's a sexy secretary outfit. What do you think?"

"Babes, didn't you get my message?"

"Yeah, come dressed up for the day which was or is the happiest moment of your life."

"So, that's why I'm dressed in my riding gear because the happiest days are when I'm on my horse. Jess is dressed as the Easter bunny because..." She looked at her. "Loves chocolate?"

Jess answered casually. "Only happy with chocolate."

"Bethany over there is wearing a fleshy see-through suit thing because the greatest day in her life was the day she was born, naked."

"I got that," Melyssa replied.

"So why are you dressed like a secretary?"

"I love my job."

Jess interjected. "Really? The happiest moment in your life was getting a job as a PA? Nothing else more exciting than that?"

"There was one other moment of happiness, the day I moved in with Kiya."

"I thought it was when you moved out."

Melyssa took a look at Jess. She wasn't impressed by her words. "What's that supposed to mean?"

"You know exactly what it means."

Sasha flicked her hair and eyes to Melyssa. "One step and one day at a time, babes."

Jess twitched her nose and changed the subject. "How is work anyway? Haven't seen you since you moved in with…" She paused.

"Michael," Melyssa finished for her.

"Yeah, Michael, that's it. Why do I keep forgetting?"

Their eyes mimicked each other in slowly closing in distrust.

"Anyway, how are things with him?" Sasha asked.

Melyssa's eyes lit up, making Jess seem more uneasy. "Love it, love being with him. Everything is so much better."

"Everything?" Sasha asked, one eyebrow raised.

"Everything."

"Isn't he like 100 or something? How can it be any good?"

"He's 40."

"Tomayto, tomato."

Jess nudged Sasha with a careful prod to her side.

"What? I'm just saying."

"It's not just about sex."

"No?"

"No, some nights I just lay with my head in his lap, and we just talk about everything, the world, politics, films, all sorts."

Sasha wasn't convinced. "Babes, look at you. You're beautiful, and he's old. He'll talk about anything just to keep you; the shorter the skirt, the shittier he talks."

"It's not like that." Melyssa's eyes glared at Sasha.

Jess crossed her hands with suspicion. "Why couldn't you do that stuff with Kiya?"

"Kiya didn't want to talk, at first we travelled and went on holiday, which was nice, but then she was just all about work and nothing else."

"So someone who wants to work and provide for their girlfriend, what's wrong with that? Most people would kill for a partner having a decent job. What does she do again?"

Melyssa readjusted her eyes directly at Jess. "That doesn't matter, I just fell out of love with Kiya. I mean, I still care about her, but I'm with Michael now."

"You had an affair with your boss. That's a funny way of showing that you care about Kiya."

"Do you have a problem with me, Jess?"

"No, just don't think it's fair your badmouthing her when it was you having the affair."

"Why don't you date her then?"

"Maybe I will."

The girls stood aside as some more party people stumbled past.

Sasha jumped up to break the tension. "Come on, babes, this is meant to be a celebration of Zara's last weekend as a single lady. Beyonce was right, put your hands up." Sasha waved her hands in the air and went back below deck.

Jess stood awkwardly next to Melyssa, both missing the boozy antics of their mutual friend.

"Where'd you get the outfit?" Melyssa asked.

"My cousin, she let me borrow it."

"That's sweet of her."

"Well, she's gone to prison, so doubt she'll be using it anytime soon."

"Maybe when she gets out?"

"She's doing time for armed robbery, doubt she'd want to dress up as the Easter bunny when she's released."

Melyssa leaned back against the boat's railings, completely ignoring what Jess had just said. "You fancy Kiya, don't you?"

"What do you mean?"

Melyssa's eyes dropped and she shook her head in disbelief. "You don't have to pretend now, Jess."

Before Jess could answer, Melyssa reassured her quickly. "I get it. I know you liked her; you were the only person to come for dinner in our flat, even when you knew I was cooking."

"I was just being friendly, and Kiya was always nice to me."

A girl suddenly rushed out from the dance hall deck and threw her head over the side of the boat; projectile vomiting followed. Jess rubbed the girl's back and moved her hair out of the way from the copious amounts of sick. Melyssa watched Jess tenderly look after the drunk girl. The girl then whooped with excitement and found her second wind. She hugged Jess and apologised quickly before moving back into the dance deck.

"You really did like Kiya," Melyssa spoke softly.

"She was just nice to me, that's it," Jess repeated.

Sasha came back from the main party group and cast her eyes over her two friends.

"You two still waffling on about Kiya? For god's sake, Melyssa, she was nice, but you're better off without her anyway."

"Why?" Melyssa asked with a smile of bemusement.

Sasha grumbled under her breath. "Like I said, she was okay but just so dull. I have livelier conversations with my Nan, and she's dead. I mean, all the holidays you went on, she suggested it, and it was you who booked them. She couldn't organise panic on a sinking ship."

"Why would you say that?" Melyssa's confused smile dropped.

"Apart from not being true, we are actually on a ship, boat thing, it's not good to be talking about sinking."

Sasha ignored her. "I do feel sorry for her in one way."

"What do you mean?"

"She's probably at home sticking forks in her eyes, thinking, *How the hell did this happen? She left me for a guy in his 80s who uses Botox*."

"I told you already he's 40, and it was just the once."

"Babes, I'm just telling you the truth. You really are better off without her, so now you're dating Alan Sugar, and you're his trophy girl. Who cares? You're happier now than you've ever been, so can we please find Zara and get back to partying?"

Melyssa beamed. "I am happy, and thank you, maybe you should try dating an older man."

"No thanks, babes, unless he's rich. I'd rather eat glass covered in crap than date anyone the same age as my dad."

Sasha started tapping her feet and moving her shoulders in rhythm to the new song playing from the speakers; she whipped off her shades again. "Why am I wearing shades when I've got these to show off."

She batted her expensive false lashes to the girls and then tried the same routine to a young waiter who had ventured out to the top deck to see if any other girls wanted some drinks. His eyes focused on Sasha first and flicked to the others.

"Can I get you ladies anything?"

Sasha eyed him back and confidently walked up to him. "If I ask you a general knowledge question and you get it wrong, do we get free drinks for the rest of the night?"

"I can't do that, I'm afraid," he replied, looking confident.

"Seeing as it's my friend's hen night, I'll make it easy for you. Free drinks all night is a bit of a piss-take, sorry. What if we say the next three or six, maybe nine drinks maximum are free."

"Depends on the question."

She swayed slightly more cocksure than booze, and after an astonishing amount of leaning back and forth, Sasha was ready. "What is a purlicue?"

"Oh." The waiter paused and then slowly started to laugh.

"Something funny?" Sasha asked, steadying her heels.

"Purlicue is the space between the thumb and finger."

She looked at him incredulously. "How did you know that?"

The waiter stopped laughing but kept his grin. "I also watched the repeat of the *Chase* game show this afternoon; that question was on it."

"Damn," Sasha hissed.

Jess stepped forward. "So are you saying that my friend only knew that question because she had seen it earlier on a game show and didn't have the brains to actually know it anyway through studying?"

He gave her his best smile. "Yes, you're right, I was being presumptuous, and I apologise."

"No worries."

He turned back to Sasha and raised his hand. "In Greek mythology, how many labours did Hercules have to perform?"

Sasha's eyes darted everywhere, trying hard to avoid the waiter's own. "Twelve," she spat the answer out.

"What's the capital of Peru?"

Sasha's forehead creased. "Lima."

The waiter had a smug delight all over his face. "So the last question which I heard on the *Chase* repeat this afternoon was 'Rome Wasn't Built in a Day' was a hit in 2000 for which UK band."

"Morcheeba," Sasha answered calmly.

"I rest my case." The waiter winked.

He turned around and was heading back to the party deck.

Jess spoke the quickest. "So, if I get this right, if you had got any of those questions wrong, we possibly could have had a few free drinks tonight?"

The waiter looked at a dejected Sasha and then back to Jess. "Possibly."

"What religious festival are those fireworks for?"

The waiter looked to the sky, unconcerned. "No idea."

Jess pointed to Sasha, who was playing with her false nails. As soon as the waiter failed, she concentrated.

"Diwali?" she said, the word came out so unsure.

"Correct." Jess nodded.

"Fair play," he chuckled. "Let's get some drinks for you, three of the same?"

"Three of the same, babes." Sasha winked.

"No worries."

He walked around the girls as they all slapped hands triumphantly.

"Right, we keep on drinking and find that wedding bitch."

Melyssa and Jess whooped and slapped hands again and returned to the party.

There were almighty cheers coming from the girls in the lower deck as someone else dancing on a table collapsed on the floor like Haley did earlier. Sasha looked around the room, many girls wiggled past her, dancing and drinking, but there was still no sign of Zara.

The waiter came back quickly with their drinks. Sasha took hers and swung her hair back around to him. "Hey, have you seen Zara?"

"Who is she?"

"The one whose hen night this is, even though I'm bankrolling this."

Some more shrieks from the party girls made the waiter duck down instinctively. "No idea. What's she dressed like?"

Sasha took a long drink from her glass. "What's your favourite time of the year, and I don't mean football or sport nonsense, birthdays, anniversaries, valentines, funerals, weddings, Queen's speech or getting your bins emptied on time?"

The waiter hummed. "I have always liked Christmas Day."

Sasha laughed and did a perfect twirl with her drink in hand.

"Zara too."

* * *

The toilet cubicles on the ship were quite small but were extraordinarily tight for two people. The girl was on her knees, a man sat on the toilet, one hand trying to keep the door shut, the other keeping her head at groin level. She felt sick, the vomit was coming, but she kept going.

"The lock on the door is broke."

Ignoring the man's whining, she stuck at it. Bile was rushing up her throat; his voice meant nothing.

"God," he gasped and pulled at her hair, knocking off her Santa hat.

The other cubicle doors kept opening, girls heading for them really needing to pee or be sick.

"Christ, those bitches are loud."

"It's a hen night," she sighed.

The girl brushed the dirt off her knees, looked at the man disappointedly and felt to open the latch on the door, even though it was broken.

"Wait, before you go, let me give you something." The man adjusted himself and pulled out a wad of notes from his wallet. "Let me give this to you."

The girl took the money and hurriedly put it in her purse. Her anxious eyes were now more determined. "Thank you."

"I have to get back to work."

"What do you do?" she feigned interest.

"I run this boat. Technically I'm in charge, the captain."

Some more drunk girls charged through the toilet door, making the captain wince even more. "For god's sake, can't those noisy tramps be quiet?"

The girl prepared herself to leave the cubicle, hurrying as she was tired and growing bored. He watched as she tidily made herself ready.

"What's your name anyway?" The words left his mouth swiftly, trying hard to care.

"Zara, it's my hen party."

The man looked at her, puzzled. "Your party?"

Zara replied quickly in a mocking voice. "My party? Yes."

The man struggled to get to his feet, but his legs were numb, and Zara easily blocked his exit. From where he feebly tried to stand, all he could see was that the quiet young, frightened girl he had taken to the toilets had somehow changed into Wonder Woman and was keeping him locked in, with no lock.

"Now I hope you'll entertain all of my guests properly as we're paying quite a bit to party on this boat. I take it there'd be some sort of reduction in price for us, or there could be a review online which would include your very little extras."

She wriggled her little finger and finally smiled.

"You wouldn't dare," he snapped.

Zara opened the cubicle door. "Why not? I mean, I'm just a noisy tramp at the end of the day; nothing to lose on my part."

She looked at the deflated face of the guy as he pushed past her, muttering.

"That's good; now off you trot."

As the main toilet door closed, Zara walked out and headed for one of the many mirrors placed over expensive wall-hung basins. Adjusting her outfit accordingly, she noticed a glass of something left on the basin next to her; it looked like wine which an eager partygoer had left in haste.

Zara took the glass and sipped it gingerly. It was a dry white wine. Confident that the drink was good to go, she downed it with fierce haste. She stared hard at her reflection and raised the empty glass to herself.

"Congratulations, slut."

* * *

Melyssa was back on the top deck, along with quite a few of the party girls. There was no sign of Sasha, but Jess pressed through the crowd to see her friend. She noticed Melyssa swiping away at her phone. Judging by the look on her face, Jess knew exactly what was wrong.

She whispered behind Melyssa's ear. "You okay?" she asked.

"Oh god!" Melyssa jumped, clutching her chest.

"Sorry." Jess jumped back as well, smiling.

Melyssa's eyes recovered quickly and went back to her phone.

"Who are you on the phone to?"

Melyssa ignored Jess and kept her fingers pressing on the screen.

"Trouble in paradise?"

Finally putting the phone down, Melyssa turned to her friend. "He's giving me the silent treatment."

"Why?"

"He didn't want me to come tonight. He still thinks you lot are a bad influence on me. I was going to lie and say I'm going to a work conference for the weekend."

"He's your boss, Melyssa, not a good one either if he hadn't realised you were lying."

Jess picked at an eyelash and held a shrug. "Why give him spurious information?"

"My mum sold our Scrabble board for dog food when I was ten, so I have no idea what you mean."

Jess stared intently at Melyssa, reached for her hand and tenderly stroked it. "Well, he is right about the bad influence."

Melyssa pulled it away. "Stop it, Jess."

Embarrassed, Jess leant against the ship railings and took some more of her drink. "I know, I'm sorry." Her eyes flared up to Melyssa. "Why?"

"Why what?"

"Why don't you like me?"

Melyssa swallowed and turned to her friend. "I do like you."

"But?"

It was Melyssa's turn to take a long swallow of Prosecco. "Not that way, you know that."

"It didn't before," Jess softly rubbed Melyssa's arm.

Under the fireworks, Melyssa kept Jess against the railings. "That didn't happen, Jess, just forget it."

"It did happen, so why are you denying it?" Melyssa held Jess tight, squeezing her arms.

Jess's head bent towards Melyssa. "You treated Kiya like dirt; she deserves better."

"I cheated on her with you."

"But you lied to her again and said it was with your boss to spare her feelings."

"I did sleep with him."

"After me."

Jess's eyes never left Melyssa. "So sleeping with me meant nothing?"

"It didn't, but it would have crushed Kiya if she'd known the truth."

"The truth? You obviously don't know the meaning of the word."

Melyssa felt frost from Jess's eyes and voice. "I know I messed up, and I shouldn't have lied to any of you, but what's done is done."

"So cheating with a guy, you could tell her, but cheating with a woman, you couldn't."

Jess watched Melyssa hesitate and shrugged her shoulders. "You're a real piece of work."

Before Melyssa could answer, Sasha appeared, legs still wobbling. "Look who I found, bitches." She walked up from the lower deck, hand in hand with Zara. "Finally found this hen night whore."

Zara broke free from Sasha and strutted confidently in front of her hen night friends. She held up a glass of wine and did a twirl in front of her guests. They all cheered and clunked their glasses together. Then for a brief moment, everybody froze; time seemed to stand still.

Nobody could move but only watch as a giant red tentacle rose from the sea and swiped off Zara's head. It was a swift blow, connected well, sending her head to the other side of the boat. As soon as it landed and rolled gently, the screaming began.

"Jesus," was all Sasha could say, with drunken curiosity more than fear. Only a few droplets of Zara's blood were on her outfit; she brushed them off quickly and turned to a screaming Melyssa and Jess.

The whole hen night girls joined them in unison.

Before they had a chance to run, the boat suddenly lurched to one side, throwing all the girls to the floor. It began to tilt slowly, and the girls slid across the deck to the opposite end of the boat. A pile of partygoers were crushed against the back railings.

"Hold on to me!" Jess reached out to Melyssa's extended hand as the boat continued to rise.

Melyssa clung onto her friend and watched in horror as some girls were sent hurling over the barriers into the freezing waters below. "Where's Sasha?! Where's the crew?!"

Melyssa's words were drowned out by the terrified shouts. "Grab on to something!" she tried again in vain.

Wine glasses flew through the air, striking some girls in the face, followed by tables and chairs.

All of a sudden, the boat stopped moving, more tentacles wrapped themselves easily around it and it was now being held up from the water in an unbelievable position.

The sea quickly became quiet again, and the only sounds were the girls screaming hysterically and fallen debris making their journey's end against the crumpled girls' bodies.

It was like the beginning of a water slide ride at a theme park, rising high, and the inevitable big drop was looming. The boat was suspended in the air, the fireworks still lit up the night sky, and the girls hoped somebody would see them on dry land.

Nobody could see beneath the boat; the myriad of giant tentacles had wrapped themselves along the bottom.

The bombardment of fireworks suddenly stopped, plunging the sky into total darkness. Melyssa's eyes were frantic. Looking around, she tightened her grip on Jess but still couldn't see any sign of Sasha. Melyssa struggled to talk; she was trying hard but only mumbled in fear.

Jess spoke, watching Melyssa's head sway silently. "Melyssa?"

No reply came from her friend. She tried again as tears began to form.

"I can't see Sasha."

Finally, Melyssa's groaning became louder. She leaned forward to Jess, her grip held firm and spoke, "We're going to die, aren't we?"

The boat wobbled slightly, causing more screams and making Jess pause before answering.

"We're going to drown," Melyssa added.

Jess tried to stop trembling. She was aware of what Melyssa had just said but couldn't answer right away through fright. "I don't know what is happening or what I saw happen to Zara, but we will get off this boat alive."

Before she could add any more, whatever was keeping the boat semi-aloft slowly twisted it to the side. An uncontrollable spasm of fear hit Melyssa and she clutched onto Jess harder.

Some other girls weren't as fortunate and slid slowly across the deck and over the barriers into the sea. Their screams were deafening as the cold waters welcomed them. The vessel kept turning as more girls dropped into the sea, dropping off like fleas from a newly treated cat.

Melyssa twisted with panic and made a full launch into Jess as they finally fell into the water.

The tipped-up boat soon followed. The waves it made on impact sent the girls further out to sea. Jess and Melyssa were swept out from the boat, still holding hands; other girls tried the same, most were successful, holding onto people they had only met that night, but all had a common goal in trying to survive. They steadied themselves against the rough motions of the water.

"Melyssa, look at me, look at me!" Jess struggled to keep both their heads above the freezing waters, pulling her friend up hard as each wave passed over them.

"It's cold. I'm so cold!" Melyssa's eyes began to sink, and she began to drift away from her friend.

Jess shook her, trying hard to keep them both afloat. The sea had a different look on its surface, scattered with the floating dead bodies of some of the girls.

"They're dead. Everyone's dead." Melyssa's voice was quavering but on point with the facts.

"Don't look at them. Look at me," Jess said, gasping for air. She looked around and eased Melyssa's head towards her own. "Some of the rescue dinghy things have come loose and are floating away. If we swim over to them, we have a chance of getting out of here."

Melyssa was too scared and ignored her.

Jess blinked the water from her eyes. "Stay with me." Jess kept her eyes focused on Melyssa.

"What was that? That thing in the water," Melyssa looked through Jess.

"I don't know, but whatever it is, we have to get out of the water in case it comes back."

"It will come back," Melyssa moaned. "It's the Loch Ness Monster."

"It's not the Loch Ness Monster." Jess shuffled her position, not really wanting to take part in those wild theories.

"You believe in dinosaurs, right?" Melyssa stammered.

"Yes."

"Then it is the Loch Ness Monster."

Ignoring Melyssa just for a moment, Jess looked around at the water, the ship's debris scattered on its surface. "Plastic bottles." Her eyes darted around the wreckage.

Melyssa turned away just to look at the floating rubbish. "What?"

"Grab the plastic bottles and empty them." Jess left Melyssa's side, making her speak some more.

"Don't leave me." She instantly reached out for Jess's hand underwater.

"I'm right here," Jess assured her.

"Stuff the empty bottles up your clothes. Put them anywhere they fit, as they'll keep us afloat."

Melyssa, trying hard to keep breathing and stay afloat, did what Jess said. This wasn't how she thought her sexy secretary's outfit would end up. She'd planned on surprising her man when she got back home, walking into the living room on a Sunday evening to seduce him as she knew getting him away from watching the *Antiques Roadshow* would take a Herculean effort.

That sweet idea she had on her return from the hen night seemed great at the time. Stuffing empty water bottles up her new outfit to keep afloat while trying not to drown wasn't on her weekend itinerary list. Melyssa vomited into the water, turning away from her soaked outfit and Jess. Throwing up on a hen night was something she was expecting to do, leaning over the boat's barriers and having friends support her, keeping hair from her vomit-stained mouth. But freezing slowly in the water after the boat capsized and being attacked by a strange creature which would make even David Attenborough's eyes spin was something she never envisaged.

She hesitated and stared at Jess placing empty bottles with determination in her own outfit, trying to ignore how cold the water was. Melyssa slowly lifted her eyes and arms. "Sasha will come back, I know it."

Jess dipped slightly in the water, surprised by the optimistic tone of Melyssa.

"She was looking forward to watching the new series of *The Real Housewives of Luton* next week."

Jess nodded without hesitation and a confident smile, just to put Melyssa at rest.

It didn't work.

"This isn't happening; this isn't real."

"It is real, Melyssa, this boat is sinking, and we're a long way from the harbour."

"What about that creature?"

"Don't care what that thing was, the tide is rising, and the temperature is dropping; we have to make it back before we die of hypothermia."

"What if it comes back?" Melyssa moaned.

"Then it comes back," Jess said quickly.

She could tell that she wasn't getting anything else from Jess apart from survival, and that was enough in her eyes. Melyssa gulped in some water, spitting it out and panicked more. "Okay, I'm tired, Jess. I just want to go home."

"Just stay strong, and with me, we'll get home." Jess continued to scan the water, the empty bottles helped, but they were still struggling to stay afloat, her head rose high, and her mouth dropped open for breath. "I see some lifebuoys over there."

"What?"

Jess moved her arm out to point with difficulty. "Those red rings in the water, we have to get them to keep us up."

Melyssa turned her head, making more of a struggle than Jess. "They're miles away," she said in dismay.

"We can't stay by this boat for much longer. We have to swim for it."

Their heads bent towards each other and touched. "You can do this," Jess reassured her. Melyssa wasn't convinced.

"So we have to swim further out to sea, grab those ring things and then swim back to shore?" Melyssa blinked rapidly, her eyes still set on Jess, waiting for an answer.

"That's the only option."

"No, we wait until somebody comes." There was a defiance in Melyssa's voice.

Jess didn't reply.

"Did you hear me?" she pressed.

"Yes, and something else."

Both girls stayed silent and listened to the short waves.

"There's something out there," Jess whispered.

"I know, it's that octopus thing," Melyssa said.

"No, it's not that."

The waters rippled in a different way. Jess stared at the new surface and prepared herself for whatever was about to break through. She clutched Melyssa's hand and closed her eyes, and expected a strange death as the water broke open.

Sasha suddenly burst through the surface; she shook her hair and slowly made her way to the sinking boat. "Christ, you bitches are hard to find."

"Sasha!" Melyssa screamed. She gave up one hand for a hug, to do both would end up in her drowning.

Jess tried to move around Melyssa to also try for a hug. Sasha shook her head, knowing it was too dangerous for her to try. Jess gave a thankful nod and kept a desperate hold of the boat.

"As you can obviously see," Sasha said firmly, taking in water before speaking again, "we should have gone to Thorpe Park."

"Worst hen night ever." Melyssa raised her head, thankful she got her view across.

The three girls shared a brief chuckle before Jess's smile went back to concern. "You booked this night. Surely somebody must know we're here."

Sasha tried to look anywhere instead of Jess's prying eyes, it didn't work. "I met some guy on Tinder. He was an idiot, full of crap, he worked as an organiser or captain, can't quite remember, but for party boats, and he said we would get a discount, a huge discount if we would do some favours for him."

Sasha shivered. "So cold."

Jess didn't care. She just wanted answers from Sasha. "What favours?" Jess asked, her eyes tiring by the second.

"What do you think? I met him on Tinder."

"So what did he promise you?"

Sasha didn't want to answer; she was struggling to kick her feet. "Remember I said earlier that we had no food thanks to a cheap deal? This ride was off the books, under the radar; we get a party boat for half price for—"

"Cheap sex?" Melyssa rose to the conversation.

"Yes, the reason your drinks were as cheap as chips was down to me because I slept with a moron."

Jess looked around, watching the remaining few girls trying to swim to land but then disappearing below the surface, taken by fatigue. There weren't many girls left.

"So if this trip was planned behind closed doors."

Sasha stepped in for Jess. "Nobody knows we're here."

"What about satellites and drones? What about ship tracking stuff? Somebody must know we're sinking!" Melyssa wailed.

"Like I said, nobody saw us leave. Nobody knows we're here."

"Oh my god," Jess whispered. "How could you have been so stupid, Sasha?"

"You weren't complaining when you were getting drinks for free."

"That was before a monster tipped up our boat and left us to die in the water!"

Sasha opened her mouth to reply to Jess but stayed quiet and looked around. "Where are the others?"

Melyssa raised her head wearily. "They're dead. Everyone's dead."

"What?" Sasha shouted.

"Some drowned when the ship tipped, others tried to make it to shore."

Jess moved one arm from the boat and slipped it beneath the water. "I can't feel my legs."

She reached further, and a moment of relief hit her as she felt both her legs, rubbing them soundly before quickly moving her hand back up to the boat and spoke with difficulty. "The creature stopped them from making it."

"Some giant octopus appears and ruins our hen night? I'm not waiting around here to be on the menu. I eat calamari. It doesn't eat me."

Melyssa groaned but had information. "Actually, calamari is a type of squid, not octopus."

"How do you know that?" Sasha asked.

Melyssa didn't answer.

Jess went back in for Melyssa's hand underwater. She felt it and squeezed tight, not for the first time. "Still think it's the Loch Ness Monster?" Jess asked.

"Don't care what it is anymore, squid, octopus or a Scottish monster." Melyssa's voice was emotionless. "I just don't want to die tonight."

"So what do we do?"

Jess heard Sasha's sullen voice and pointed out to sea. "Those lifebuoys over there, I say we swim out, grab them and then head back to shore."

Sasha wasn't convinced. "If we try to reach them, that creature is going to get us."

"We are going to drown if we stay here." Jess was trying to remain calm as she froze.

Melyssa's eyes flicked from the lifebuoys back to Sasha. "Plus, thanks to rent-a-skank there, nobody knows our location."

"You should look in the dictionary and search for the word *slag* before you lecture me on morals."

"I'm not interested in burning hot metals, so what do you mean by calling me a slag? And yes, I did look the word up in a dictionary."

"Not the first time, eh?" Sasha puffed.

"Not now, please?" Jess pleaded.

"No, sod that! She's lecturing me about morals after she slept with you and that old guy while being with Kiya."

Nobody said a word as Sasha continued. "You think I didn't know about you two?"

"I'm sorry," Melyssa said breathlessly.

"Don't apologise to me. Apologise to that poor girl you cheated on."

"This didn't mean to happen." Melyssa's words became slower.

Jess shook her head. "Now isn't the time for this."

"Well, my diary is kinda free right now."

"What's wrong with you, Sasha?" Jess demanded.

"You both think I'm stupid, thought I wouldn't have guessed. Christ, it's so obvious you like Melyssa."

"Look, I know what Melyssa and me did was wrong, but now isn't the time. You're scared, we all are, but we have to stick together if we are going to survive."

She tried to feel her legs again, all of her body was turning numb. "We can't stay here. We need to go."

"Yes, boss." Sasha's tone turned from angry to sarcastic in a heartbeat.

Jess glared back at Sasha, taking time out from her changed breathing technique to register the rudeness in her reply. "I would quit while you're behind, Sasha. I still haven't forgiven you."

"Will you both shut up!" Melyssa found some energy and put it in her voice. "You two want to fight? Go ahead, but Jess is right. We have to get those buoys and leave before we get more tired and can't swim. So yeah, Sasha, I cheated on Kiya with Jess and blamed it on my new man. We'll discuss it when we all get back home."

"Really? Didn't know that part."

"Sasha," Melyssa said stiffly.

Sasha checked her balance as she trod water.

"Yes, seriously, let's forget about it."

Jess looked at the shore again and then to Melyssa. "Those water bottles I gave you to float on. Were they completely empty?"

Melyssa took one from the top of her costume and shook it. "There's a little bit of water left."

"Drink it, drink whatever's left in the others and put them back; you have to float to live."

"I know."

"I'm serious."

"I said I know, Jess."

Jess stopped the conversation. "It's time to go."

Sasha took a chance and huddled up to Melyssa, fiddling with her drink bottles for the second time for the night. "I'm sorry, babes."

Melyssa's voice was colder than her whole body. "It's fine."

The lifebuoys were drifting further out to sea.

Jess twisted her neck around slowly as if she was warming up for a hot yoga class. "You two ready?"

Sasha and Melyssa looked at each other; their faces were a far cry from how they looked when they first arrived on the party boat. Their earlier fun looks were now tired, worn and scared, but their eyes were united in survival.

"Let's go," Jess grunted. It wasn't an epic voice, just a moan to get things done quickly, and they all kicked off towards the lifebuoys.

Sasha swore under her breath as soon as they left the boat. Melyssa tried to follow as quickly as Sasha had kicked off, but she struggled with the relentless water entering her mouth and the sad realisation that Sasha and Jess were stronger swimmers than her. She let the current sweep over her again before she tried speaking. "A soaking wet jodhpurs outfit. Got a receipt?"

"I have a horse, babes, so not wasted," Sasha replied vaguely.

"Get back home, wash, rinse and then look absolutely stunning." Sasha spat out more water and paused. "That's all I want to do."

Melyssa wasn't sure if Sasha meant her horse or herself. Either way, it had slowed her swimming down, giving her a chance to catch up.

The sky had some light due to the full moon, which helped the girls; the rippling effect of their every stroke had its face across it. Jess looked up at it after every few strokes, hoping to see it again on dry land. A full moon was so blasé to her in the past, a quick glance from her car on the drive home from working late or sitting at a pub garden near a canal on a warm summer's evening.

Things which she took for granted seemed ages ago now. Cramped travel on a train, sitting next to someone who had just bought all the meals on Burger King's menu or driving all the way to Leeds for a business meeting last week really annoyed her so much that it went straight to all of her social media pages, but she would give anything to be stuck in gridlock right now and eat a vegan double whopper.

The lifebuoys were still slowly heading out to sea, a concern for Jess.

"Everybody still okay?" Her voice trailed off; she was trying hard not to cry in front of the others.

Jess didn't get a reply, but the continuous splashing behind her gave her slight ease. It was in rhythm and not frantic, which would have been a concern. Wherever the creature was, it was not focusing on them at the moment.

Sasha was swimming well. She even slowed slightly to allow Melyssa to catch up. She hesitated as Melyssa drew closer.

"So did you care about Kiya before cheating on her with Jess?"

Melyssa wasn't sure if it was the saltwater in her mouth that made her sound so bitter.

Frowning in the water was hard to do, but Melyssa gave it a go. "What do you mean?"

"From what I gather, you like using people, first Kiya, Jess, and now this current old guy."

"You don't even know his name."

"Because it won't last; it never does with you."

Melyssa appeared shocked, which slowed down her kicking. "Why would you say that?"

Sasha was right behind Jess and knew she was out of earshot, the water in Jess's ears helped. She tried hard to catch up. "You just get bored quickly, and you use people, it's what you do. You don't know it, but it happens every time you date; everyone is a project, not a partner."

Melyssa was instantly defeated by those words, making swimming a lot harder. "Why would you say that?"

Sasha snorted, trying to stifle laughing, which was a strange sound to hear in the water and something she thought she'd never do in this situation. "It's true, babes, it had to come out sooner or later."

"Why now?"

There was a silence, a long silence. Melyssa failed to notice Sasha shrug in the water.

Jess, unaware of the conversation happening behind her, had reached the first lifebuoy. She took a mighty gasp of air as her head broke through the surface; her head spun around immediately to check on the progress of her friends. "You okay?"

A quick head nod came from Sasha. Melyssa didn't bother to reply.

"Melyssa," Jess called out again.

"I'm fine." She had a constant gaze on Jess's back.

The lights from the harbour boats were beginning to disappear, and the guide to land was beginning to fade. Sasha watched Jess grab hold of the lifebuoy and reached out for her own. Melyssa struggled but finally clung onto her lifebuoy; relief swept across her face as she hung on tight. She looked at the others, her eyes finally wide.

"That's it. Can we go home now?"

Jess nodded. She reached again under the water to feel her legs; they had worked so well for her as she kicked ferociously to reach the lifebuoys.

Her legs were tired but fine, and they started again as she turned around towards land.

All three of them now held on tightly to each individual ring in a line.

Jess reached over to grip Sasha's arm. "You ready for this?"

"I'm aching all over. Now I know how my grandma feels when she waffles on about her bad back."

Melyssa interrupted. "I thought you said she was dead."

"I had two; it's quite common."

Melyssa looked squarely in the eyes of Sasha, ignoring her comment. "I'm sorry for what I did," she whispered.

"Your eyes are leaking," Sasha said, her voice dropped.

"It's water."

Jess was right beside her, which Sasha acknowledged.

"No worries," she silently mouthed back to Melyssa.

Jess was swimming at a steady pace, kicking steadily. Sasha followed, picking up some speed. Melyssa's head cautiously looked around, looking for survivors for once and not the creature.

The mix of Prosecco and Pinot Grigio on an empty stomach wasn't going well for Sasha. She had already urinated in the ocean and didn't really want to be sick. She just gripped her lifebuoy and kept up with Jess. Something else grabbed her attention, making her gasp and wobble.

Melyssa spluttered out water. Her eyes looked at what had made Sasha freeze. A figure was struggling in the water; they had made some distance from the boat but were now drained of strength.

"Haley!" they both screamed. Jess turned her head to see what her companions were shouting about.

Haley had somehow managed to survive the boat flipping over and sinking. She froze instantly in the water when she heard the voices of the others. Her eyes rolled over to them. "What's happening? What's going on?" Her voice shook due to coldness and fear.

"Doesn't matter, just stay calm." Melyssa tried to reassure her.

Haley relieved herself in the water and then felt scared again. "Help me," she moaned. It then turned to a cry. "Help me, please?"

"Swim to us. Just swim, Haley, now!" Jess yelled.

"I can't do it. I'm tired." Haley continued to cry, her sobs becoming more frantic. Between the cries, the water was becoming increasingly quiet. Something was sliding through it, just about visible to Sasha. She turned her attention back to Haley and screamed with all she had.

"Haley, don't look back. Just swim as fast as you bloody can!"

All their hearts began to thump harder, and Haley's strokes feebly slowed down.

"Swim faster!"

Haley stopped swimming completely. She just about managed to stay afloat, her breathing slowed down, and she was rooted to the spot. A horrified look appeared on her face as she looked below just in time to see razor-sharp teeth take her under.

"Haley!" Sasha screamed directly into the empty spot where Haley once was.

"Where is she?" Jess yelled hard.

Sasha didn't respond.

Melyssa did instead. "It took her! It took her!"

The three struggled again in the water, just moments before they had found their rhythm and were seemingly heading home.

Confused and scared, Melyssa tried again. "Haley! Where are you?"

The calm water unsettled them.

It was finally broken by Haley. Her body shot back through the surface like a champagne cork, and her head was violently thrown backwards and forwards. She screamed for help as the girls watched, unable to grasp what was happening, let alone help. She thrashed around wildly as her body was being shaken left to right like the waltzers on a funfair.

"Haley!" Jess yelled again, wanting so much to help but not knowing how.

A tentacle moved further up her body, and the girls finally saw the horror from the deep. Wrapping itself neatly around Haley, the creature dragged her under.

Melyssa watched the empty spot carefully. The others were shivering, awaiting Haley's return.

It didn't happen.

"It killed her! She's dead!"

Jess looked to Melyssa, who was wailing hysterically. "It's not fair!"

All she could remember was Haley struggling for help in the water.

Melyssa's cries snapped her out of her forlorn trance. "We have to go," Jess said quietly.

"Go where? That octopus thing, yeah, not the Loch Ness Monster, is going to get us wherever we swim."

Jess was shivering harder, with coldness and shock.

Melyssa turned her anger and fright to Sasha. "You happy now? You happy now, you stupid slut!"

"This isn't the right time for this," Jess stuttered for once, her confidence draining.

Melyssa's brow creased. "When is the right time?!" she spat back.

Jess hesitated as more water moved up her nose.

"This stupid cow has killed everyone on the boat. Haley and Zara died in front of us, and for what? So she could get a better deal on a shit show of a party boat and sleep with some nobody?"

Waiting patiently to get a word in, Jess found a gap in Melyssa's words. "Sasha didn't know this was going to happen."

"Getting attacked by a giant octopus, yeah, who knew?"

"Difficult to miss," Jess said slowly.

"This is not funny. People are dying," Melyssa replied. She corrected herself. "Our friends are dying."

Jess's face grew tight, and her breathing grew more difficult. She was finding it harder to use the lifebuoy. "I just want to go home," was all she could muster.

Melyssa stared at Sasha and refused to budge her eyes. "Just keep her away from me."

The boats at the marina still had their lights on; they were still quite a distance away, but it gave Jess some hope. She gave a faint unsuccessful wave to the shore, hoping somebody would catch her dainty hand.

"We have to tell all their families." The quiet voice from Sasha took Jess by surprise.

She opened her water-filled eyes but kept them focused on the marina. "What did you say?"

"Everybody who died, the ones who drowned or got taken, we have to tell their loved ones what happened."

Melyssa was still keeping afloat, fairly close to Sasha and heard every word. "So you have a conscience now? You were a dick who should be investigated by *Watchdog* for how you conned us into this trip; our boat has gone and so have our friends!"

Sasha's swimming was growing unsteady, but she found time to turn to Melyssa. "Have you finished? Can I speak now?"

Her voice grew more agitated as Melyssa needed dealing with, more so than the freezing water.

"I'm a lot of things, bit ditzy, bit stupid, but not a hypocrite." Sasha's eyes were closing; she tried hard to keep them intense. "I'm everything that you thought I was, ever since you knew me, I was the party girl, a bit dim, the easy skank, tramp, sleep-around girl, whatever the girls called me, and I know they all did."

"Nobody thought that," Jess said, getting right in with the conversation with great effort in speech.

"Yes they did, maybe not you, babes, but the others always thought I was just some girl who was mad on horses, had a lot on top, and I don't mean brains."

Jess looked at Sasha's tired grim mouth. "I'm sorry."

"Like I said, wasn't you, babes."

Jess's head tilted and dipped deeper in the water. She attempted a smile when she resurfaced.

Sasha moved her head forward towards the shore, she gave a fleeting look back to Melyssa. "I've never had affairs and lied to my friends. I know what I am, and I'm glad it's not you."

Melyssa couldn't stay silent. "Screw you."

Sasha ran a tired hand over her watered face. "I'm not 40 yet, babes."

Jess rubbed her eyes. She was too tired to care what Melyssa's response would be. The cold water was clinging to her more tightly than before. "Whatever happened in the past, we'll deal with it when we get home."

"Will we?" Sasha frowned even deeper.

"Yeah, course, sit down over a nice meal and discuss everything; all of us will."

Sasha looked to the horizon, where the dark blue of the water met the star-riddled sky. "We're not going home, that thing has killed all of our friends, and we're next. It just tore apart Haley and wasted Zara in an instant. We're dead, end of, babes."

Melyssa and Sasha stared at each other for an instant.

"I don't care what you think about me, dying in a giant octopus or drowning," Sasha's voice faded. "Still didn't get my kebab, either."

Jess suddenly erupted with a roar of laughter, ignoring the numbness all over her. "Kebab houses aren't shut yet. We'll get one."

"Chicken doner for me." Sasha shivered.

"Mixed doner." Jess blinked readily.

Melyssa fiddled with her lifebuoy and turned around to face the others. "Vegan kebab for me."

Sasha and Jess looked at each other, and then both shot a quick look to Melyssa.

She smiled with difficulty as the cold grew more intense. "It's on me. I'm buying."

The others gaped at her, and then all three laughed.

"I'm making it back just to see you put your hands in your pockets for once."

"Not in this outfit," Melyssa replied to Sasha.

"Okay, let's try and get back. If we keep together, huddle and look big, the octopus may leave us alone."

A sarcastic smile appeared on Melyssa's lips. "Piece of cake."

The three girls held their lifebuoys tightly and continued towards the shore. They bobbed their heads up and down in the water, and all of them continued in a strained rhythm. It was a strong concentrated effort; no words were spoken as the lights from the shore grew closer.

Jess was slowing down for the first time and broke up the tight trinity. Sasha waited for her and then pointed confidently to the shore. "Almost there," she huffed.

Jess shivered, her breaths became increasingly erratic. "I could do with a long nap right now."

"Don't start now. Kinda defeats the purpose of getting home safely."

Jess bubbled up more water, fear had set in ages ago from the moment they had all entered the water, but this new anxiety was the fact that she was closing in on finally being safe. Sasha smiled weakly at her. "People don't die in their naps, do they?"

"That's a bit random," Jess said, closing both her eyes as the cold set in further.

"Well, you hear of people dying in their sleep all the time. I've never heard of anybody dying while taking a nap. Nobody has died after finishing work and taking a quick nap after watching Judge Rinder."

A sudden yelp from Jess took Sasha away from her train of thought.

"You okay, babes?"

"Yeah, just caught my leg on something, bit of a pinch, all good."

"Cool," she whispered and carried on with her usual pace.

Jess tried to keep up again but instantly felt a moment of weakness, more than anything she had felt before. She was struggling to keep her head up now and felt dizzy and lethargic. Melyssa and Sasha were now in tandem and making a beeline for the shore. Jess was faltering and didn't know why she couldn't keep up, unable to swim the way she did so well previously.

Something caught her tired eyes as her head dropped. It looked like a piece of driftwood was floating past her. Whatever the object was, it looked like it was wearing one of her shoes. She was gradually forgetting about going home; the shoe had her full focus as it now sunk into the deep.

The cold was lingering over her, and she reached down to give her legs another rub.

Her arm found her right leg and rubbed it soundly. She tried to rub her left leg, and her arm passed through water where her left should have been; it was missing.

Jess felt the water lap over her shoulders, sinking slightly. She was losing grasp of her lifebuoy, confused and scared but not in pain. She was spending more time underwater than she would have liked.

A mixture of white and red lights illuminated the deep, heading towards her. They were attached to a number of brilliant tentacle arms which calmly waved themselves in front of her, making a beautiful lighted display. Jess was still transfixed as a number of them came closer; she held her right arm aloft as the lights were becoming more blinding.

The tentacle wrapped itself around her outstretched arm and freed it from its socket. Jess didn't feel anything; she was still fascinated by the wonderful light display. She really wanted to tell the others about it, but they were far away now. Annoyingly, the lights were beginning to fade. Jess thought she'd close her eyes for a moment and wait for her friends to come back for her. She had been in the water for ages, so didn't mind waiting for them for a bit longer as she sank further into the depths.

Melyssa was focused on the shore; she knew that Sasha was on one of her sides but hadn't checked on Jess for a while. She did a quick flick to her left and instantly panicked. "Sasha! Where is Jess?"

Sasha splashed around frantically, still trying to keep hold of her lifebuoy as she tried to find her missing friend. The two exchanged terrified glances as they scanned the water for Jess.

"I can't see her!" Sasha's panic began.

"Jess!" she shouted out to the waters. Melyssa tried her own turn at shouting.

"Jess! Where are you?"

Sasha held her head up from the water and swallowed hard, hoping it would help her calm down.

"No, no, no, no, it's got her!" Melyssa wailed. "Jess, Jess!"

The water was quiet, and Melyssa still heard no reply. Her tears were instant. "She's gone, she's gone, no, no, no!"

Sasha concentrated on the waters around them, looking for any movement. She turned to her crying friend. For a long, sad, frozen moment, Sasha held her concerned stare at Melyssa. "We have to go."

"No! We have to find her." Melyssa's head was still spinning around, looking.

Sasha's voice grew deeper. "She's not coming back."

Melyssa's head desperately swung back to Sasha. "Yes she is. She will come back to me!"

Sasha was fighting back her own tears. "Look, that water monster got her, we have to move or it will get us next."

"God no! I'm sorry, Jessica, please! I'm so sorry!" Melyssa's mouth twisted angrily.

"It's not fair. I didn't mean it, please come back!"

Sasha moved closer to her; she managed to keep her lifebuoy in one arm and pulled Melyssa in and held her tight.

"I need to see her again. I have to make things right."

They held each other for a long time, both knowing they should start again for the shore but clinging on to each other felt so much better.

"She knew how you really felt about her," Sasha whispered.

Melyssa had another frozen moment. She finally looked up at the sky, the moon and down to the water as the waves brushed against their ruined outfits. "I didn't tell her myself."

Sasha kept hold of Melyssa until the continued stillness of the water began to bother her. She snapped to attention. "Hold your lifebuoy, not my hand. We need to leave here quickly."

Melyssa sadly tilted her head, looking at the now attainable Torquay shore, her legs felt useless, but she had to try and get them moving for one last time. She gave a hesitant, quiet sigh. "On the count of three, shall we go?"

Sasha gave a complacent nod and waited for Melyssa's countdown.

"One…"

"Two…"

Melyssa paused to look at the safety of the harbour. She stopped her crying with another wipe of her shivering hand.

"Don't act so uptight," Sasha said.

Melyssa's countdown went out the window. "Sorry?"

"Jess is dead."

Sasha gave an almighty cough. "She loved you, she really did, babes, and you treated her like crap." Another dirty cough came straight afterwards. "You were bored with Kiya, so you slept with Jess and messed with her feelings, and then jumped into bed with Gandalf."

Melyssa stared at the empty, tired eyes of Sasha. "I'm sorry," Melyssa moaned. "I'm so very sorry."

"So you said."

Sasha's third cough was enough to clear her throat, but her voice was still emotionless and dry. "Like I said, Jess is dead. I invited her on this boat, I invited everyone and messed up; it's all on me, babes."

"You weren't to know."

"All my friends are dead. If I make it back, I'm handing myself in to the police."

Melyssa's face turned down, and she lifted it up for a chance to catch Sasha's eyes. "Not all of your friends are dead."

Sasha straightened her back with great agony, her face scrunched up in pain, her eyes slowly turned away from Melyssa. "All of my friends are dead."

Melyssa let out a startled whine. "You don't mean that."

"Three..."

"What did you say?"

Sasha's face hardened. "Just finishing your countdown."

Melyssa tried to right herself in the water. "Okay."

There was an awkward silence as they continued their swim to shore. The lifebuoys had drifted off slightly, but the two strained friends managed to keep a direction to the shore. As they swam in silence, the moon had changed but still lit up the ocean; its light was easily guiding them to safety. They had made a good distance without speaking, concentrating hard as the harbour lights loomed closer. Ignoring the pain and tiredness, they kicked on, slowing but still on their way to making it home.

Melyssa pressed her lips together, so eager to reach land. She couldn't swim any faster, but she had easily overtaken Sasha, who had slowed down considerably.

She was concerned but also so close to reaching the steps of the wharf.

Melyssa looked back to check on Sasha, but the sight of people moving around in the boats spurred her on. She was so close to reaching the harbour that she began to cry out and shout for help; ladders leading towards the mainland were in sight. Turning again to check on Sasha, the waters grabbed her attention.

It was a strange sight. The dark, dreary waters were illuminated by some sort of light beneath; it was the only time in the night when she wanted to stay looking at the lovely surface. Sasha was oblivious to the bright water behind her slow strokes, her eyes were closing, but she also was focused on the harbour.

"Sasha!" Melyssa cried out. "The water's moving!" She sounded terrified.

"It's always moving," Sasha mumbled back. She then looked at the fright in Melyssa's eyes and followed them to what they were focused on. "Oh, it's you," she whispered to the creature.

"Swim!" Melyssa screamed.

The waters began to part as the red tentacles rose to the surface. Sasha paused briefly at the magnificent sight of multiple lighted limbs heading towards her; she tried to feebly move her useless legs.

Melyssa swam frantically towards the nearest ladder, still screaming for anybody on the boats to help her.

Gritting her teeth through the pain, Sasha had earlier resigned herself to dying in the water when the boat capsized, but she was still alive in freezing waters and was so close to getting back home. She let out a cry of dread as the creature gained on her.

Melyssa had made it to the first ladder and hauled herself onto the first step; she climbed up each one painfully, and water from her soaked secretary outfit dripped on each step.

"Help me!" she shouted; the anger replaced the fear as nobody was coming to help from the boats.

Sasha twisted her head back fearfully. The octopus was still making a move forward. "Shit," she hissed.

Melyssa was close to the top of the ladder. She could have easily rolled herself to safety out of reach. She froze for a moment mid-step and then gave a frightened look back at the water. She then climbed back down to the water's surface and submerged herself again, something that was unthinkable after tonight's events.

Holding out her hand imploringly, she screamed again. "Sasha! You swim to me right now!"

Sasha had ditched her lifebuoy and was now struggling strongly towards Melyssa's ladder. "I can't!" The panic in her voice urged Melyssa on.

"Yes you can! You're the toughest bitch I know. Swim to me. Don't you dare leave me!" Melyssa's words were direct and sincere.

The octopus was spreading out its tentacles. It seemed to be assessing its prey and the best way to capture it.

"Swim, Sasha!"

She swam harder, trying hard to gulp back the fear stuck in her throat. Sasha was close to the ladder and Melyssa, the darkness on the water had almost disappeared as the calming lights of the octopus were almost upon her. The hypothermia didn't matter now as she reached out for Melyssa's free hand.

There was no time to hug as Melyssa pulled her up, then made her way back up the ladder. Sasha's gaze flicked from Melyssa to the row of tentacles behind her.

"Yes!" Melyssa shouted as Sasha gripped hold of the ladder in agony and made a pitiful attempt to climb up behind her.

Melyssa swallowed hard. She had done this before, and making her way back up was easier than the first time.

She got to the top and again made a familiar reach out to Sasha. "Give me your hand!"

Tearing herself away from Melyssa's crying eyes, Sasha looked over her shoulder and back at the water; it swirled neatly as the lighted tentacles moved gently through it.

Melyssa was still screaming for help, but her eyes were fixed on Sasha. "Climb to me!"

Sasha took a deep breath, her mouth finally free of water. Each step was a pain for every one of her muscles, her bleary eyes focused on Melyssa's hand, and she slowly moved up. Her whole body was numb, but Melyssa's concerned eyes kept her going. Sasha noticed Melyssa's shouts getting louder and saw her body shaking with more fear than she had seen all night. She couldn't move any higher; something was preventing her. She looked down a few steps and saw a tentacle wrapping itself around her waist.

Sasha's only strength left was to scream.

Melyssa's was louder.

The tentacle pulled Sasha away from the ladder and hoisted her in the air. She feebly beat at it with her tired fists. Her squeals grew quiet as more tentacle coils moved up her body and tightened. Sasha's mouth filled with blood as her ribs were broken and splintered her internal organs; the tentacles kept squeezing Sasha as her beating hands dropped to her side.

Melyssa was used to the cold now; the waters and whipping wind had been around her all night. Her face was suddenly splattered with warmness, and the shock knocked her back a few steps. The lovely warm feeling stayed on her face until it dripped over her eyes; she took hold and pulled it off, it was a part of Sasha.

The prolonged scream from Melyssa made a few more lights from the docked boats turn on. Melyssa stood shivering on the dock, covered from head to toe in Sasha's blood.

Sasha's crushed body and the tentacle responsible dropped in the water and didn't resurface. Another lighted tentacle rose from the sea and hovered above the shivering Melyssa. It hesitated for a brief moment. Melyssa stood still and shut her eyes, anticipating the killer blow. The tentacle swayed gently but didn't move towards Melyssa's head.

A voice made her open her eyes as more tears made their way through the blood on her face.

"Hello, is anybody there?" A man's voice came from one of the boats.

"Hello?" The voice became louder.

The tentacle stiffened as soon as the hatch to the boat opened. It just as quickly went limp and made a return to the water with a quick splash.

A middle-aged man appeared onto the harbour. His eyes moved around in the dark until they locked on to a shivering Melyssa. He couldn't take them off of her blood-soaked face and clothes. "Jesus Christ," he whispered.

She gave a little jump at the sound of his voice.

"Are you alright?"

Melyssa backed away from him. She had been shouting for help, but when it finally appeared, she was fearful.

"What happened to you?" he asked, approaching her tentatively.

She couldn't speak. Sasha's blood and shock stopped her. Melyssa simply whimpered.

The man turned back to his boat and shouted. "Natalie! Call an ambulance and the police."

A woman's voice spoke next from the boat. "What's going on out there?"

"I don't know," he said, unable to take his eyes away from the sad sight of Melyssa covered in blood.

"I'm coming out," Natalie said.

Suddenly Melyssa started screaming.

She was still screaming by the time Natalie made an appearance.

* * *

Kiya sat quietly behind a desk at her workshop. It was very late, but she was transfixed with watching her laptop. The room had huge lights running across the ceiling, but the only illumination came from the computer. Various film posters littered the walls of the room.

She frantically pressed buttons and swiped away on a tablet to her left. The tablet was controlling a drone; its view was showing the remnants of the stricken party boat.

Suddenly the lights above her began to flicker, and then they lit the room. Latex rubber monster masks littered the room, masks and models were dotted everywhere, Werewolves, Zombies and other fantastic creations. Models with grotesque features and bloody perfect textures. Some were colourful and complete, the others still needed work. The creature designs were magnificent.

A young woman entered. She was in her mid-twenties, her hair was brown, her face filled with stunning freckles. They startled each other.

"Oh, Kiya! Didn't see you there. What are you doing?"

Kiya slammed the laptop down and shared the surprise. "Shelly, hi. What are you doing here?"

"I came in to get my sketch pad, remember. I'm off next week, so thought I'd make a start on those creatures for that new CBBC series."

"Ah yeah, *Minors vs Monsters*, how's that coming on?"

"Not bad. I've got an idea for the leader of the monsters, a giant ape. I've called it Margaret Scratcher."

"Is that wise? I feel a lawsuit coming on."

"It's just a nickname. The writers will give it a final name from their script."

"Ah, good."

Shelly stared back with an odd expression. "What are you doing here?"

Kiya kept her eyes on Shelly as she walked between the workstations. "I'm just, I'm just…" She hiccupped. "I'm just going over the final details of the new 20,000 leagues under the sea film project."

Shelly clapped her hands excitedly. "Oh yes, you're testing out the movements for that giant creature, right?" She glanced over to her laptop. "Have you got it out? Can I see?"

Kiya slowly slid the laptop further away. "No, I mean not yet. It's got some niggling issues to sort out before we test it."

Shelly moved closer, adding to Kiya's anxiety. "Please? I want to see it."

"I said no, Shelly!" she snapped, which shocked Shelly and herself. Shelly stood back.

Kiya paused for a moment and then waved her finger in a fake rebuke. She brightened to relax Shelly. "Sorry, listen, you know me, I want things to be perfect, always have been a stickler for detail."

Shelly eyed up the empty wine bottle by Kiya's side. "You sure you're okay?"

"I'm fine, honestly, it's all good here." She relaxed back into her seat and flicked a worried look at the laptop. "All good."

Shelly nodded slowly, collected her sketch pad from her worktop and made her way out of the door.

Kiya sensed the tension and waved her hand to grab Shelly's attention. "Listen, the test run tomorrow will be fine. I'll have most of the team with me."

Shelly swung back immediately. "Did you do the tentacle extension test?"

"Yes."

"What about the suction cups and the light effects?"

"I think so."

"You were joking about adding hallucinogens in its beak as well, right?"

Kiya nodded vigorously and instantly changed the subject. "Was there anything else?"

"Have you hired the vans to put the creature in?"

"Yes, we'll take it apart, put the pieces in the vans and reassemble it at..." Kiya's voice trailed off, and she looked to the ceiling in deep thought as Shelly spared her.

"The swimming baths in Turgan Road. I've booked the pool for the evening, and I've emailed the address and booking details to you."

"Thank you."

"You are most welcome," Shelly said obligingly.

"What would I do without you?"

"Stickler for detail?" she said with a grin.

"Good one," Kiya replied, laced with sarcasm. "What would I do without you, Shelly?"

"You would struggle as always, Kiya."

Both women gave genuine chuckles.

"On that note, I will leave you to it, boss."

"Thanks again, Shelly."

She got to the door and made another turn to Kiya. "Just one more thing."

"What's that, Columbo?"

"Who?"

"Doesn't matter," Kiya sighed at wasting a good gag.

"When you get the octopus in the pool, can you film it and send me the link? Practical effects over CGI will look great in the film. I really want to see it in action."

Kiya shifted uneasily in her chair and took a moment to answer. "Me too."

Shelly smirked. "See you in two weeks, and remember, I want pictures."

She headed out the door and didn't return, turning off the lights on her way out.

Kiya sat in the darkness and opened her laptop. Again she punched every button on the keyboard, but nothing was responding except the live feed coming back from her drone over the water. As she pulled the drone away via the tablet, she failed to notice an ambulance and police car parked up on the edge of the harbour. She gave up on the laptop and shut it again, sitting in total darkness.

"Shit."

Suddenly there was a beep from her phone. She opened it and found she had a notification from YouTube, a new video, 12 seconds long.

Kiya pressed play.

There was music playing and raucous laughter from a group of girls. One girl with incredibly high heels was dancing on a table. She leaned back and fell off, crashing onto a chair but kept her phone in her hand.

Kiya cracked a slight smile. "That is pretty funny."

Lose the Ethnic

Ben Butterworth
29 Steel Paddock Lane
New Chelsea
Humberfield

"Driver! Driver! Don't go pissing off, and get back in your cab!"

Ben Butterworth looked up from his phone and saw his colleague lead a confused driver back to his lorry.

"You stay in your cab until we finished unloading you," the angry man barked.

"Please, I need toilet," the driver said; his lorry and trailer were from Poland. It was hooked up to a docking bay, and he obviously had thought the unloading process was finished.

"No! You stay in cab until we tell you to leave." The angry man was using hand signals to the driver, but his efforts were wasted and embarrassing as the poor man held his urine inside and returned to the vehicle.

The annoyed worker headed towards the back of the docking bay where Ben was leaning against a forklift truck.

"What the hell, man! Get off your phone and finish unloading this bloke."

Ben put his phone away and got back onto the forklift truck. He strapped himself in and continued unloading the Polish vehicle, riding up the ramp. A few lifts later, he was done, driving the forklift back into the warehouse. The angry man pressed a button on the docking bay, and the huge ramp lifted from the trailer and retracted into the bay; he walked back off the dock and to the cab.

"Stay in your cab, driver, documents in ten min." He held out both hands to show all his digits.

The driver nodded. "I have time for toilet now?"

"Yeah."

The man's anger had subsided, and he pointed past the lorry. "Walk down that path, past the car park, and it's the portakabin on the left."

The driver left his cab and hurried away.

Ben sat forlornly on his forklift truck, still looking at his phone.

"What's happening with you? This idiot shouldn't have taken that long." With still no reply from Ben, Jason came closer. "Ben, man!" he clapped him on the back. "So that girl you took out last night, she hasn't got back to you yet?"

Jason was the same age as Ben, both in their 30s, both had a working life in logistics, but that's where the similarities ended. Jason was a lad, an older, short, bullish lad, but still the misogynistic views he had 10 years ago didn't die out like page 3 did in the tabloids.

Ben didn't want to be there at all, he joined a local theatre group in his teens and had some background artist roles in some soap operas, but even that work dried up, and his girlfriend Melyssa left him soon afterwards. He was still a minor celebrity in the distribution warehouse, mostly just for piss-takes with his colleagues, especially when one of the soaps he appeared in was on the television at break time. He knew he was a failure at work but didn't want to be with the opposite sex, but dating was hard for him; he would over analyse any situation which wasn't appealing to anybody.

"I said did your date get back to you?"

Jason's words and the slap on the back bought Ben back to earth. "No, she hasn't replied yet."

"Why not? Did you bore her to death or something?"

"No, we went out for a meal and had a lovely time. I made her laugh, she made me laugh, it was nice, we finished the meal, and I offered to drive her home, which she accepted."

Jason got excited. He moved closer to Ben on his forklift truck; his eyes demanded more.

Ben noticed how dark the skies had become in seconds, and he noticed a few drops of rain hit the side of the Polish driver's lorry. "It's starting to rain."

"Who cares? What happened?" Jason wanted date answers.

"Well, after I dropped her off and she invited me in for coffee, plus she said her flatmate was away, which I didn't think was relevant."

"Yeah, go on."

"So I thanked her for a good night and left."

Jason's eager beam dropped. "You what? You just left her?"

"Well, I didn't leave her; she was on her doorstep. I waited until she walked in, and then when I got back home, I sent a text to say what an enjoyable evening I had with her."

Jason shook his head in expected disappointment. "What's wrong with you?"

Ben looked at Jason.

"What do you mean? I had a nice time, we both did, and if she doesn't fancy me, at least we may be friends and speak on social media."

Jason sucked in a huge breath. "This girl invited you into her flat, she was all ready to sit on your face, and you just binned her off, saying how you just want to be friends? You doughnut! She offered you a better end of your date than you could possibly imagine, and you just threw it back at her. You've pissed her off, you will never speak to her again unless you get drunk on a weekend and text her, and that is just being a prat on your part. Texting an ex-girlfriend when you're pissed up is bad enough, but texting a girl you just went out on a date with is social media suicide."

Ben waited for a gap in Jason's speech. "So you think I should have gone in?"

Jason beckoned for Ben's phone. "Let me see a picture of this girl you took out then."

Ben swiped and pressed buttons on his phone and then handed it to Jason. "This is her."

Jason's eyes widened, impressed. "Punching well above your weight there, mate. I'll definitely have a slice of that cake."

"Good god." Ben sighed and snatched the phone back. "Well, looks like she isn't going to get back to me."

"That's your fault, should have gone in when she invited you in. Any other tarts you looking at?"

"Don't call them that."

"Don't give a toss. Is there anybody else?"

"One or two girls have caught my eye, obviously. Nicki was the one I took out; don't think she'll get back to me."

"Plenty more fish in the sea. Pass me your phone again."

Ben repeated the phone entry process and gave it back to Jason.

"Oh Christ," Jason murmured. "Plenty more whales also, it seems."

"Please don't body shame. It's rude and disgusting."

Jason ignored Ben and carried on scanning each profile, his thumb swiping quickly. "Look at this one, Sally. Says she works at the post office in the returns department, looks like she could do with returning a few dinners."

"What the hell is wrong with you, Jason? Stop being a dick."

Jason whispered something Ben couldn't hear as he looked at the next girl. "This one is called Helen. Says, 'Believe it or not, I'm still scared of the dark.' Looks like she's scared of mirrors too."

"Have you finished yet?" Ben asked.

"No, mate, this is fun."

Jason went through Ben's phone and took pleasure in insulting every girl who appeared on his dating app. After he'd finished, he took glee in Ben's disapproval. Jason raised an eyebrow in a 'Roger Moore' James Bond way. "None of these birds are any good."

"Stop calling them that, and I'm sure to meet a lovely person online."

"How's that working out for you? Listen, I just don't understand why girls can't just go to a pub or club, shut their noise for five minutes while blokes chat them up, why? Because you're getting in their personal space, and it offends them."

"So you think we just have to club girls over the head like a caveman?"

"Worked for him. He was always with those three birds in the cartoon."

Ben got off the forklift and leant against it. "That's captain caveman."

"So?" Jason said without looking up.

"You still have my phone."

"She's alright. I'll have a go on that."

Ben could only sigh as Jason continued. "Hey, this Chinese-looking girl is a tasty sort as well."

Ben angrily snapped the phone back; he hoped for the last time. "What's wrong with you? You can't say stuff like that. How do you know she's Chinese?"

"Calm down, Mr Sensitive; it says so on her profile."

There were many nationalities who worked on the shop floor, mostly eastern Europeans and only three black men. Ben was the only black British person in the warehouse. There was racism within the workplace, Ben would have been naive not to think so, but it was a subtle racism and not in your face, not like the rife sexism that oozed throughout many of the male workforce.

Unfortunately, it was many of his eastern European colleagues that caught the flack of hushed tones of begrudgement from his British-born workmates. He knew if this was the 70s, it would be him that people would be blaming for 'taking their jobs', but as it stands, he was one of the lads, albeit extremely liberal.

Jason's soft laugh was what Ben heard next.

"Break time, soft lad. Let me know if your date gets in touch."

He flicked through his phone for a few more positive swipes before climbing back onto his forklift and following Jason to the drive for the break room.

* * *

The canteen where the warehouse staff took their break was a big one. There was a pool table near one corner and a tattered old dart board on the opposite side of the room. The kitchen served many foods on a tray, handed out by a tired and overworked staff. A small number of workers sat on chairs behind tables scattered around a huge TV set placed on a wall directly in the centre of the room.

Breakfast was the busiest time for the kitchen staff; the shop floor workers piled in with their plates on trays waiting to be given their break time food.

The TV was playing a rolling 24-hour news channel, and it was showing highlights of a women's football game. England were playing in the World Cup. Ben went to the communal fridge in the corner and took out a small bag of grapes with a banana, and then found a seat in front of the TV.

Jason soon followed and went straight to get a full English breakfast from the canteen.

Their table had two other chairs filled by Nick, a quiet, tall man who was in his sixties with heavyset glasses and a mane of grey hair. He was reading a newspaper and seemed oblivious to the noise around him; he was looking forward to retirement more than anything else. In the other chair was the team leader,

Frank, a short man the same height as Jason but more sturdy. His bald head and face showed scars, battered from a life before becoming the head of the current shift. His eyes were small and extremely close together, it seemed unnatural and a strange sight to see on first meetings, but eventually you got used to it; nobody ever bought it up or used it as a joke at his expense.

Frank watched as the two sat down. He eyed up the screen and turned to Jason. "Did you watch this rubbish last night?"

Jason glanced up at the screen, still reporting on the women's football and picked at his breakfast before answering his boss. "Yeah, I saw it, we were down to ten men."

Jason corrected himself quickly. "Ten women at half-time, one got sent off."

"Why, what happened?" Frank asked.

"Someone had to go off and make the tea!"

Jason and Frank exploded into heavy laughter as Nick and Ben stayed silent, carrying on with their breakfast and paper reading respectively.

"I'm just waiting for them to swap shirts at full-time." Jason rocked back in his chair, hysterically laughing at his boss's comment.

"I mean, did you actually watch the game? God, it was so boring. If it was being played in a back garden, you would close your curtains."

Frank noticed Ben's silence. "What's wrong with you?"

"You can't say those things anymore. It's like living in the 70s."

Frank stared at Jason.

"Don't worry, he's been like it all morning. At least it's now the 70s, it was the Stone Age earlier, so we're improving."

Jason turned back to Ben. "What you upset for? It's just a bunch of dozy mares running around a field, trying and failing to kick a ball as good as blokes do. They should stick to what they're good at and stay in the kitchen."

Ben felt himself cringe. "You do know what century this is, do you?"

"All I'm saying is that I'd rather watch a bunch of men play than a bunch of old cart-horses run around. Listen, I was watching *Match of the Day* the other night, and they had some woman commentating on one of the games. I mean, really? It's not netball. What the hell do they know about football? It's a joke having women talking about it."

Ben tried hard not to laugh, thinking that his colleagues were messing around until he noticed their faces in a tight scowl. "Are you for real? I can't believe I'm hearing this! That woman you're talking about has a degree in sports science and is also a football coach, qualified by the FA and played professional football where she was nominated for a young player of the year award by the PFA."

Frank blinked quickly and looked into Ben's stunned eyes. "Yeah, that sounds good and fair play to her, but if she can't make a decent bacon and egg sandwich for me, then what's the point?"

"You're disgusting," Ben said.

Frank didn't answer.

One of the women from the football team was being interviewed on the screen. She was South

American and attempting to conduct the interview in English. Struggling with some words, the footballer made a decent effort.

Frank and Jason laughed at the screen and imitated her accent. Ben opened his mouth quickly. "How many languages can either of you two speak?"

They both went quiet like scolded schoolchildren.

Nick didn't stir from his newspaper, and Ben just shook his head in pity. He had to say something. "You do know there are girls in school right now who want to be professional footballers, girls I'm guessing who can play better than the guys you pay extortionate prices every weekend to travel to watch home and away."

Frank didn't answer. He knew when Ben was in this mood, it was great to wind him up, but you had to let him breathe every now and then.

"You really think I'm a dinosaur, don't you? An old-fashioned throwback to the men of the 70s, don't you?"

Ben didn't answer; he wanted to but also wanted to have a break of some sort.

"You think I'm thick, an idiot, that I don't know anything?"

"I doubt you can have *Babestation* girls as a specialised subject on *Mastermind*."

Frank smiled, waited for a moment and then spoke again. "So how's the dating going, Ben? Met anybody yet?"

Ben clutched his forehead. "It's fine, I'm meeting really nice people, and it's all fine, thank you."

"Mate, you don't join dating apps to meet nice people, you go on there to meet your next missus or at least get some."

Ben looked annoyed. "That's just wrong. I'm not on these dating sites for sex."

"So why are you going on them then?

"It's not all about sex; it's about friendship and meeting kindred spirits."

Frank laughed and didn't want to stop, so Jason took over. "Most of the girls on your social media sites are failed dates, admit it."

Ben chewed on a fingernail, still listening to Jason.

"That to me is useless and a waste of time. If I have a date with a girl from a dating site and by the end of the night she's not in my bed, I would want my money back."

"For heaven's sake!" Ben moaned.

Frank's eyes stared hard at Ben, keeping their look as Ben's own eyes turned to meet them.

"By the way, when you do go out on your next date, make them laugh. Women don't forget anybody who can make them laugh."

Jason nodded in agreement.

"Plus, don't forget to use the old black boot polish."

Ben shook his head again in disbelief on hearing Frank's comment. "Why would you say that? That's completely inappropriate and racist."

Frank looked confused. "What are you talking about?"

"Oh come on! Use boot polish? So what this is a blackface gag now? Just scrub it on my face to look like the *Black and White Minstrel Show*. That's just plain wrong and ridiculous, Frank."

Frank hesitated but then spoke with a reasonable calmness. "Mate, it's common knowledge that women look at men's shoes on a first date; the cleaner the shoes, the better chance of a nice night, just so long as he's not a dick."

The whole table went quiet.

A news report came on, and most of the heads turned back to the screen when it was local and heard a familiar place from their area. A face flashed on the TV, and a young boy's mugshot appeared. He had attacked another youth with a knife and had been charged and convicted. His previous offences were mentioned, including drug dealing and GBH.

Frank's little eyes studied the picture and then turned to Jason. "Another one off the street."

"Good, dirty bastards."

Frank's mouth twisted in disdain as Jason continued. "They should round them all up and kill every one of them."

"Line them up against a wall with a firing squad. Yeah, that sounds about right."

Frank was well into his stride now and shifted in his chair, pointing to the screen and waggling his finger at Jason. "What gets me is that lot, that scum shouldn't even be over here; they should go back to where they come from."

Ben sat in his chair, shocked at what he'd just heard. He managed a stutter. "What the hell are you talking about?"

"You what?" Frank said.

"You do know I'm black, right?"

"I have noticed, thanks."

"Yet, you're willing to spout out that racist stuff in front of me."

Frank held his arms up in defence. "Racist? I'm not a racist, but—"

"Let me stop you right there." Ben slowed his speech down and gently lowered his voice as he was still speaking to his boss. "The moment someone tells me that they're not racist and add a 'but'... 9 times out of 10 are the most racist people I've met in my life."

Frank moaned and rolled his eyes; they didn't have far to go.

"Another one off the street? And they should be lined up against a wall and shot? Sounds pretty racist to me."

"Drug dealers, Ben."

"What?"

Drug dealers, not addicts. I believe in rehabilitation and hope they get the help they need, but drug dealers should be taken off the streets permanently."

Jason nodded in agreement.

Ben reclined in his chair, not convinced. "Okay, what about when you said 'they shouldn't even be over here' and they should 'go back to where they come from' – sounds racist."

"I still agree with that."

"Thought so." Ben let out a quiet, triumphant puff.

"Yes, they shouldn't be over here and should go back to where they come from, back to south London or any part of London that deals in drugs. I don't want them coming here to Humberfield and selling drugs to our kids, do you?"

"No," Ben admitted with a glum expression.

"While you were getting on your high horse, I was paying attention to the news. Listen, mate, the whole world isn't out to get you, there are some evil bastards in this world, and some happen to be black. Does that make me a racist if I say that?"

"Yeah, but..."

"Listen, Ben, he was scum, that lot always are. He got what he and all of those filth deserve. Job done, case closed."

Jason took a sip of coffee, observing and agreeing. He then nudged Frank to look at the screen, the weather report was on view as was the young female meteorologist. "That's a nice bit of slice."

Frank agreed with a smile, and the pair were now fixated on the screen. It seemed the past conversation was now instantly forgotten, and Jason and Frank had moved on with ease, and the svelte figure of the weather presenter had their complete attention.

Ben was working with Jason for the rest of the shift, he had done for years. Even though he was incredibly sexist, Jason was a good worker when he wanted to be. Both he and Ben had started working in the warehouse at the same time as temps. Ben did all the overtime going, plus weekends when needed, while Jason lounged around the offices with the bosses cracking jokes and sexual innuendo. He fitted in naturally with the male sexist *Carry On* style humour in the workplace.

Jason was made permanent within a year, and Ben was entering his tenth year as a temp. Others had come and gone and had also been taken on within their time with the company. It hadn't really bothered Ben until after his fifth year, anyone who strolled into work with a right-wing redtop newspaper under their arm was guaranteed a full-time job, whereas if you listened to Radio 4 and watched any arts channel, you were considered too highbrow and a work leper.

"She'd get it." Frank followed up on Jason's observation on the weather girl.

"What do you think, Ben? Is she worth a bit?"

Ben couldn't understand his boss. One minute he was talking about his support for victims of drug abuse, and the next he had turned into a caveman and ogling a female presenter on TV. He stared unbelievingly at the two and then rose to his feet, picking up his bag of remaining grapes and his peeled banana.

"Where you going?" Jason giggled.

Ben looked out of the window of the canteen and saw a brilliant sun rising in the distance. "I'm going outside."

"It's freezing out there," Frank said without looking up from his full English breakfast.

Ben took a slow and soft bite from his banana and headed towards the door. "It's colder in here," he replied.

Ben left the room, leaving Jason and Frank cackling like hyenas, his phone beeped and he checked the message. It was from Nicki, his last date.

Hiya, fancy a McDonald's later?

As he walked out, Ben's spirits slowly began to rise.

* * *

The cars queued patiently in the road to exit the building. It was 2pm, and the early shift workers were leaving site to head home or wherever they needed to be after work. The security staff in the building checked every car as they left site. Employees left their car boots open to be inspected. Once satisfied, the safety barrier would rise and the car would leave.

Walking beside the cars was a young man in a very baggy tracksuit wearing an orange hi-visibility vest.

He was pulling a wooden pallet with a pump truck; on the pallet was an empty washing machine box. The first security guard acknowledged him straight away.

"Hello, Henry. What's in the box?"

The young man spoke with a soft voice, barely a whisper. "Hello, boss, just an empty box, nothing in it, just dumping it in the second skip around the building."

The security guard looked in the box and confirmed it was empty to his colleague with a thumbs up to raise the barrier.

"Thanks, boss," Henry said with a contented smile. He waited for the barrier to rise and then pulled the pump truck away from the building.

The security guard watched the cleaner walk away, and the barrier closed as a car pulled up. Ben got out of his car and opened his boot for a check, he also saw Henry disappear around the building.

"Not doing overtime today, Ben?" the security guard asked.

Ben slammed the boot shut after he got the-all clear. "Nope, not today, have a date this afternoon."

"Ah nice." The guard was genuine.

"Going anywhere special?"

"McDonald's."

"Ah okay, different, have fun."

His smile wasn't so genuine now.

* * *

Ben rarely had a second date with anybody, but when they did arise, it was going bowling, a visit to a zoo or even a day out at a theme park. All of the dates came to nothing, so he was up for a change. However, a meeting in a fast-food restaurant was not what he'd expected.

Casually dressed as he was last night when he met Nicki before, Ben sat at the table in his local McDonald's. It was 4pm, and he had finished his 6am-2pm shift to scramble home and change, refusing overtime which he hated to do, but a date would always come first. It was busy at the restaurant, it was filled with children who had finished school and just wanted some junk food before they went home.

Ben sat nervously at his table, more anxious than last night. He had used up all of his gags and quirky anecdotes yesterday, Nicki laughed at all of them, but now he needed some new material to keep her entertained. He was quickly scouring YouTube after work for jokes from comedians which he could use on his second date, he had enough for the afternoon.

Nicki walked in before he could recite any of the stolen gags he'd remembered. She nimbly eased past the tables with shouting kids and tired parents, wearing knee-high brown boots and a camel-coloured mac coat.

Nicki waved at Ben and seemed impressed with her date's reaction. "Hello, you. Thanks for turning up."

"Hiya, sorry about last night."

Nicki sat down, and her eyes turned huge at what Ben said. "What last night? No need to apologise, you were the perfect gentleman."

Ben struggled to relax with all the kids running around him. "Yeah, but you invited me in and I left."

Nicki held her eyes towards Ben and smiled. "Gives us more time to get to know one another then."

She looked around. "You hungry?" she asked.

"Yeah, I'll get something. What do you fancy?"

Nicki left the table no sooner than she arrived, and before Ben could give his answer. She went to the order screen and swiped away like she was on a dating app, not even looking at him. Ben watched as she scanned the menu and seemed to take an age making her decision. Nicki finally turned to give him the thumbs up and returned to the table with her receipt.

"All good?" he asked.

"Coolio," she replied, waving the receipt.

Ben sank a little, that was what his ex-girlfriend, Melyssa, used to say all the time and he hated it. It may have been the big age gap between the two, as she was 10 years younger than him."

"We're number 195."

A little boy ran past and knocked her leg on the way.

"Hey, careful little fella!" Ben nervously laughed.

He watched the boy dart in between a number of legs queuing up at the serving desk.

"Some kids, eh? Little terrors."

Nicki didn't respond right away. "Well, I know you're not a vegetarian or vegan so I ordered you a Big Mac meal."

"With water?"

Nicki's mouth hung open, and then she spoke tentatively. "Yes, because you hate Coke."

"You remembered?"

"Not hard. Anybody who doesn't drink Coke is a nut and easy to remember."

Ben stifled a laugh. "Just don't get it, full of sugar, ruins your teeth, makes you burp, don't see the point."

"Double JD and water sounds much better." She quickly grinned and then it left. She was already waiting for her number to appear on the screen and wasn't concerned if Ben had an answer.

The outpouring of children running around was a growing concern for him, they were everywhere, and he was becoming more agitated as each child accidentally hit him as they ran past; some apologised, most didn't.

"Woah!" Ben craned his neck around and watched the little kids run to the crayoning table. "These kids are pretty wild."

Nicki kept her eyes on the screen and didn't attempt to move them. "Does that bother you?"

"No, just think that the parents should be keeping a better eye on them."

"Totally agree," Nicki said nonchalantly.

She shifted away from the order collection screen and looked at him. "Did you watch the *Big Brother* catch-up last night?" Her eyes locked onto him finally.

"Yeah, I watched it. The show is so awful, can't believe people are still applying to get on that show." Ben gave another glance around, hoping the kids didn't run back again. "Because it's now having to spend a whole year in a house full of wannabes and Z-listers."

Nicki nodded, her eyes straying back to her waiting food list. "Three million pounds, though, to waste a year of your life for a shot at turning on the Christmas lights in Dunstable or hosting a Sunday morning cookery show?"

Ben folded his napkins, which he'd acquired earlier, onto his lap. "Not sure I could do that, living with all those people running around naked in front of the camera."

He pulled his foot in quickly as another kid ran past. "Bloody hell."

Nicki gave a quick eye flick to him. "I like your shirt, by the way."

"Thank you."

"Did you sleep in it?"

Ben shook his head in laughter. "No, I just don't have an ironing board."

"Really?"

"Yeah, just don't see the need to iron anymore, I wash and put the clothes on an airer, and that's it."

Nicki looked with concern at his eyes. "It's not working."

Ben made a shivered smile, slightly confused.

Nicki went back to the order screen. "You aren't going to impress a girl wearing a shirt with more creases than…" She paused. "Bugger! Can't think of anyone who has an old face on TV."

Her angelic face looked fun while she was thinking. Ben studied her more as she was in deep thought.

"Doesn't matter." She shrugged.

Ben left his seat and headed for the condiment table. "Do you want any sauces?" he asked.

"Yeah, could you get some Bee Bee Q sauce?"

Ben quickly shifted his neck back to her and slowly leaned in. "You what?"

"Bee Bee Q sauce, don't you like it?"

"Don't know it?"

"Of course you do."

Nicki stood up. "Watch our seats."

They passed each other as Ben returned to his chair. Nicki rummaged through the packets of condiments and came back to the table, her hand filled with sachets. "These, see?"

"Barbecue," Ben said politely.

"Yeah, spell it."

"B-a-r."

"No, what does it say on the front of the sachet?"

"It says BBQ." Ben held his eyes to her.

"There you go," she said flippantly.

Nicki peeled off the wrapper and stuck her finger in, swirling it around and offering Ben a lick afterwards. He put his hand up in a mock defensive way. "I'm fine, thanks."

Nicki's eyes switched back to her predatory target of the collection screen. Happy that the wait for their food wasn't too long away, she decided to talk to Ben. "Thanks for a lovely time last night, really enjoyed myself." Her voice was brighter and more casual.

Ben swallowed slowly and very visibly upbeat. "I had a great time too."

"No, seriously, you were so funny and listened to me."

He cocked his head, confused. "Doesn't everybody?"

"You'll be surprised."

Ben appeared shocked. "So guys really don't listen to you?"

Nicki's eyes were back to Ben. "I'm not constantly out dating, you know."

"Yeah, sorry, just that—"

Ben rested his arms on the table and saw Nicki was back to being preoccupied with their upcoming order. "Well, I had a lovely time, too." His voice raised slightly to get her attention, his eyes dropped as he realised he'd already said that.

It worked anyway as Nicki hadn't completely ignored him. "Relax, Ben, if I didn't want to see you again, I wouldn't."

Her words were direct, not loud, but it made him take note.

"Thank you."

"We haven't finished yet."

Nicki slipped back into fun mode as their food number appeared on the screen. "Yay!"

Her happy gaze bore into Ben as she left the table and went to collect their order.

Ben watched as Nicki seemed genuinely happy to get the food. She looked so sweet and cheerful as she returned with a tray. As soon as the tray hit the table, Ben rummaged through to check his goods.

Nicki watched him sort through his order. "All good?"

A mouthful of chips and a thumbs up was all she needed to know from him. Nicki gave a laugh and waited for Ben to finish. "You're still nervous, I can tell."

Ben gobbled up the fries which had spilled onto the tray and looked up. "Well, like I said last night, I don't really date that much since Melyssa left."

"Ah, yes I remember, your ex-girlfriend. You said she had a wandering eye, awful when partners can't stay faithful."

"No, she didn't cheat. Her wandering eye was her left one; it pointed in a different direction to the other. I think it's fixed now, and she's met someone else, a girl, I think."

Nicki didn't speak, thinking that it was information she should have remembered from the first-date inane talk from last night. She slowly looked up and whispered. "Nobody cheated. She just got bored and left you, right?"

"I guess so."

"Are you sure she didn't cheat on you?"

Ben shrugged. Nicki leant in with inquisitive eyes. "You alright?"

He quickly tried to change the conversation. "Yeah, I'm fine. We had a nice time, didn't we?"

"It couldn't have gone better," Nicki replied.

Ben offered her a solitary chip. Nicki snapped it up and swiped a few more from his tray.

"So you had my attention last night, Ben. What can you do now to keep it?"

He looked at her as she played around with the chips in her mouth. Her tongue twisted them as if she was playing with a Rubik's cube.

"I'll surprise you," he said. "When you least expect it."

"Looking forward to it." She beamed with a mouthful of chips.

Ben didn't seem to mind. However, the kids buzzing past him were becoming more annoying. "Whoa! These kids are everywhere."

Nicki just about finished her chips. "What was that?"

"Just the kids running around."

Nicki took a sip from her milkshake. "Are they bothering you?"

"No, just wondering where the parents are. Anything could happen to them."

"Agreed," Nicki said firmly. Her head spun around, not as far round like the girl in the *Exorcist* film, but it was pretty close. "I'll tell them myself."

Nicki targeted the boy nearest their table. "Jamie! Stop running around and sit down!"

Before Ben could speak, Nicki spun back around in her seat. "I thought you were meant to be looking after them!"

Ben's eyes followed Nicki's voice to a man sat in the corner. The man looked up from the meal he was eating. "You looked like you were having fun, I didn't want to disturb you."

The little boy, Jamie, ran up to him as did another young girl and sat at his table.

Nicki threw her arms up in the air. "One day, Mark, one day I asked you to look after the kids, we both agreed."

Mark pushed his tray of half-eaten food to the children. "I know I said I'd look after them, but they just wanted to see their mum."

"Who's that?" Ben asked, confused and offended.

"That's my ex, Mark."

"Your ex?"

"Yes, ex, as in no longer together and father of my kids."

"Those are your kids?" Ben's voice rose in surprise.

Mark gave a polite wave and sympathetic smile, which Ben reciprocated.

"You never said you had children."

Nicki shook her head. "It shouldn't be a problem."

"It wasn't."

He felt her eyes on him. "It isn't a problem. I just thought something like that would have come out last night."

Nicki's eyes widened. "Something like that? So my children are just 'something' now?"

Ben went quick on the defensive. "Wait, hold on, I've done nothing wrong. You never mentioned them."

"Mentioned them? Keep digging that hole, Ben."

Ben glanced over to Mark. He was still smiling over to them; it was turning into a smirk as he was obviously anticipating it.

"Nicki, I don't know what you want me to say? Yes, it's a shock to see your kids running around in McDonald's, but it wouldn't have bothered me if you had told me yesterday. I thought we were getting on?"

"We were until you dissed my kids."

"Dissed? What are we back in the 90s?"

Before Nicki could react, he grabbed her hand. "Just listen for a minute. Whether you had children or not, I had a great night yesterday and am loving an even greater afternoon in McDonald's."

Nicki wasn't convinced. "Really?"

Ben took another look at Mark, but he was playing with his children at the table, and for once the kids were content; he didn't get a smile this time.

He switched back to Nicki, looking deep into her eyes. Ben's soothing tone continued. "Let's start again, right at the beginning of this delicious meal, which will probably give me the shits tomorrow morning."

Ben put his hand over his mouth, lowering his head; his guilty eyes looked left to right quickly. "Sorry, bad language when there are kids around, not cool."

Nicki's voice became less serious. "It's fine, don't think they heard it. Swearing is completely off-limits to my kids, though."

"I get it and completely understand."

He was getting ready to accept another rejection speech from a failed date. Nicki picked up a chip from her tray and slowly made sure it entered Ben's mouth smoothly.

"Thank you," he said, loving the surprise.

"Don't mention it."

"Wasn't going to."

"I like you, Ben."

She looked around and smiled mischievously. "Mark should have the kids for the night." Nicki kept the smile up as she eventually took a sip from her drink. "I can really make you swear hard if you want to come over to mine?"

Ben considered her offer, hoping she didn't notice him slightly shaking. "Yes please."

"Good."

Folding her arms across her chest, Nicki thought for a moment. "Well, let's put this stuff into a bag, and you can come back now or wait until later?"

Ben was hit hard now, the dilemma of going back to her place for what was looking to be a sexual encounter or declining and still continuing to be the upstanding gentleman she was attracted to in the first place. He didn't want to embarrass himself with a cheesy joke he'd heard from a panel show comedian. Nicki wasn't waiting and unfolded her arms.

"When I get back home, I'm going to unwind for a bit, take these clothes off and relax in a lovely bath with scented candles all around me, do you like candles, Ben?"

"Only for birthdays and power cuts."

Nicki's mouth opened wide like an egg-eating snake, and she emptied the rest of the chips from the carton. She licked the salt from her lips and pretended not to notice Ben's eyes on her. "So, what do you think?"

He wiped a trail of sweat from his forehead. "Now, please. I mean if that's ok with you?"

"Perfect, you get the food. I'm just going to say goodbye to my little munchkins."

Nicki reached for his hand. "I know this may seem a little bit quick, but after last night's date, I think we get one another."

Ben shook his head and laughed. "So my jokes weren't that bad?"

"Baby steps." She grinned.

Across the other side of their seating area, Jamie watched his mum getting ready to leave. She had hardly spoken to him or his sister today, and her new friend was getting all the attention. Jamie slid off his chair, ducked beneath the table and slid out between Mark's legs. Stretching out, he saw his mum and Ben still holding hands as they stood up. Just wanting to say 'Hello', Jamie waited for his moment... and then acted quickly. Gathering speed, he easily avoided the other kids in his way and caught a look at Ben's eyes.

Jamie smiled as he saw them widen in surprise; he'd perfected his jump just right. Landing heavily and right on Ben's toes, this was a fun chance to introduce himself. A scream shattered the air, a scream followed by an extreme obscenity. Diners' heads all turned to see the car crash Ben's mouth had left.

The next 49 seconds were a blur for him. Nicki had already grabbed Jamie away from him and was heading for the exit, grabbing her daughter on the way. She stumbled on a step and almost fell down, but her two children kept her balance. She couldn't leave McDonald's fast enough; it was her date who let her down, not the food.

Ben whipped off his trainers and rubbed his sore toes. He watched Mark follow his ex out of the door. Mark was smiling again.

* * *

It was late evening and Ben was back home. Nicki was ignoring his messages and two phone calls. He was already on the Pinot Grigio and unfortunately had sent most of the messages way after he started his second bottle. Looking past his sent messages, Ben hoped to hear a 'ping' and a reply from Nicki.

The wine was starting to kick in hard, and reading was becoming a struggle. Ben was resigned to being alone again for the night, so he started his drunk routine. Settling back on his sofa, he put on a 90s playlist from his phone and began watching TV. Something quickly entered the room and made him jump slightly. A black cat confidently strode in and jumped on Ben's lap.

"Hello, Stir Fry."

The cat turned around a few times before making itself comfortable. Reality cooking shows with Gordon Ramsay shouting at Americans made up a few hours of viewing. As time and booze went on, the music got louder, bringing out the air guitar and imaginary drum kit. Stir Fry had long since departed due to Ben's constant toilet breaks; he found a better place to curl up further down the couch.

Ben stopped the MTV nostalgia trip on his phone and craned his neck to look at the big clock on the wall. He opened his mouth to yawn and did a double take at the time, it was really late now, and he was still working early tomorrow. If he was at Nicki's tonight, then ringing in sick was an option in the morning. That wasn't happening now, as she hadn't returned any of his messages.

It wasn't enough for him, especially what may have happened at Nicki's tonight. Ben blinked slowly and pulled his laptop towards him and logged on to various social media sites, he looked at the profiles of ex-girlfriends and various past dates and saw that each and every one of them was now in a relationship.

He slammed the laptop shut. "Typical," he moaned.

***

Ben had managed to make it to work. No sore head from the wine, and still no word from Nicki. He dumped his petrol station sandwich into the communal fridge and went to his forklift truck. His eyebrows raised as Jason headed towards him.

"How'd the date go?"

Before Ben had a chance to answer, Frank tapped him on his shoulder. "You got a minute?"

"Yeah, um, yep."

"Take a seat in my office. I'll be there in a minute."

Ben simply nodded and walked through the double doors which led to Frank's office. He took a deep breath before he entered. The office was like any other, flow charts on a whiteboard showing how the company were performing this year. Some first aid and forklift truck certificates were on one wall. Advertising posters with over-smiling models using washing machines and vacuum cleaners littered the other walls.

Ben took one of the two seats opposite Frank's desk. He was nervous, not first-date nervous, but usually when people are hauled up into the boss's office and it's not Christmas bonus time, then somebody has made a mistake on the job.

The chair felt quite cheap and obviously on offer, but Ben tried to make himself comfortable until Frank arrived. Twenty minutes had passed and there was still no sign of Frank. Ben got up to have a closer look at the whiteboard, he didn't particularly find it interesting, but it was just a chance to stretch his legs. He wandered around the whole room and then to Frank's desk.

He knew he shouldn't, but it seemed there was no chance of Frank coming back any time soon. Not moving with a purpose, Ben browsed through Frank's desktop. Nothing really stood out, his laptop was open and had his football team's colours on the front, nothing seemed out of the ordinary until he noticed a list of things to do with today's date at the top.

1) *Meeting with Polly from the temp agency at 11am (Rescheduled from Jess, unavailable)*
2) *Order more white Euro pallets*
3) *Take the piss out of Ben*

Ben's stomach dropped when he saw the third. He stood there looking at the pad, a mixture of disappointment and anger. Breathing hard and heavy, Ben backed away from the table and headed for the door. Opening it slowly, he peeked around the corner. There was still no sign of Frank, and Ben was tempted to walk out and head back to work or maybe just walk out for good. He hesitated at the door, thinking about his options should he decide to leave his job. Before he could make the decision, he heard footsteps coming up the stairs to the left of the office and hurriedly sat back in his seat, whipping out his phone to put his supporting acting skills to good use.

The office door opened and Frank briskly entered. Seeing Ben sitting in his office gave him a little shock. "Hello, what are you doing here?"

Ben's frown deepened. "You told me to go to your office."

"Yes, sorry, I completely forgot all about you." Frank's face softened. "How long have you been here?"

"Twenty minutes, 30 at a push."

"Oh dear, sorry again, mate."

Clearly flustered, which was odd for Frank, he sat down at his desk and moved the mouse on his computer, fixated on the screen; his eyes looked up and down various screens until they stopped blinking and focused. Frank turned the screen towards Ben; it was a picture of a lorry attached to a 40-foot trailer.

"This delivery went to a Curry's warehouse in Guilford, but unfortunately it was meant to go to Nottingham."

Ben was unsure where this was going and kept listening.

"You loaded this delivery, but you put it on the wrong trailer, number 101, not 001."

He stared at the screen as Frank continued.

"Your name was on the loading document. It was a big mess."

"No, I didn't."

"Excuse me?"

"The paperwork said 001; that's why I loaded it on that trailer."

Frank opened the first drawer of his desk and pulled out some paperwork, showing it to Ben. "Is that your signature on that loading sheet?"

Ben looked down; the paperwork did say trailer number 101.

"Yes, that's my signature, but I loaded the right trailer; it didn't say 101 when I got the paperwork."

"In all honesty, this isn't the first time this has happened."

"I'm sorry?"

Frank wasn't even looking at Ben. "You've loaded quite a few trailers wrong over the past few weeks. I didn't say anything as I'd thought your work would improve, unfortunately it didn't."

Ben bent his top lip in and blew on to the bottom. "This is all new to me."

"Obviously."

"Why didn't you tell me before? If I had known I was making a mistake in my work, I would have stopped or at least hoped someone in charge would have told me about it?"

Frank finally peered at Ben from behind the laptop. "We're mates, have been for ages, that's why I kept quiet."

"Kept quiet? Why would you?"

Ignoring Ben's tone, Frank rubbed his teeth with a prying tongue. "I don't know, you seem quite distant recently. Is everything alright at home?"

"You know I live alone."

"Well, whatever is bothering you, it's affecting your work."

"I'm fine."

Ben took a look at Frank's notepad for just a few seconds; he hoped his boss would catch him staring. "So what now?" Ben asked nervously.

"Well, unfortunately, your loading errors will go against you with regards to achieving your full bonus this year."

"Wait, I thought my review was next month?"

"May as well do it now since you're here."

Ben was fighting hard to sit still in an already awkward chair. "Right, let's get this over with. Give me the bad news."

He couldn't believe he had said that so directly to his boss. Something was on his mind; he was still thinking about Nicki and her lack of contact.

"We've decided not to give you a full bonus this year."

Ben folded his arms and waited. Frank went through the tried and tested routine of explaining why and how Ben didn't receive his full bonus for the year.

As soon as he'd finished, Ben unfolded his arms and laid them on the table. "Wow, great."

Frank sensed a tinge of sarcasm from Ben, so thought he should wrap it up quite quickly. "Is there anything you would like to say?"

Ben sat motionless in the rubbish chair, not wanting to stay there any longer than needed. It wasn't just the conversation. Frank's breath stunk, not through cigarettes or drink, just a horrendous natural stink, like a diseased goat chewing on cheese.

"What about me being taken on full-time? Is that going to happen? I've been here for years and still temping."

For the first time since the meeting started, it was Frank who was slightly apprehensive. "I'm afraid we're not going to take you on as a permanent member of staff."

Taking a look at his watch, Ben wasn't interested anymore. "Listen, I've heard this all before, nothing's changed I guess, I've been working here for years and still won't get taken on."

"Don't you want to know the reason why?"

"Not really, I don't want to be rude or anything, but if there's nothing else, can I go now?"

"Just a moment; there is one more job I would like you to do."

Ben was in mid-rise from his chair but slowly sat back down. "Go on."

He was still taking the conversation relatively seriously, but the little respect he had for Frank was ebbing away.

"We had some new chest freezers delivered, model E500X, but unfortunately the instruction manuals inside were for a different model, the now redundant E300."

Frank paused, and their gazes finally locked longer than a second.

"They all have to be opened up, replace the old booklet for the new and then sealed back up again."

"When are they going back out for redelivery?"

"In two weeks."

"So you want me with a team to sort this out?"

Ben saw a strangely familiar look in Frank's eyes, never good. "No, you'll be doing it on your own."

His own eyes couldn't comprehend what Frank had just said and stretched wider. "On my own? How many freezers are there?"

"Eight hundred-ish."

Ben's neck craned forward. "How can I replace 800 chest freezer manuals in two weeks by myself?"

"Overtime, weekdays and weekends, it's down to you."

"I've got a life out of work, you know?"

"I wouldn't bet on it after yesterday."

"What's that supposed to mean?"

"How was McDonald's?"

Ben leaned back in his chair, and he answered with caution. "Fine, thanks. How did you know about that?"

"You really have no idea what I'm talking about, do you?"

Ben shook his head quickly.

Frank suppressed a grin and went to his phone. He swiped and pressed quickly before showing it to Ben, a chuckle finally made an appearance.

"Might be better to switch to Burger King if I was you."

Looking hard at the screen, it took him a while to take in what he was seeing. It was a video of the incident yesterday at McDonald's. Somebody had caught the exact moment Nicki's son jumped on him, and his swearing was used in a continuous loop with some comedy music for added effect. His contorted face was zoomed in on for the finale.

"It's all over social media."

He waited for Ben to respond, he didn't at first, so he kept talking. "I wouldn't look at the comments, mate." Frank smiled, knowing full well that Ben would.

Ben swallowed quickly, trying to picture what exactly he was looking at. His jaw clenched as his eyes followed the comments down the screen. Some were comedic, but the majority of them were insulting, abusive and toxic.

Frank saw Ben's eyes flutter and look away, staring blankly at the wall. "Okay, that's enough." He motioned for the return of the phone. There was a twinge of uneasiness on his face, the same shift which Ben's stomach was experiencing.

"Who's seen this?" Ben asked, eyes still wall bound.

"Everyone has. It's the Internet."

"I mean from work."

"The same, I'd expect. The lightning's out of the bag now, mate. You're an internet sensation, will probably be having interviews on breakfast television soon."

Ben's voice trembled. "Are we done here?"

"Yeah, look, I think it will get a few people laughing and pointing at you, but it'll soon blow over. Now, are you going to be alright?"

"Yes," Ben sighed.

"Do you mind telling your face that?"

Ben didn't answer.

Frank looked down at his laptop with a slow smirk. "Besides, you people are quite resilient and used to hardship."

Ben looked up and waited to catch Frank's eyelift from the screen. "You people? What do you mean by that?"

"West Ham supporters, what did you think I meant?"

The sick sensation in Ben's stomach didn't go away. "Nothing, it's fine."

"Right, so can you get started on those freezers now?"

Checking the time on his watch, Ben simply nodded.

Frank went back to his screen. "Well, Nick will bring out the freezers to you and lay them in the loading aisles for you to sort out. Sections A to F are ready for you to start, when you've finished each section let Nick know, and he'll start loading them onto delivery trailers, understood?"

Ben nodded in quiet agreement.

Frank didn't speak straight away afterwards, so Ben truly knew it was time to leave.

"Next time, try going out on a date with one of your own kind." Frank's smirk came back.

Ben spun around quickly. He let out an irritated sigh, and his voice rose. "Come on, why would you say that? Why would you actually say that to me?"

"No idea what you're talking about, mate."

"That's just racist, man, and you know it."

Frank was genuinely surprised by the bitterness in Ben's voice. "Yeah, one of your kind, you know, like another geek, a nerd girl, you know, one of those sorts who dress up like spider girl and go to those comic conventions you go to."

Frank laughed it off as Ben stood dumbstruck.

"You really have to get this chip off your shoulder, man. It's getting pretty tiresome now."

"I heard what you said, Frank."

"Yeah, and you've got it wrong again."

After a moment, Ben spoke. "Alright then."

Frank moved forward in his seat. "You're a funny man, Ben, but you're imagining things in that conspiracy theory head of yours."

He clapped his hands twice by his head. "Chop, chop, get those freezers sorted."

Ben shook his head as he left.

Making his way down the corridor, he sadly looked behind at Frank's office and then imitated a poor African American man from the 1920s.

"Shoe shine, boss?"

* * *

It was a long morning for Ben. True to his word, Frank had laid out large numbers of chest freezers on the loading bays for repacking and inspection. Ben had exchanged the old instruction manuals for the new one, resealed the freezers and then waited for Nick to load them onto the trailers with lorries waiting.

Continuous checks on his phone had shown that the clip was still very infamous on social media; the comments were still appearing, not as quick as last night, but still enough to make him perturbed.

Nick pulled over in his clamp truck, its body was like a forklift, but its attachment was a hydraulic clamp, like two big metal hands capable of lifting an assortment of white goods. He gently lowered the clamps to the floor and safely stepped down from his truck.

"Nice dismount." Ben smiled.

"You won't be smiling when it's your turn at my age."

"I doubt I'll be working here when I'm your age, mate."

"We'll see." Nick grinned.

"So we all done for today?" Ben asked.

"Yes, I think so. Frank wants to see us in his office tomorrow morning."

"Again?"

"I'm sorry?"

"I mean me, not you. I saw him earlier." Ben paused as if listening for a response, it didn't come. "Not in a bad way." Ben steered away from fluttering. "It was just to talk about these freezers."

"Ah, right."

Nick always liked Ben, so he didn't want to pry but knew him well enough to know when he wasn't fully on board with the truth, especially when he stammered. "Well, that's the last of the freezers going out for today. I'll get one of the other lads to lay some more out for you."

"So I can do it all again tomorrow?" Ben huffed.

"You love it really, Ben."

"No, I don't." His voice was serious.

"I'm never leaving this place, am I?"

"That all depends on you, my friend."

Nick was like the 'Obi-Wan Kenobi' of the warehouse. He'd worked on the shop floor and had more knowledge than everyone, including the supervisors, about most of the logistical procedures. Everybody came to him for advice, new starters to the old guard.

"I suppose you saw the video of me at McDonald's then."

Nick put his tongue in his cheek and moved it slowly. "Some of the other guys were talking about a video." He corrected himself. "Laughing at a video."

"That was probably at me, Nick."

Nick stared at him with curious eyes and backed off with a smile. "It's not my place to pry, but these videos are fun for a few seconds, and then tomorrow everyone has moved on to the next joker in the social media pack, no offence."

"None taken, mate." Ben smiled back and watched Nick walk away. "See you tomorrow."

Nick raised his right hand in the air in acknowledgement. "Just one thing, though." He shuffled around. "Might want to try Nando's next time you have a date."

Ben gave a broad grin, his first for the day.

"Good one."

As the cars from the early shift queued at the security barrier to leave, Henry the cleaner weaved his way through the cars again, dragging a pump truck attached to a wooden pallet behind him. On the pallet was a box which had earlier contained a washing machine; it was now filled with black bin bags.

The security guard stopped him at the closed barrier. "You alright, Henry?"

"Yes, boss, just dumping this rubbish."

The security guard took a slight look inside the box and pulled away instantly in disgust; the smell of dirty toiletries and stale food was enough. "Okay, off you go."

Henry nodded and smiled. "Thank you, boss." He pulled the pallet past the queue and trundled on.

Ben arrived next at the barrier and got out of his car for inspection. Opening his boot, he waited for the security guard to give a fleeting look at his belongings.

"He's a good one, that lad."

"What, Henry? Yeah, he's cool, always smiling."

"Haven't seen you smile for a while, plus Spurs are playing well, so why the glum face?"

"I'm not a Spurs supporter, I'm West Ham."

"Ah, right, no wonder you're always miserable, try supporting a local team next time. Things that bad?"

Ben picked at his dry lips and pulled off some skin with satisfaction. "Sometimes life doesn't go according to plan."

The security guard watched Ben get back in the car. He tapped on the driver's window and stood back as Ben unclipped his seat belt and rolled down the window.

"Next date you go on, maybe try going to Subway."

Ben shook his head, and a smile emerged in the process. "Splendid."

* * *

Back at home, Ben still couldn't keep off his phone. He'd had more interest from a single 10-second video than years of being a supporting actor on soap TV. Many of the comments were from anonymous users, no profile pictures, just jokers cracking on to the lasting embarrassing video trending.

He recognised the profiles behind a few of the posts. It was former colleagues and failed dates who were all suddenly coming back into his life. They were laughing at him and completely destroying his character. Ben knew he'd never see any of his former dates again, they did the polite thing knowing they were just going to remain online friends and barely exchange personal social media details. Their laughing emojis and memes hurt more than the stares he got from eating steak with his hands at a restaurant; that particular date excelled in her putdowns for the video.

He thought about what Nick had said earlier, these videos were fads, but some did tend to stick in the mind longer than others, and it seemed his was taking its time to fade from online humiliation. The video was being thrown around the internet like clothes in a tumble dryer. So many trendy sites were showing the video now, and Ben was still concerned.

His phone was buzzing with messages from people he actually would see again. Family and current work colleagues wanted to know how he was, and he answered them all sporadically and thought about going to bed. He still hadn't heard from Nicki since their date. It was an immense effort not to message her while drunk, he had made the mistake of being inebriated when trying to send friendly catch-up messages to his last dates and it never turned out well. It was always embarrassing apologies from him the next day. So it was no wonder that they were now laughing at him online and taking great pleasure in doing so.

Ben had had enough and thought about going to bed, his cat was out for the night, and there was nothing worth watching on TV. Bed was probably the best idea. After making sure all the lights were off and doors locked, he made his way to his bedroom and got ready for some sleep.

The only light illuminating Ben's room was from his phone. He stared at it in disbelief as the video was showing no signs of stopping for comments. Ben put the phone on his bedside table and waited for it to go off. Finally lying in darkness, he pulled up his t-shirt and scratched his belly. His stomach was getting bigger due to eating so much crap. It was another thing his exes had noted.

* * *

"It does."

"No, it doesn't."

"I'm telling you, it does."

Ben sat in the canteen at work. He'd managed to get through his first break without too many people mentioning his exploits in the video at McDonald's. It seemed finally that the video was no longer the talking point. A discussion with Jason was currently what the canteen occupants were interested in.

"Jason, that isn't true; it can't be." Ben crossed his arms and leaned back in his chair against the wall. "So you're telling me that Frank has a cat the size of a lynx and trained it to get sausages for him from the butchers."

"Yes," Jason said confidently.

"I think he's winding you up, mate."

"I don't think he is, Ben."

As implausible as it sounded, Ben couldn't help but laugh as he imagined a large cat carrying a basket in his mouth filled with sausages from his local butchers.

"Did anybody tell you that you were funnier when you were on that video?"

"Oddly enough, no, but they did ask me, why does your mate have a mouth bigger than a thief's pocket?" Ben answered.

He let out an audible sigh and continued eating his breakfast. "Where is Frank anyway?"

"He's talking to Nick, something about those chest freezers you were sorting out."

"Oh yeah, I was meant to be there." Ben immediately moved from his chair and left his food. "I have to go."

Jason spoke before he left. "You still getting crap from that video on social media?"

There was concern in his voice now.

"Yeah, some people are still commenting about it." Ben had to lie next. "On the plus side, some ex-girlfriends have been very nice and commented; they said we should hook up and go out sometime."

"I don't think that's wise, mate. The past is the past, you should just let it go and move on."

"I don't know, they've been very supportive."

"Mate, a noose is supportive, doesn't mean it's good for you."

Jason made his point and his eyes were slowly looking upwards, and his lids began to close. Ben knew that look, Jason's mind was wandering like an unsupervised toddler in a supermarket, but it finally gave Ben time to catch up with Frank and Nick in the meeting.

***

Ben quick-stepped towards Frank's office for the second day in a row. Slowing down his hurried walking, he reached the door and noticed it was ajar. The voices inside were those of Frank and Nick, as expected, and Ben was about to knock. He hesitated for a moment and held his head to the door, listening intently. Frank was speaking, and Nick was agreeing with him, probably nodding his head as he did that a lot when paying attention. The next words he heard made him stumble back from the door. His stomach was twisting in knots, and breathing wasn't happening as easily as normal.

Ben ran a hand through his slightly greying black hair. His thoughts were all over the place.

Did he just say that?

His face was confused.

That's not right, that's not right.

Ben stayed still and recounted the words from Frank.

'*Lose the ethnic. I want rid of it straight away, make it quick and simple. If you need support, I'm willing to help, but we have to make it look professional, or I'm going to have to bring someone in to finish the job, but it has to go as soon as possible. I don't ever want to see that black shit in this warehouse after tonight.*'

Both men were quiet, and Ben could only assume Nick was nodding again. He turned around to see if anybody was watching. Satisfied he was alone in the corridor, Ben moved his head to the door again, but the room was still silent.

"Can I help you?"

The voice startled Ben, and he jumped back.

A young girl carrying a shedload of paperwork held her awkward position in the corridor. They stared at each other for a moment. She craned her neck forward and raised her eyebrows, waiting for a response.

"I'm just going for a meeting with Frank, waiting outside until I get called in."

A voice spoke from within the room. "Is that you, Ben?"

Ben kept a look at the girl and offered a nervous grin. "See? That's him, that's Frank. He wants to see me now." His words spilled out.

"Ben?" Frank asked again.

"Yes, I'm coming."

He walked into the office, leaving the girl with her paperwork.

"How long have you been standing out there for?" Frank asked.

"Long enough," Ben replied sharply. An odd silence hung in the air. "I mean, I didn't want to disturb your meeting."

Frank ushered him in further and to take a seat. "Did you catch any of that?"

Ben lied easily. "Should I?"

"No, it's cool. Well, I was discussing these chest freezers with the old boy over here."

Nick chuckled and took his glasses off to rub as Frank's lips moved to a grin. "The deliveries are going out as normal. We could probably end the run if we had some more numbers to start a bit earlier?"

Ben looked around the room, back to acting nervous. "You want me to come in early tonight?"

Frank swung a look to Nick and then back to Ben. "If you could? If you can't, it's not a problem."

Ben's head buzzed with questions. "Will you be starting early as well?"

"Yeah, of course." Frank beamed. "I'll be here to help you out in any way you need."

He's going to kill me.

Ben thought hard and his shoulders started to tremble; coldness wasn't the issue. "So, just you working with me then."

Frank nodded with enthusiasm. "Yep, me and you. Can't really ask old Nick to start work that early."

Ben missed his chance to reply as Frank carried on quickly. "Plus, if we get these freezers changed and pushed out quickly, this could really go down well for you finally getting taken on full-time, better money."

A pay rise is a pay rise, just have to not get killed. Sweet.

Ben looked at the gap between Nick and Frank at the table. "Okay, I'll come in," he said nonchalantly.

Frank's eyes left Ben briefly to check on Nick, who just nodded again. "Great, so you continue with the freezers for today, and then I'll join you early tomorrow morning, and that's when I'll help to finish you off." Frank corrected himself in a heartbeat. "Help you to finish off these orders."

His goat breath wafted over to Ben. He didn't react to the stench as it may help him to keep his life. "Right, see you tonight then."

Ben got up from his seat and headed for the door, trying hard to keep the horrible sensations in his mind and stomach in check. He turned around and watched Frank and Nick grinning at him like twin Cheshire cats.

His exit was hurried.

***

The work day was achingly long for Ben. His chest freezer orders were shifting well, but he apparently had to still come in early later tomorrow morning. He got a row of freezers ready to start with for when he returned later. Skipping all the quick conversations he would usually have with colleagues on the way out from work, Ben just went straight to his car and headed for the security gate.

A new security guard came out to inspect Ben's car.

"What happened to Wayne? Doesn't his shift end tomorrow?"

The security guard gave a quick look into Ben's car boot, and without even looking up, he grumbled an answer.

"He's got the sack."

"What! Why?" Ben was genuinely shocked.

The guard lifted his head from the back of the car and sighed; he'd been asked the same question all morning and was becoming increasingly tired. "He was let go because management thought he may have been complicit in a spate of thefts happening."

"Wayne? He's as straight as they come; nothing gets by his eyes."

"Unless it's pallet trucks."

"Sorry, am I missing something here?"

A slow, steady queue of cars were starting to build up behind, and the security guard really didn't have time. "Henry the cleaner was nicking pallet trucks every day. He was taking them out with a box of rubbish on top and Wayne failed to spot them."

Ben sat in his car, motionless as the security guard hoped he would move sooner rather than later. "What happened to Henry?" Ben asked.

"Long gone, he's disappeared, nobody can get hold of him."

An impatient car horn from behind shook Ben from his thoughts but was welcomed by the guard. Ben drove out of the complex, shaking his head. The security guard shook his for a different reason.

* * *

Ben had tried to get some sleep on his sofa during the afternoon before his early start later on. It wasn't working; his head was all over the place, tightening his grip on his cushion. Thinking about the inevitable and what Frank had planned for him was enough for him, and he hauled himself up. He needed to start being busy to take his mind away. Going to the gym, where he hadn't been in months but was still paying the monthly fees for was an option, or doing a thousand star jumps. A long jog was another idea and was the one he opted for.

Two hours later, Ben returned to his doorstep, gasping for breath and dripping with sweat. Back inside, he went straight to his fridge and gulped down a bottle of water like a premature lamb taking milk from a farmer. Ben checked his heart rate display on his watch monitor, it was higher than usual, but he put it down to the massive run he'd just had. He looked at the time and instantly began to worry about later; he started taking deep breaths and tried to calm himself down. Thinking about his boss talking about killing him would bring stress on anyone.

His anxiety was getting worse.

Twenty minutes later, Ben was feeling fresh from a well-needed shower, and a ready meal for one was his dinner. His appetite was shot, and he left half for tomorrow, hoping there'd still be one for him. "Good grief," he sighed.

Ben left the other half of the meal in the oven; it was caked in grease and dried food and was overdue an intensive clean. The whole kitchen was a state, dirty pots and pans in the sink, the floor was covered in crumbs. The whole place was a mess, but Ben didn't seem to care anymore; he never had many visitors anyway.

He rubbed his forehead more times than necessary and went to his fridge, taking out a bottle of white wine, he plonked it on the table. Ben grabbed the bottle and tightened his grip on the cap to give it a twist. He threw the cap away instantly, knowing full well the bottle would be finished tonight, filling up a wine glass and rolling his eyes with guilt at the state of the kitchen.

Ben's stomach wasn't empty, but it still gave a growl. He downed the whole glass's content in seconds. His stomach had stopped growling, but Ben filled up his glass with more wine and was drinking it just as fast as the last. Making his way slowly to the sofa with glass and bottle in hand, Ben picked up his laptop with his free hand and sat down heavily, happy as he'd made no spills.

Easily flipping it open, he immediately logged on to see what his ex-girlfriends were up to. The glass was almost empty, and Ben glanced at the time again as he poured more wine in. He could easily do two bottles before it was time to have limited sleep and start work. Pinot Grigio, watching his ex-girlfriends' social media pages and immediate death afterwards at work later was far too easy.

Ben raised a glass at the profiles of every past girlfriend.

"Cheers, girls."

* * *

It was 2am, Ben usually started work at 6am this week but was in earlier due to Frank's request. The night shift team were going about their routine business and gave Ben a head nod acknowledgement as they drove past in their forklifts, watching as he exchanged the old instruction manuals for the new in the chest freezers. Ben rubbed his eyes in tiredness; having little sleep and two bottles of wine wasn't the best start for work, using his car also shouldn't have been an option. He'd added another bottle before work and drunk it all too easily. Rows of freezers were ahead of him, and he kept a quick hand motion with the manuals.

Frank arrived on his forklift, slid out quickly from the seat and looked around at the quiet spot. "So this is nights? There's nobody here."

Ben just looked up and smiled faintly. "Good morning, Frank," Ben said pleasantly.

"Good morning, Ben," Frank replied with a sarcastic smile.

Frank watched Ben carefully replace each freezer manual with a new one and slowly began to follow suit. "Is this what we'll be doing all night?"

"Yep." Ben didn't even look up.

"Sorry, man, if I'd known it would be this boring, I would've never given you the job."

Ben let a small silence hang before smiling back. "You'll get used to it after a while."

"Don't want to, mate."

Regardless of his boredom, Frank was adamant about holding it in a little longer to help Ben. The night shift crew drove past in their forklift trucks sporadically, honking their horns in amusement, even though there was a team leader present, f-words and abusive hand gestures followed with laughter. Both Ben and Frank remained focused on swapping the manuals in the freezers. They carried on for an hour, silence between them; the less talking, the more easily they would finish their work on time. Frank had picked it up quickly whereas Ben was slowing down on each freezer, he usually knew his limit with his drinking but not when he was starting work so early.

Finally, Ben broke the silence, speaking slowly. "How are you getting on?"

Frank's face drooped slightly. "Losing the will to live if I'm honest, mate."

Ben looked at him, a hard stare behind his back. The wine was still buzzing in his head, staying quiet hadn't helped as much as he'd thought, but the drink pushed something out of his mouth. "Have you got something against me?"

Ben didn't regret it as much as he'd thought, knowing Frank was grimacing as he turned around.

"What did you say?"

"I meant, why haven't I got a full-time job yet?"

Frank gave Ben a look of disapproval.

Ben rolled his eyes. "No, that came out wrong, well not wrong, just not how I'd thought it would."

"Why would you come out with rubbish like that?"

"It's not rubbish, just the wrong time, granted."

A gasp of dismay was on Frank's s face. "Why is it always the wrong time with you."

Ben had started and couldn't backtrack now, the wine may have played a part in his words, but he had to keep going. If this was to be his last night on earth, then he needed to get some things off his chest.

"Actually, it's not the wrong time. I've worked here for years, more than most of the idiots who you took on, listen, it's just you and me here, no office talk, just tell the truth."

Frank had a twitch of irritation. "Maybe, just maybe, some people don't like you, and you aren't good at your job, despite the colour of your skin."

Ben couldn't let that go. "You're wrong and you're a racist."

Frowning, Frank shook his head. "Listen, mate. It's a stupid time in the morning, can we just crack on with this job?"

Ben swayed slightly and held on to a nearby freezer, expecting a response. Frank gave a puff of annoyance.

"Not denying it, are you?" Ben continued.

Frank's little eyes shut slowly as Ben waited for an answer, they sprung open, and his eyebrows bent. "I'm not racist, Ben."

"So why am I the only person not to have a full-time job?" Ben got the impression that Frank was avoiding something.

"You really want to go there?" Frank asked.

"Yes, please." Ben closed his eyes and waited until his stomach had stopped shifting white wine back and forth.

"Mate, let's not go there and just get this work finished."

Looking at his watch, Ben was already prepared. "You don't like me because I'm black."

There was a slight hesitation. Frank glanced around for the night shift; they weren't around to hear him. "Dull."

Ben hesitated to reply.

"People can be racist, sexist or homophobic, but these usually are through upbringing with an idiot family, dipshit friends or nut jobs online, but that can hopefully change through education. I say that stuff at breakfast and lunch to wind you up. I make notes on a piece of paper to myself as well, Ben, to rile you for the day because it's the only time you show any emotion. Maybe not my greatest idea, granted. I'm guessing nobody is born racist and sexist, but there are some people in life who are just born dull as hell, and nothing on earth can change that."

Ben suddenly felt uncomfortable as he knew there was more to come.

"That's the reason why you haven't been taken on. There's nothing there in you, no drive, no enthusiasm, you are just boring, and I'm sorry to say that, and yes, some people can be dull but bring something to the table. You don't even do that, I'm afraid; you lack everything we need to bring you on board with this company because you are just too dull."

Blood pressure beginning to boil, Ben kept listening.

"Like I said, you can be dull and do stuff good, mate, there are loads of dull people who work here, but the others get on with it quietly and don't make a fuss. You constantly moan, bicker and whine about everything and everyone; you never have or never will say anything interesting."

Frank was tired but didn't stop.

"In life, there will be people who just don't like you, it doesn't matter what colour or race you are or if you are a gay person, sometimes people just don't like you, that's just how it is. But if I was to say, right in front of your face that I didn't like you or you aren't good at your job, I'm suddenly called a racist. It's not about race, it's facts about your work; you aren't that good, that's why we haven't taken you on, as I explained to you earlier. I'm not racist, Ben."

"Yes, you are."

Frank threw him a quizzical look. Ben rubbed his eyes through tiredness and irritation, and his boss got a decent look at his face.

"I mean, Christ, you look like you've been sleeping under a bridge for months." The words came out harsher than he'd intended, but Frank noticed Ben had difficulty standing when not leaning against a freezer. "Are you drunk?"

"No, just been taking lessons on slurring. How am I doing?"

Frank shook his head solemnly. "Right, sorry, mate, I can't have this at work."

"It was a joke."

"Which part? Look, come into my office and we'll speak about this."

Ben immediately became more agitated. "I'm not going anywhere with you. I know what you've got in store for me."

"You're drunk at work, I can't allow this. Can you come with me, please? This is serious."

Ben knew there was no going back from this now. He was thankfully still breathing, but his job was gone; the wine had won. "Piss off, Frank, and you can stick your job."

Frank moved closer to him. "I advise you to think very carefully before you speak again."

"What are you going to do, Adolf?"

Frank kept walking towards Ben. "You need help, Ben."

"Not from a racist."

"Stop calling me a racist."

"You are, though, and I'll say it again, you don't like me because I'm black."

Frank took a nibble on his lip. "You know what? I had a lot of respect for you before, you'd turn up for work every day and take shit from me and Jason and gave as good as you got, but you've overstepped the line now. If you continue with these accusations, I'm going to have to let you go."

"Now it comes out!" He was swaying more freely now; the wine had finally made all his inhibitions leave him. "I've known what you had in store for me all night, you dozy shit! Well, it's not going to work."

"Okay, I'm afraid I'm going to have to let you go, Ben."

"That would suit you, wouldn't it? Getting rid of the only black guy in the warehouse."

Frank frowned after a few seconds of silence had passed. "I can say this now as I'm no longer your boss." He wrinkled his nose. "I don't like you, Ben, not because you're black, and this is the thing, this is the actual truth now." Frank wiped his nose to stop it itching. "It's because you're a fucking dick!"

Ben swung an arm out. His elbow struck hard and he heard two sickening thuds. Ben's eyes had been shut and he opened them slowly and turned around. There was a blood stain on the corner of one of the freezers. Frank's body lay motionless next to it.

Panic flowed through his body quicker than the alcohol ever did, and he bent down immediately to check on his boss.

"Frank? Frank, get up, man!"

There was no movement, and Ben shook him, each shake harder than the last. Ben shot up from the ground and looked around for support. The night staff were on their break and would be back in around 15 minutes, Ben could have easily gone to get help from them or just rung for an ambulance, but he just stood rooted to the spot, unable to move.

He was drunk at work and had struck his boss with seemingly devastating consequences; he could cope with not having a job but could do without going to prison. The trail of blood from Frank's head to the floor had stopped.

"Wait a minute." Ben meant to think but spoke out loud.

Bending down, he picked up Frank's wrist and felt for a pulse. "Yes," he said triumphantly through gritted teeth. Frank's pulse was faint, but he was alive.

A gasp of relief came from Ben; he wasn't a murderer, not yet. He still hesitated from contacting his workmates. Frank had been attacked by him, so he was still in trouble, but only if Frank remembered. He was probably suffering from concussion and wouldn't remember anything.

Ben got to his feet, eyes wide and mind racing.

If I could get him to hospital, just leave him there and not have to explain anything to anyone, maybe just say that's how I found him.

Ben shook his head quickly.

No, not good. I'll take him to hospital and explain everything to the medical team. I won't be coming back to work ever again, but nobody here needs to know. Get him in the car and go from there. Yeah, that sounds good, he's alive, and that's the main thing.

Men talking in low voices in the distance pulled Ben out of his thoughts. The night shift had finished their break and were heading back to work. He eyed the crowd and mumbled slowly, "Okay, okay." The panic he felt at the start had returned. Forklift trucks were being switched on, and he only had seconds before they headed his way.

Swallowing hard and without thinking, Ben lifted the lid of the chest freezer next to Frank and tried to haul him upright, he weighed more than he looked. Ben struggled more and immediately felt dizzy with the strain. "Come on!" he grunted.

With a final Herculean effort, Ben managed to shove Frank into the freezer and slam the lid shut. He grabbed a packet of microwave and freezer wipes included in the freezer package. Frantically tearing it open, he wiped down the blood from the corner. His heartbeat matched the speed of his hand rubbing.

Ben looked to the ceiling and blew out a sigh of relief as the last traces of Frank's blood disappeared. His eyes locked on something directly high above him, and he froze once more, allowing himself only a rapid eye blink. The fixed security camera made Ben's heart flutter, he put his hand over it, still beating fast, and he stumbled back, holding on to a chest freezer for the umpteenth time tonight for support. The wine wasn't to blame this time.

Trying to control his heavy breathing, he lifted his head again to look at the camera. His image had probably already been caught on camera, so there was no point in hiding his face now. Moments passed as Ben's head was filled with explanations and excuses for his upcoming arrest, past conversations with people raced through his mind as he thought of a way out.

He shot to his feet as one chat flashed through and stuck. It was a banal conversation he'd had with Wayne the security guard as he was leaving the site once. Wayne was moaning as the team had to do more security walk-rounds as the cameras in that section were down.

"No cameras," he whispered.

Ben had just enough time to let out a calm breath before a forklift truck drove up to him; the driver slowed down and poked his head out from the unit. "You alright, mate?"

All Ben could do was nod vigorously. "Yeah, all fine here."

The driver looked around from his truck. "Frank about?" he asked.

Ben's stomach fluttered. "No, toilet, I think."

Shaking his head, the driver mumbled under his breath. "Just let him know he owes me £20 from that snooker result last weekend."

"I'll tell him for sure when he comes back."

The driver rubbed his tongue around his mouth, keeping his eye on Ben as he drove away.

As soon as the driver left, Ben clutched his stomach. He felt sick, but also his bowels were moving. Ben's jaw went slack as he really needed the toilet. He looked hard at the freezer containing Frank, and his stomach churned over again.

"Oh no, not now."

Ben looked to Frank's forklift and eased himself onto the seat. There was no way he was able to run to the toilet unless he wanted his bowel movements to make a quick appearance, so a steady drive was the best option. He looked more panicked. Frank was unconscious in a chest freezer a few chambers away, but Ben really needed to go to the loo.

Making it to the truck parking area, Ben slid off the chair and scuttled to the toilet. Just about making it to the seat, his body relaxed as did his bowels. It was quite a removal session from all of the contents of his stomach. After cleaning up all the faeces from the throne, Ben sat back, leaning against the cistern. His eyes were heavy, and he wiped them with the back of his hand as the front hadn't been cleaned yet.

Thinking about what to do about Frank in the freezer, Ben stayed on the toilet. It was comfortable in an odd sort of way, he looked sideways and above in the cubicle. The purple ceiling and grey doors seemed warming for once, and he didn't want to move.

Ben couldn't take the weight on his eyelids anymore and drifted off to sleep. For the first time that night, he felt good. Nobody was laughing at him in there.

* * *

"Hello? Ben, are you in there?"

Ben rolled his head up and shook it instantly. The banging on the door didn't seem to be stopping anytime time soon. Instantly straightening all his limbs, he remembered where he was, and the panic soon followed.

"Yeah, I'm in here," he replied, his voice lighter than usual.

Ben waited for the reply. He recognised the voice, it was Connor, a young guy from his own day shift. "Hey! Is Frank in there with you too?"

Ben was too busy wiping his eyes to notice the lame gag from Connor. "No, just me."

"Everybody thought you'd gone home." Connor laughed. "Couldn't find you for a long time," he added.

Ben mopped his forehead frantically, trying hard not to make his voice quaver less. He stared at the ceiling, his eyes taking in nothing, and then looked at his watch. "No!" He leapt from the toilet seat.

"Are you sure Frank's not in there?" There was a giggle in Connor's voice.

The cubicle door opened, and Ben pushed past Connor and ran out of the toilet. He kept running towards his current work chamber; safety protocols went out the window as he sped down the warehouse, dodging quickly around the working forklift trucks, not caring too much if they hit him or not.

Ben reached the loading chamber, holding his stomach as he ran too hard. He clutched it harder as he saw the floor was empty, every chest freezer was missing. Bulging with sickness, his eyes looked around the empty floor. The clock in his head was ticking hard on what to do; the sound was growing louder and louder until the alarm bell went off as Nick drove by on his clamp truck.

"You alright, lad?"

Ben couldn't move. He just spoke, which came out as a stuttering whisper. "What happened to the chest freezers?"

Nick craned his head forward to hear properly. "What?"

"The freezers, where are they?" Ben's voice was louder but still shaky.

"Gone, mate."

Ben breathed out quickly. "Gone as in where?"

Nick flicked his head to outside of the warehouse, and Ben's eyes followed.

"Well, Frank asked me to come in early as well to finish off this order of chest freezers. We had the trailers waiting to be loaded, I couldn't find you or Frank, so I just boxed them up and loaded the ones you had ready."

Ben sucked his lips in. "Oh God!"

Nick was wondering what was going on as Ben ran outside to the loading bays. He came back even more flustered, his arms were flapping around desperately.

"The trailers are gone, the yard is empty."

"Yes, because the trailers have all been taken. They've all left."

Ben felt his stomach rolling, he took a step back, still looking at his now empty workspace. "No, that's not right, that's not right."

Ben's behaviour was a concern for Nick. "Are you okay, lad?"

Completely ignoring him, Ben's ranting continued. "How many trailers did you load?"

Nick let out a thinking puff of breath. "Well, the team on nights helped out with the loading. We took what freezers were left here, added them to the ones which were already completed in the picking bays." He bit his top lip in thought. "We loaded about six tonight, and they joined the ones we completed earlier today."

"How many, Nick?"

"About 12 left here tonight," Nick said without hesitation.

Ben felt wobbly on his feet. "Where have they gone?"

"Everywhere, you know that, some up north, Leeds, Newcastle, Sheffield, some in Scotland, I think, plus the other way in Portsmouth and Southampton."

Only half listening, Ben's face grew more fearful as the veins in his neck stood out.

"I've got to find something. I've got to find someone!"

"Right, what's wrong with you? You better sit down, lad." Ben was becoming more frantic by the second, worrying Nick even more. "Where the hell is Frank? He'll know what to do."

Ben groaned as soon as Nick mentioned his name.

Another colleague drove up and slowed down to poke his head out of his forklift.

It was Jason. "Is he alright?" he asked, pointing at Ben.

"No, he's not feeling very well."

"Frank is the only first aider. Have you tried to find him?"

Nick shrugged. "He's nowhere to be seen, can't find him anyway in the warehouse."

Jason frowned slightly. "His car is still parked up."

Ben's breathing started to become erratic and he bent over.

"God, he's getting worse. Maybe he's popped to the shops on foot."

Nick shook his head. "No, I checked with security, he hasn't clocked out. He's here somewhere."

Ben was getting worse. Jason stepped down from his seat and helped Ben to sit down. "Just breathe through your nose out of your mouth, slowly."

"How'd you know that?" Nick asked.

"The missus loves watching *Casualty*."

Jason had a moment. "Actually, that's not a bad idea."

Nick kept an eye on Ben. "What do you mean?"

"Well, we can speak to Gillian, Frank's missus."

Nick was listening avidly as Ben suddenly perked up. "What did you say? Frank had a wife?"

Jason stared at Ben in surprise. "No, he's *got* a wife."

Ben went quiet.

"Oh, I don't think you followed Frank on social media."

Jason pulled out his phone from his pocket and swiped around quickly. "Here she is."

He showed it to Ben, who scanned the screen with a pitiful look. 'Women never forget a man who makes them laugh' was the header on his profile page.

There were pictures of a black woman with her arms wrapped sweetly around Frank's neck. He was looking lovingly into her eyes due to their height difference. She was considerably taller than him, maybe she was standing on a box or he was kneeling, but either way the picture showed that they were in love and happy. Nobody could fake that feeling.

Ben's stomach felt like a rollercoaster beginning its ascent as Jason swiped through the pictures on Frank's page. Two girls of mixed race who looked around 10 and 12 were also in many of the photos. Laughing around with their parents in holiday pictures, picnics, on the beach, and even posing with Frank in their football kits. But the picture that stood out most was the two girls as very young bridesmaids at their parents' wedding.

"Do you think it's wise to contact Frank's wife about his whereabouts? If she thinks he should be at work, then it would only cause worry for her."

Jason agreed with Nick. "Yeah, that's probably a good idea."

He put the phone away as Ben's head shook like a cat smelling food in a kitchen bin, his lip was quivering.

Jason pointed hard at Ben while looking at Nick. "Right, get him to the canteen, give him a cup of tea.

There's something stronger in my bag, but that stays between us."

Everyone knew about Jason's drinking so it wasn't a shock to Nick. "What did Frank say to you before you left yesterday?"

Nick thought hard about what he was supposed to notice in the meeting with Frank. He looked up slowly. "All he said was if I was available to come in early last night to help move the chest freezers."

"Are you sure? Anything else?" Jason pressed.

"Not really. Oh yeah, he wanted me to move all the stock out of one holding chamber to use as a new parking bay for the forklift trucks."

"Really?" Jason was interested in this more than Ben's shivering.

"Yes, he wants to keep holding chambers A to E and then to get rid of F."

"What?"

"Yep, he said to lose the F, Nick."

Ben spun around quickly to Nick. "What did you say?"

"I said Frank asked me to get rid of the F chamber."

"No, what did Frank say to you?"

"I just told you, plus to paint it yellow and get rid of the black paint underneath, black shit he said."

Ben held up his hand towards his head; it was shaking hard and turned into a frantic finger waggle. "His exact words."

Nick pushed his glasses higher up his nose and continued, his eyes never leaving Ben.

"Lose the F, Nick."

Ben threw up all over the steering wheel of Jason's forklift. "Really?" Jason sighed.

"No, no, no, no, no, no," Ben moaned.

He rocked back and forth on the truck, his breathing was verging on hyperventilating again, and he began to cry uncontrollably. "I'm sorry, I'm sorry, I'm sorry," he whispered.

"I take it all back. He's not ill, this bloke's a nut."

Nick calmly waved Jason to stop, not convinced.

"Listen, Ben, I'm going to take you to security. They definitely know first aid and can help you."

Ben threw his head back, his eyes alert and wandering and heart still pounding. "No, I have to go." He made his way off the truck, slipping on some sick as he got down.

Jason put his hands to his face and pulled them down slowly as the sick was more evident as soon as Ben left.

"Ah come on, man."

Without even looking back, Ben suddenly sprinted away and headed towards the admin office.

Jason watched him take off and snorted to Nick. "I don't think he's coming back."

"You might be right. He doesn't look good." Nick rubbed his chin. "Do you think he's messing around?"

"What do you mean?" Jason asked.

"Well, him and Frank are always winding each other up. Frank can be a bit of a complete pranker sometimes."

"A what?"

"A complete pranker."

"Sorry, I thought you said something else."

Hand on his head to rub his thinning hair, Nick went to follow Ben in his own truck to check up on him. He gave a slight grin to Jason, who wondered how he was going to clean up the mess from Ben's stomach from his truck.

"Are the cleaners still here?"

"Do it yourself, Jason," Nick huffed.

As Nick started his truck back up, Jason called to him. "Almost forgot to tell you, one of the trailers you loaded isn't going out yet."

"Why?"

"The break chamber has gone; there's a van coming in later to mend it."

"Which one?" Nick asked.

Another forklift drove by, momentarily distracting Jason. "Trailer 001, I think?"

"The one Ben loaded wrong."

Jason shook his head. "He didn't. It was admin's fault, they messed up, not him."

"Does he know?"

Another head shake came from Jason. "Don't think so," he replied.

Nick frowned. "That's a shame. Ben took that quite bad."

Jason didn't care too much; the stench of sick on his truck was his only concern. "Anyway, the trailer is going to the John Lewis warehouse in Humberfield, just five miles away."

Nick drove his truck away, and the smile returned as he glanced back at Jason.

Ben sat in his car fiddling with his sat nav. His breathing was fine now but nowhere near calm. He had a list of warehouses that all of the trailers with the newly loaded chest freezers were heading to, warehouses all over the UK. Finding Frank was his only priority.

Wiping his sweating brow, Ben typed in a postcode for a warehouse district in Aberdeen. It was going to be a very long trip from where he was in Humberfield.

He took a swig from some bottled water which had been lying in his back seat for months and then headed towards the security gate. Once the security guards had done their checks, the barrier lifted, and Ben was free to go.

Ben took another sip of water before concentrating hard and driving away. He prayed at the same time.

The day crew were busy loading and unloading various trailers from the yard. Only trailer 001 remained, waiting for its repairs. Its cargo of chest freezers remained steady and secured. Inside the freezer with serial number 150641, something moved.

Just a little.

Where is Molly Holiday?

Kathy Moran
Flat 6a, Peddlers Way
Newcross
Humberfield

Day 1

The young woman stared at the ceiling from her position on a bed, she had been lying on her back for ages, and she yawned, trying to feign interest in the conversation. She wanted to politely cover her mouth as she had grown up with manners, but that was an issue at the moment.

"Are they too tight?" a man asked.

"No, they're fine, well not obviously fine, but not hurting." A cat was meowing outside. "Aren't you going to let him in?"

The man wasn't interested in her question. "Thank you for not screaming, by the way."

"Well, I've seen those films when a girl is taken hostage by some maniac and tied up. Screaming doesn't tend to help."

The man hummed nervously under his breath. He wore a black balaclava, and his clothing was also dark.

The look was like a ninja, albeit one who was missing his five-a-day of vegetables. "I'm not a maniac."

"You're doing a good job imitating one."

"It won't do you any good to scream. I've told all my neighbours that I'm making a short film about a girl who gets kidnapped by her boss, so they know to expect screaming and shouting, so if you do, nobody is coming to help you, they'll think it's all part of the film."

"Usually when anybody gets kidnapped, I'm assuming their abductor doesn't bring them back to their own house."

"It's not mine," he said confidently.

"What about the neighbours and the film?"

"Point a film camera at anybody and they will become your friend."

The girl wanted to rub her wrists, and the man noticed it. "I've been talking for too long. I apologise for that."

"You've got a lot to apologise for, but talking isn't one of them."

The man nodded knowingly.

She gave him a mock stern look, and the man corrected himself, avoiding eye contact with her. "Are you thirsty?"

"No."

His movement made her look at him intently and slowly. She listened, focusing on the eyes stuck on her.

"Are you sure?"

"I'm sure, can you give me a phone? Need to check in with my followers."

"We both know that's not going to happen."

"I may need to take a pee soon."

"Well, let me know if you do."

"I won't, I'll just pee and maybe defecate on your bed, and you can clean it up."

"I don't live here, I told you."

Her eyes flicked back to the ceiling. "Let's just get this over with, shall we?"

"I don't know what you mean? Whatever you think, that was never my intention."

She eyed him up with suspicion and looked at her legs and arms. "Much as I love a duvet day every now and then, you've kidnapped me and tied me to a bed."

He shook his head as the woman shifted, waiting for a response.

"You've been quite the entertaining host, but let's not forget about the elephant in the room."

She looked around. It was a small bedroom, perfect for a child but lacked space for an adult. The windows weren't boarded up with wood, just had curtains drawn. Plasterboard was on some of the walls, the rest had carpet underlay attached to them. The floor was covered in plastic bags.

She was tied to a sturdy single bed, a huge wardrobe took up most of the room, plus there was a television set at the foot of the bed. Her handcuffs were attached to a metal bed head, and her legs were tied with rope. She still had the ability to swing them towards her captor, but she didn't want to enrage him, so she kept them firmly on the bed, not knowing how long she would be here for, and she still needed to eat.

"What are you going to do with me?"

The man looked at her scowling face. "I'm not going to hurt you. I just wanted to talk to you."

"So you do that by kidnapping me? I've got a million followers on social media. You could have reached out online."

"Really? Do you really speak personally to all of your followers?"

"No, as that would be impossible."

"Listen, like I said, I just want to talk to you, and then I'll let you go."

"As soon as you release me, I'm going straight to the police, and then your kidnapping days are over, babes."

"No, because I'll be heading to a place where nobody will find me."

"What? You planning to head abroad, Cuba or Mexico?"

"Milton Keynes."

"Milton Keynes? Who goes to Milton Keynes?"

"I rest my case."

"Good one."

She knew that listening was the best option. "So what do you want to talk about?"

The man smiled and moved closer. "Why don't you like me?"

The girl wanted to get to her feet but only could manage a tug at her handcuffs. "Are you going to kill me if I tell you the truth?"

"I didn't bring you here to kill you."

"What are you going to do then? Take pictures of me and send them to my parents for ransom money or blackmail me? Put all these pictures online or something?"

He rubbed his right wrist. "That was never my intention, although it is a good idea, one I never thought of."

The woman struggled again as she wanted answers. She knew not to scream but was becoming more frustrated as it seemed the guy holding her hostage didn't have a clue about what he was doing. She had been kidnapped by a rank amateur.

"There are enough pictures of you online anyway. You're a travel blogger and constantly on trips abroad and in this country, over one million subscribers want to know 'Where is Molly Holiday?' I like the name, sounds like a kids' cartoon show, but all your fans love it, the glamorous lifestyle you lead, jumping from country to country—"

"While you're stuck here," she cut in quickly, throwing the man off guard.

"Excuse me?" he said.

"You're jealous of my life, my work. What I do for a living is far more glamorous than your job, whatever it is you do, and so you thought you'd teach me a lesson by bringing me up here and tying me to a bed, well it worked. I'm sorry for being successful, can I go now?"

"You're not going anywhere, Kathy Moran."

"What?"

"Like your name is really Molly Holiday, who just happened to have a job as a travel writer? That's like someone called Terry Tyre, who just happens to work as a car mechanic."

"I never said that Molly Holiday was my real name, it just fitted into what I was doing as a job. Would you follow a travel writer called Kathy?"

"It wouldn't be a lie. That's what you do best."

Kathy sighed sadly. "What is your problem? You obviously know who I am and what I do; you even know my real name, which is creepy. Why are you doing this?"

The man was looking at Kathy's eyes where tears were beginning to form, she had kept up the bravado for a while, but now she was scared. The man began to pace around the small bedside, albeit it didn't take long, but still left Kathy feeling more nervous. His teeth strangely clicked when he spoke.

"You lot, you are privileged from day one. You lord it up and look down on normal people; you've got a silver spoon in your mouth, trust funds, university."

"Anybody can go to university."

"Well I didn't. I couldn't." He scowled.

The man was becoming more anxious, and Kathy snorted. She couldn't wipe the snot from her nose, so she breathed out and spoke. "What happened to the geese that fell down the stairs?"

"You what?"

"They got goosebumps."

The man didn't even smile.

"You see? I can be just like you and tell stupid gags. I'm not privileged and no different to you. I'm like anybody else, so please let me go."

"So you think telling a stupid gag from your expensive Christmas cracker makes us the same? God, you're deluded."

"Then tell me, please?"

The man glanced over his shoulder and back to Kathy. She was becoming more worried now and spat her words out.

"You asked, 'why don't I like you?' I can tell you now, I can tell you anything you want."

"Much as I love to be disappointed again, I have to go to work. Now I suggest you take some water as I'll be gone for most of the day. I'll turn the television on for you and will be back as soon as I can."

"No, please don't leave me. I'll do anything you want!"

"Please take some water."

Kathy nodded hard. The man took a bottle of water from a low shelf on the wardrobe and unscrewed the cap. "Drink this."

He poured it down Kathy's throat and stopped when she began to gag.

Turning on the television set, he flicked to a channel with a documentary about unscrupulous landlords. "This looks good. I'll turn up the volume a little bit so you can hear it."

The tears from Kathy's eyes now streamed down her face, more so when she saw what else he'd taken from the shelf.

"Right, I'm off now, don't panic, breathe easy and relax."

Kathy violently shook every limb in her body, all chains and rope staying firm. "Will you let me go, please?"

"I wasn't going to gag you, but something tells me you won't be staying quiet, despite the movie-making tale I told you, and you are quite right to try and scream for help."

Kathy shook her head in terror. "I won't scream."

"I don't believe you, and you have every right to."

He tried to smile to put her at ease, and Kathy spat in his face.

"I'll allow that only once. I'm going to gag you now."

The man tied it around her mouth before she could spit again.

"I'll be back soon."

He hurried out of the room, making an effort not to look at Kathy.

As soon as he shut the bedroom door, Kathy looked to the ceiling and struggled frantically.

She tried to scream anyway.

Day 2

Kathy knew what time it was due to the television set and the channel. The normal programming schedule had finished and was replaced by a late-night betting show. A hostess took calls on a roulette wheel spinning throughout the night.

Kathy suddenly heard footsteps from outside her closed door. It opened, and the man turned the light on. Kathy turned her head and closed her eyes from the brightness.

A ginger cat followed him in and jumped on the bed. The man walked in, and Kathy pulled hard at her cuffs, almost dragging the headboard from the bed.

She became more frantic as the man approached. He took off her gag.

"Please, I need to pee," she cried.

"Okay."

The man was seemingly prepared. He picked up an empty vase from the side. "Use this," he said calmly.

"I can't."

"Ah, yes, of course."

The man was flustered for a second, and the cat jumped down at being disturbed. Taking hold of Kathy's jogging bottoms, he pulled them down from the waist. When it came to removing her pants, the man looked away and fumbled nervously. He put the vase in between her legs and didn't have long to wait to hear the vase begin to fill with urine, his head still looking in the other direction. When Kathy was finished, the man took the vase and left the room. She heard a toilet flush and waited for him to come back.

"Are you okay?" he asked.

"What do you think?"

"I'm sorry, I didn't know."

"You didn't know? You're keeping me tied to a bed for hours now, and you didn't think that I would need to pee?"

"I'm sorry, I forgot." He kept looking at her. "Do you need anything else?"

"Like do I need to use the toilet for the other thing?"

The man put a hand over his mouth. "Oh my god, I haven't fed you."

"Nope."

"Are you hungry?"

"Have a wild guess."

The man stuck to being nervous. "I've got some stuff in the fridge."

Kathy kept her eyes on him.

"What would you like to eat? I've got some ham, bacon."

"I'm a vegan." Kathy sniffed.

"Okay, but you can eat eggs, right? Egg laying is natural and doesn't hurt the chicken, so I can just boil some eggs, no fats, just water."

Kathy nodded. Right now, she would have eaten anything. "Vegetarian then."

"Fine, I'll put some on."

As soon as he left, Kathy pulled her cuffs against the headboard again. Nothing but the same result as before.

She turned her head to the television and waited for the man to return.

Ten minutes later, he walked back in with a bowl and two boiled eggs. "I'm sorry, couldn't find any egg cups."

"This is your place, and you can't find any egg cups?"

"This isn't my place.

"Oh, of course, you did say." There was a tinge of ice in her voice. "So, where do you live then?"

He smiled. "This isn't about me. It's all about you."

"Okay, this is getting sad. Eggs, please."

"Yes, sorry."

Despite kidnapping her, Kathy saw that her captor was extremely polite, but he still obviously had major issues with her. She watched as he cracked open the top part of the eggshell and spooned out the insides.

"Open wide."

Kathy closed her eyes and swallowed the boiled egg quickly. "It's like being a kid again." She giggled nervously, allowing just a little laugh to calm them both down. She took another swallow, carefully fed by the man.

"You hate me, don't you?"

He continued feeding Kathy. "I don't like what you stand for," he replied.

"But you still want to date me, right?"

His hand began to shake, the egg almost fell from the spoon. "I just don't like what you stand for," he repeated.

"Which is?"

"Travelling around the world, showing off your photos on the beach."

"I'm a travel blogger; it's my job."

"You have almost a million people following you. Those sycophants hang on to every word you say, anything you do, anywhere you go, they love you, even though their lives aren't great, they still hang on to everything."

"And that bothers you?"

"Yes, it does, because we can't have what you have."

Kathy pulled away from the upcoming egg. "Anybody can, I'm not Wonder Woman."

"No, because she doesn't actually exist." The man put the remaining egg on the wardrobe side and stayed by the door. "I just don't really like your kind, the way you think that everybody should love your lot and bow before you, the voice people should listen to."

"Your lot? You have a problem with women?"

"I meant northerners."

"Must be tough business being an idiot."

"Don't forget where you are, Kathy."

"Oh, you're a big brave man, aren't you? Kidnapping me. Take these cuffs off of me, and we'll see how much of a man you really are."

The man looked sheepish and held down his head. "I know what I did was wrong and shouldn't have done it. I just wanted to get past all of your thousands of followers so you could get to know me, get to like me."

"Never going to happen."

Kathy's words hurt as he left the room.

Day 3

The man came into the room much earlier than yesterday. He carried a tray of sandwiches filled with cucumbers and tomatoes. Kathy looked tired; her eyes were drained of any sparkle they used to have.

"Can I go now?"

He gave a disapproving look. "We spoke about this. I can't let you go yet."

"I need to go to the toilet."

"Right, okay, right, okay."

The man put the tray down. "I'm going to release you from the bed and walk you towards the bathroom. You've been on this bed for hours, so your legs will be numb, so it's no good trying to run. You're double-cuffed to the headboard, so I wouldn't go trying to strike me. Is that clear?"

Kathy just nodded, too tired to try and escape.

The man went into one of his trouser pockets and took out some keys. He unlocked both handcuffs and gently helped Kathy to her feet. She collapsed in his arms, and he tried to make her steady again. Kathy was like a newborn foal, unable to walk properly. The man took her down the short hallway and into the bathroom.

"I'll leave you here, and you can do whatever it is you have to do."

"Can you lock the door, please?" Kathy asked.

"No can do. I've taken the lock off so you can't shut me out or shut yourself in, plus I've rented some cheap film cameras; they are outside now pointing towards the bathroom window. If you open it and start to scream, people passing by will just think it's part of the fake movie being filmed, and I wouldn't try breaking the glass – your hand will break before it does."

If Kathy heard what her captor said, she didn't respond. "Does that shower work?"

"Yes, it does."

"I've been here for days. I need a wash and my hair as well." She softened briefly. "I don't know how long you intend keeping me here for, but I feel terrible. I need new clothes. I need to get clean."

"That wasn't part of the plan, I'm not sure."

Kathy swung the door back open, her face had gone back to hard. "You're not sure? You break into my flat and kidnap me, drive me miles away, I'm guessing, and have me tied to a bed for days, and all I want is a new set of clothes, and that's too much for you?"

He backed away. "Right, I could buy you some new clothes and bring in some perfume."

"Why would I want to smell lovely while I'm held up in this dump?"

"I just thought."

"No, dipshit, you didn't think." Kathy breathed in and composed herself. "I'm going to take a shower, and when I come out, I think we have to discuss where we go from here."

The man closed his eyes and focused on how confident Kathy was becoming. "I'm going to have to think about this."

"I need my phone."

"We spoke about this. I can't give you your phone back."

Kathy rubbed her stomach to stop the uneasy movements. "I'm a travel blogger, my job is to travel, I get paid to travel, and while I'm tied up in your bed, I'm not travelling, so people, my followers, my sponsors would want to know why I haven't been on social media for the last few days."

The man stroked his chin. "There's no way I'm giving you your phone back. Do you think I'm stupid?"

She didn't answer, which surprised him.

"All it takes is one phone call to the police, and I'm done."

"I wouldn't do that."

"Really? You wouldn't take the first chance to put the guy who kidnapped you in prison?"

"I don't care about you. I just care about my followers."

His face dropped. "What about your family?"

"You didn't do your research on me enough, did you? You may have found my address but didn't check up on my family. I've been a travel blogger for ages, my family know if I don't reply to their messages straight away, then I'm on holiday working. They don't need to speak to me, they just need to see me."

He stared at Kathy in confusion as she continued. "Just give me my phone, a quick recording. I'll say that I'm ill with the flu and bedridden and will be back on holiday soon. Obviously take the cuffs off me, and we'll make it as natural as possible."

The man was extremely spooked now. "This is not a good idea."

That lifted her anger. "What do you want me to do? You tied me to a bed for what? What do you want from me? I've done nothing wrong to you. Why won't you let me go?"

"I just want to talk. I just want you to get to like me."

"Am I the only woman in your life then? Is there no one else?"

He didn't answer.

"I said, is there no one else?"

"My mum."

"What?"

"It's my mum. She's in a care home; she doesn't know who I am. This is her house."

Kathy looked up to his face, without blinking. "That sounds terrible, I'm sorry. Are you the only person she has?"

"Apart from the care staff, yes, it's just me and her cat."

The comment caught Kathy off guard. "When you leave me in the day, you aren't going to work, you're going to see your mum, am I right?"

"Yeah, I work part-time and spend the rest of the day with my mum."

"I'm sorry to hear that."

"Really?"

"You may have done this incredibly stupid thing to me, but your mum is ill, and that must be a horrible strain for you. She's going to love what you've done to her floor and walls."

"I don't think she'll be coming back here. I think she'll be staying in the home."

"That's so sad, so what are you going to do with the cat?"

The man was surprised that the cat was Kathy's only concern. "Mum hated that cat. She would damage the furniture, make a mess everywhere."

"Which one? Your mum or the cat?"

The guy smiled with nervous frustration.

"I asked her: Why do you keep the cat when you can't stand it?" He paused, and Kathy waited. "She said, when you live alone, it's nice to have two other eyes to look at."

"That is so sad and so sweet."

"I take the cat to Mum in the nursing home, it does make her smile; she remembers the cat and nothing else. If the cat stopped coming, it would be so much worse for her, nothing to look forward to."

"So, with that in mind, why are you doing this?"

"Like I said, I just wanted you to talk to me."

"Go to my flat and get me a change of clothes."

"Can we talk afterwards?"

Kathy peered through the crack of the door. "We'll see."

Days 4/5/6

The sheets on the bed weren't sweaty yet. Kathy lay on them, and they didn't smell. She was used to her routine now. Her captor would bring her food in the morning and disappear for some hours and then come back to give her dinner, and then he'd let her take a shower. Her gag was also removed, she had tried screaming for a whole day but nobody came. The television set had loads of channels, and she now had the remote control, but the man made sure the volume control was broken so Kathy wouldn't have the neighbours knocking to complain about the noise if she turned it up fully.

The man unlocked the door and entered.

"You still haven't got me any new clothes."

He put the food tray down. "It's soup today, vegetarian, obviously."

Kathy ignored him.

"How did you sleep?"

"Every day you ask me that, what do you expect me to say?"

"Just making conversation."

Kathy glared at his sad little face. "We've been over this time and time again. Get me something different to wear, and then we'll talk properly."

"You know I can't do that."

Kathy rolled her eyes and shifted her bottom. "At least can you untie me from the bed? Just let me walk around, not just when I need the toilet."

"Watch you walk right out of the front door, you mean? You can be quite testing sometimes, Kathy."

"I have that effect on people, especially kidnappers."

She finally turned away from him. The cuffs were longer now, the man had exchanged them, giving Kathy a little more movement on the bed. She planted one side of her head deep in her pillow. "Can't believe I actually haven't asked you what your name is. If you tell me what it is, you'll probably kill me, right?"

"I think we've established that I'm not going to do that. It is a surprise you took so long, though."

She looked back at him with tired eyes. "What is it?"

"Ronan, my name is Ronan."

"Nice name."

"Yeah, nice name, nice guy, that's all I get."

"I'm sorry?"

"Doesn't matter." He sighed.

She stared at him as if he had grown another head. "Something bothering you?"

Ronan shook it off. "Nope."

"So can I have my phone then?"

"Nope."

Kathy twisted and shook her body. "Why?"

"You know why?"

"If you won't get me my clothes, at least let me talk to my followers."

"Is that all you think about? Your social media."

"At this present moment in time, yes, there's nothing else and no one else on my mind right now."

Ronan brought the soup over and sat on the bed.

"How long had you been planning this?" Kathy asked.

"A while; obviously it's not a professional setup, but it's working."

"So you were spying on me, stalking me and waiting for your chance to talk by abduction, right?"

"I'm not normally like this. I didn't really mean to go this far. I just like you and wanted to see you, be close to you."

Kathy paused slightly and bit on her lip. "Can I have my soup, please?"

Ronan moved closer and dipped the spoon in the soup, hovering it around Kathy's mouth. "Open wide."

Kathy swallowed the first spoon of soup and pulled a face. "It's hot on the outside and cold inside." She waited for a comment. "Like me right?"

"I didn't say that," Ronan said.

"You're thinking it, though."

"Shall I reheat it for you?"

"No, just give it to me."

Ronan carried on feeding Kathy until the bowl was empty. He took out a handkerchief from his pocket and wiped her mouth.

"What grown man carries a handkerchief?"

He ignored Kathy. "Anything else I can do?"

"Could you wipe my eyes, please?"

He carefully wiped the crusted sleep around Kathy's eyes.

"Thank you." She nodded gratefully.

Kathy realised she was about to be left alone again for the day. "Have you ever had a girlfriend?"

The question threw Ronan, and his face darkened. "Why do you ask?"

"I'm guessing kidnap isn't the best start for a first date."

He began patting his pockets, trying to look away from Kathy's face. "Yes, but she left me."

"You lie! What did you do wrong, Romeo?"

Ronan ignored Kathy's sarcasm. "Why do you think that it was me in the wrong?"

"Just a hunch."

He nervously played with various fingernails before answering. "I put four sausage rolls in her oven and burnt them."

"And?"

"That's it."

"I think there must have been something more than that."

"Nope, so she said."

A smirk grew on her face.

"Women don't seem to like me."

Kathy pulled at her chains again. "Can't think why."

Ronan rubbed his eyes, preparing to open up. "I'm not very good at meeting people and socialising."

"So you've never dated since the sausages?"

Recoiling, Ronan tried to keep calm. "Yes, I've been on dates. I'm just not what women want."

"Which is?"

"They don't want a nice guy, that's all I'm constantly called, and then they leave and never get back to me."

"Maybe turn down the oven heat on the sausages."

"This is all a joke to you, isn't it?"

"Of course it is, so this is your way of getting back at every woman who turned you down then."

"Have you any idea what it's like to be me or a guy like me? We don't exist to people like you. We're something you just wipe away from under your shoe."

Kathy just blinked quickly but listened.

"Do you even know what it's like to receive a message from someone you like who isn't just replying to you? Not just being polite? They are actually wanting to see how you are? It makes your whole boring day just a little bit better, but if they don't reply to you, it hurts; waking up the next morning in your crummy life just hoping to have a message from them on your phone, and there's absolutely nothing."

Her eyes tightened on him. "Why should they reply?"

"What?"

"Well, you had your date. It didn't work out, so what do they owe you? Nothing, you move on and try again. That's what dating and life is about."

Ronan looked back and forth to Kathy; she wasn't finished yet. "These people owe you nothing at all; they're not obliged to message you after your date. If they do, it's just out of politeness."

"But why?"

"Have you ever taken into consideration what it's like to be a woman? To go on a date with someone, it not working out on the day or night, but you do the nice thing and add them as a friend on social media, and then they get bombarded with messages and texts from guys they want nothing to do with?"

"So why do that? Give men false hope."

"False hope? We're not doing anything of the sort, women, no wait, people go on dates all the time, and if it doesn't work out, then they're to blame? That's just ridiculous."

Kathy wasn't finished. "Have you any idea what it's like to be a woman and have a decent social life without the worry of meeting people like you."

"I don't understand."

"Do you know how many times I've been followed when I leave a pub or the gym by some random weirdo? How I love the spring because I can get a little more light in the sky when I'm walking anywhere in the evening? Or how I can't wear two headphones, just one, so I know who's around me as soon as the sun goes down.

"I can't really believe that." He was stammering.

"No? Okay, what about the abuse I get online, the disgusting attention."

"Wait, you are an influencer. You crave attention."

"So I deserve to have messages of filth from people, usually from men, older men who think it's okay to send me sick messages and pictures of various body parts which nobody should be seeing online. If anybody came up to me on the street and said what I hear daily from these sad bastards behind their keyboard, then they would be arrested, and rightly so, but because they have anonymity, it's fine, and I get this every day. They think I'm easy access, and they can say what they want and send what they want."

"Well, the pictures you post, the clothes you wear in your profile."

"Whatever I wear on my posts does not give you the right to send in genitalia pictures to me."

"I didn't." Ronan's forehead was gathering sweat as he corrected himself. "I wouldn't."

"How do I know that? You could be one of those hundreds of freaks out there on my daily posts."

"You know me now."

"Do I? Really?"

"If it bothers you, then why don't you come off social media."

"I shouldn't have to. Why should I get bullied off while these creeps can go about their daily lives without a concern? I can't have a go back, I can block and report, but they always find a way to crawl back onto my comments. Where's my privacy? Where's my help? Why do men think that they can get away with it?"

"Because we can, and we will never get caught." There was now a dark shift of tone in his voice.

"One guy messaged me, said he and his wife just took the kids on a day out to a theme park, and when they are back home and tucked up in bed, he's going to send me a picture of his—"

"I get it," Ronan quickly interrupted.

"I don't think your kind do. I shouldn't be made to feel frightened or threatened because I'm on social media or just going for a walk."

"Isn't that a tad dramatic?"

"What did you do to me again? I'm curious."

Ronan went quiet. "Even though you get abuse and dirty pictures online, you are still joking."

"It's a defence mechanism. I get scared all the time, and it doesn't end online either. Why do I have to watch my drinks at a bar constantly in fear that they may get spiked or have to walk home with my house keys in a fist in case somebody tries it on with me."

"Not all men are like that."

"No, they're not. I really know that. It's just you then, the kidnapping kind."

Even though she was still held captive, Kathy's words were meant to hit their target – Ronan.

"You haven't got a girlfriend, and you blame every girl you see for that, which is wrong on so many levels. I have a life. I travel for my job and see the world and get paid for it, and that bothers you? That makes you jealous of some women on so many levels."

Ronan grunted. "You don't know what it's like."

"Don't you dare go there! I get messages from loads of women, some girls as young as 12 telling me that they get the same thing, pictures and videos from guys saying dirty stuff that they want to do to them, and they have no idea what to do to stop it. These men make fake accounts or message them on loads of social media platforms and reduce these girls, these women to just objects, so don't tell me that you've had it hard. Try being me, try being a woman in the 21st century, you fucking idiot!"

"No way, you don't get off so easily. Do you have any idea what it's like to be a man in this day and age? The pressure we have to look good, told what to wear, be fit, be funny, be a good boyfriend in all departments for a woman, and if we fail in any of them in dating, we go to the back of the queue. We are made to feel insufficient as men, we're lonesome, some of us don't know how to make ourselves attractive to women, we don't know what to do."

Kathy shook her head and kept going. "Here's the thing, if you want to be respected as a man, if you want women to accept you as a decent human being, don't send pictures of the thing in your pants to us online."

"You didn't like being Kathy Moran? No one is going to follow plain old Kathy on social media, but Molly Holiday is much different; she travels the world and is exciting, is so much fun to be with. You changed because you didn't like being you or seeing the real you on social media."

"So what if I did? It's my life, not yours."

"So you're just a fraud and a liar, like everyone else."

Kathy sensed the tension wasn't easing but kept speaking. "You know there are other ways to meet people besides kidnapping them."

Ronan picked up the bowl and made his way to the door. "I'm sorry about the soup."

She held in her desire to scream at him as he left.

* * *

With the curtains drawn, the room was always dark, even in the daytime. Kathy shifted uncomfortably; her legs were hurting more now. She knew Ronan had issues, but it seemed every time he came to see her, a different man came through the door. Sometimes he was caring and considerate, and other times sad and despondent. She hoped the one who entered the door next was the former. It was time for a toilet break, and Kathy needed Ronan to let her out soon. Her anger subsided when Ronan did enter, earlier than usual.

"Did you see your mum?"

"Yes. Do you need to go to the toilet?"

"Yes, and I still need some new clothes and a shave. What's the point of allowing me to have a shower when

I'm putting back on the same dirty clothes, plus I don't know how long I'm going to be here."

Ronan looked at her with a glint in his eye. "Agreed."

"So you'll go back to my flat and pick up some clothes for me?"

"I still don't think that's a good idea. Why don't I just buy some new clothes for you."

"Have you ever bought clothes for a woman before?"

"No, but how hard can it be?"

Kathy smiled. "Let me out for the toilet and we'll discuss this."

"Do you have a boyfriend?"

The room fell silent, and Kathy's eyes moved to the left and right.

"Or girlfriend?" he asked.

"Where did that come from?"

"I've never asked that question before, it would be nice to know."

"Would it bother you if I did?"

Ronan exhaled loudly. "Can I sit down?"

"I don't know. Bend your legs and see what happens."

He sat down on the edge of the bed. "Expected, in all honesty."

"My holiday photos, I'm in all of the pictures, so who did you think was taking them?"

"I guess a friend, a travel buddy of some sort?"

"No, it was my boyfriend. I have a boyfriend. Is that what you wanted to hear?"

"What's his name?"

"I'm sorry?"

"Your boyfriend. I want to know his name."

"Why?"

"Just tell me, Kathy."

"Dean, his name is Dean."

Ronan had a smile. "Really? Okay, wait there."

"Obviously," Kathy spat.

"Sorry, just, sorry, wait a moment."

Ronan got off the bed and left the room. He came back quickly before Kathy could register what was happening.

"I have your phone, took it from you when you came here."

"When you kidnapped me, you mean."

"Doesn't matter. What matters is that I don't obviously know your phone password and would never try to find it out. However, I can see messages you get, and I didn't see any from someone called Dean, so why is that?"

Kathy fought back a sigh. "Dean was my boyfriend. We aren't together anymore."

"So you're single now?"

"Yes."

"Why lie about it?"

"Because I don't know what to do. I don't know what to say to you. I am chained to a bed because you have a crush on me, and if I say the wrong thing, I don't know what you'd do to me."

"I would never hurt you."

"Then why are you doing this?"

"I'm lonely, everything feels so lonely. I keep thinking I shouldn't have done this. I should have stopped myself."

"You need help, Ronan, some therapy or something."

Ronan was breathing heavily. He looked to the ceiling, and his eyes stayed there. "It hurts to be alone, watching the world live a life when you can't."

Kathy looked at her cuffs. "I get it, but sometimes in life, you meet the right person at the wrong time, and you love them so much, but it's not reciprocated. You want to see a message from them every now and then in the day to help you get through your awful life, and it's horrid when they don't."

"Then what can I do?"

"I'm not sure. If you were just nervous or lacked a bit of confidence, that can be worked on, but what you've done to me is just insane."

"I can change. I have changed, really."

"Leopards don't. You won't either."

Kathy went to hold her stomach; the chains kept her in check.

"You're not helping me or yourself, Kathy. You aren't who I thought you were."

"Who did you think I'd be then? Some saintly innocent lovely goddess untouched by anyone?"

Ronan looked around for support, it was just Kathy and him, and that made him more on edge. "Yes, I thought you were the one."

"What makes you think I was all innocent and saintly? Did I tell you that I was?"

"No, but…"

"I'm not some untouched saint, I travelled with my boyfriend, and we slept together. It's what most couples do."

"That's not what I meant."

"Well, so you can't blame me for not being someone you thought I would be. That's not fair."

"I just thought you would be different."

"You've chained me to a bed, and I've done everything you've asked me to do. Did you think

I would wake up after you drugged me and fall instantly in love? Life isn't like that, don't try and turn me into someone I'm not."

Ronan thought hard with his instincts. "Then what can I do?"

"I really need to pee."

"Please help me?"

Kathy felt a pinch of concern for him. "In life you have to throw yourself in the deep end and remember how to swim."

"I can't swim."

"Sounds about right." Kathy huffed.

"But I don't want to drown."

Kathy was about to let out a long-suffering sigh but paused. "Maybe I can help you."

"How?"

"Okay, I need you to seriously let me out to pee and then go to my flat and bring me some clothes."

"We spoke about this, I can't."

Kathy motioned to Ronan to sit closer to her on the bed. He was transfixed by her and didn't move, so she made an effort with her feet to reach him. She tried to rub his trousers with her toes.

"I can help you, go to my flat, bring me some clean clothes and something extra."

"Extra? I don't understand."

"You grabbed and subdued me as you were stalking me, right?"

"Yes, sorry, won't do it again."

"Well, let me take a pee, and we'll be good."

Ronan went to release Kathy, and she quickly wriggled closer. "I'll tell you what to bring me. There's a key inside a fake stone to the left of the front door.

Let yourself in and go to my bedroom, which will be the first door on your left, and just grab whatever you can."

"Grab whatever I can? Why?"

"If we are going to be some sort of couple, then I need new clothes."

Ronan clutched his stomach; butterflies were fluttering around inside. "But I thought what you said before about me being unable to change and being weird..."

"I never called you weird, but maybe you can change with my help. Maybe we can both help each other."

She rubbed his legs again with her toes. "Maybe I want to help you be the man I want."

Ronan didn't move.

"You can bring me my crotchless body outfit hanging up in my wardrobe or my black lace bra with a matching thong, plus some stockings and my heels, my very high black heels. Can you do that for me?"

Ronan nodded nervously.

"Good, then when you come back, I'll show you how to please me, make me happy, how to be a proper man."

She rubbed him again with intensity, her toes doing the work. "We'll see if you can be my new boyfriend, if you can let us enjoy each other."

"What if I can't make it happen?"

"You will. I will tell you exactly what to do, you like films, right? Going to the cinema?"

"Yes, I go on my own."

"Thought so. Well, if you could consider getting my clothes as the trailer, when you get back you can have the full feature all to yourself."

Ronan rubbed his face and the back of his head; it was more sweaty than usual. "Okay, I'll go. I'll get the clothes."

"Good, wind me up and watch me whirl."

Excitement began to hit Ronan as he turned to leave, but Kathy wasn't finished. "Wait, could you just please?"

She yet again pulled at her chains, indicating a much-needed toilet break.

"Yes, sorry," Ronan replied.

He unlocked her and watched as she made her way to the bathroom. Kathy didn't have a shower; she just used the toilet and quickly headed back to the bed. Ronan was concerned.

"Are you not taking a shower?"

"We'll have one when you get back."

"A shower together?" Ronan looked deep into her eyes. "Mrs Robinson, you're trying to seduce me. Aren't you?"

The moment was then lost.

"What?"

"It's a line from a film, *The Graduate*."

"Okay, here's the thing. I'm not a nerd or as old as you. I just want to have you. Is that too much to ask?"

Ronan looked down, embarrassed. "Right, I'm going."

"I look forward to seeing you when you get back."

Kathy settled back down in her all too familiar position on the bed.

She waited. Kathy knew that Ronan would return quickly.

* * *

Two hours had passed.

The television was on, and Kathy was settled in watching her daily input of dodgy landlords. She heard the front door open and then slam shut.

Ronan burst through the bedroom door. "Kathy! We have to go. We have to get out of here now!"

Kathy's eyes never left the screen. "What's wrong?" she asked calmly.

"We have to leave right now! Please, we have to go!"

Ronan was shouting nervously, and in a blind panic, Kathy finally looked at him. "Did you go back to the flat, Ronan?"

"Yes! We have to go now!"

Kathy looked back to the screen and the television programme. "This landlord is a cheating bastard, had no heating in the house, and still charging awful rent."

"You're not listening. We have to go now!"

"Tell me, what did you see?"

Kathy's voice was inquisitive and calm. "I said, what did you see?"

"He's dead, he's dead, I saw him!"

"Saw who?"

"A body! There's a body in the flat."

"Are you sure?"

"Yes, he's dead!"

"Who's dead?"

"A man. I don't know who it was."

"Did you check the body? Did you make sure?"

"The smell was terrible."

"Did you check the body?"

"Yes, he's dead."

"Then you better release me so we can leave then."

Ronan nodded and wiped away the sweat from his head. "Yes, yes!"

He reached into his pockets and pulled out the key to release her.

He never thought she would make a run for it, and she didn't.

"Okay, next up, I need my phone."

"Why? You're just going to call the police."

Kathy rubbed her wrists and scratched a knee through her jogging bottoms. "You drove to my flat and parked outside, right?"

"Yes."

"Plus, you opened the door with keys which weren't yours and found a body, and now your fingerprints are all over the flat and on the dead body."

"Yes."

"Okay, you're in trouble, so give me my phone, so I can call a taxi to get us out of here. I'm not sure the security cameras outside the flat work as they would have probably spotted you taking me in the first place, but I don't want anything to happen to my new boyfriend."

That took Ronan by surprise, almost more than finding the body. "Boyfriend? Do you mean that? Do you really mean it?"

"Sure, now can I have my phone, please? We can't use yours."

"Yes, but we have to go now."

Kathy switched off the television and took the phone from Ronan, still calm and rational. She easily got inside it and swiped away. "Well, that's booked. I've got a taxi app on my phone, money comes right out of my account, so we're fine."

"Good, please let's go, Kathy!"

Kathy straightened herself, giving a large stretch and coughed into the corner. "Go where?"

"Anywhere. We just have to get out of here!"

"I'm going to ask you again, Ronan, go where?"

"What are you talking about?"

"Well, I can go, but you can't, not after what you did to Dean."

Ronan became more confused.

"Dean, he's the guy in my flat, the guy you murdered."

Ronan blinked rapidly, and then his eyes never left Kathy. "What do you mean?"

"Well, when you kidnapped me and held me against my will for almost a week, you obviously killed my boyfriend, makes perfect sense."

"No, I didn't, please, that's how I found him. He was already dead."

"You expect me to believe that?"

"You do. You said you did!"

"No, I said, 'You're in trouble', and it looks like you are."

"That's not true. We're leaving here together."

"One of us is leaving soon, very soon probably."

Kathy mockingly shook her phone in front of him.

Ronan let out a shaky moan. "What are you saying?"

Kathy put her hand over the speaker on her phone and made a huge effort to whisper slowly. "We can't have anybody else listening in on us."

He rubbed his eyes with the heels of his hands. "What's happening, Kathy? Please tell me!"

"Well, like I told you before, I had to change my boring old name from Kathy to Molly Holiday, and I'm a successful travel blogger. I've been all around the world on my adventures with thousands of lovely followers and loads of sponsors. However, some of my sponsors are a little bit sneaky about how they get their funds. Dean knew this and threatened to expose me using blackmail unless I would let him in on my travel business, as a partner sharing everything, not just the guy behind the camera. I said no."

"Why would you?"

Kathy got slightly agitated.

"Because I'm the one people want to see, not him. Nobody cares about Dean; he's nobody. They want to see me; they want Molly Holiday and nothing else."

Ronan backed away. "What did you do?"

"Actually, nothing. Well, he came over to my flat to have it out with me, we had words which were very heated, he went for me, trying to grab my hand and he tripped and fell, hitting his head on the corner of the kitchen table. He wasn't moving, and I didn't know what to do, so I went outside to think, and that's when you grabbed me."

Ronan put his hands to his head. "That's not right, that's not right."

"I'm afraid so, and your prints are all over Dean's body."

"No, it wasn't me. You did this, you pushed him over."

"Not really, we had a disagreement and he fell down, but my fingerprints aren't on him at all."

Ronan was desperate to get away from the conversation and turned his head away from Kathy as she continued.

"I was jogging. It's pretty cold out there, and I had my gloves on all the time, so even when Dean went for me, he grabbed my gloves."

Kathy waved her bare hands at Ronan.

"No gloves. I was wearing them when you grabbed me, but after a few toilet breaks and woman stuff, I dumped them days ago, and you emptied the bin for refuse collection, so the gloves are gone."

Kathy took delight in waving her hand.

"You didn't even notice my gloves were missing, did you? You've got nothing on me. Whatever evidence you may have had has been thrown out with the rubbish."

Ronan tried hard to keep his face from twitching. "Why would you do this? I thought you wanted to be with me?"

Kathy put her hand to her mouth, trying hard to stifle a laugh. She took her other hand off the phone speaker. "You kidnapped me. I would say anything to stop you from killing me."

"You know that's not true."

"Really? Is that right Ronan Birchwood? That is your name, right? Here's a little hint, when you let your captive use the bathroom, don't put your bill letters in the bin, so I don't know this address. It could be this one, meaning you have your post sent here or you still live here, and that means you've never left home, which makes you even sadder."

"Please, Kathy, stop this."

"Is that your mouth wobbling? Is that a tremble, I see? Are you going to start crying? I think you are."

He shoved nervous fingers through his hair. "You have to stop doing this."

"Why? Because you asked me to? You really are quite sad. You really are deluded."

Ronan sniffed in heavily and snorted out with disdain. "Please don't be a bitch."

"Bitch? Now it comes out. Is this the true guy behind the messages? Now the real Ronan is with us, you really thought I could be with someone like you? I'm the most popular travel blogger in England. I've seen so many beautiful sights around the world, I love travelling to the most wonderful locations and meeting up with the most fantastic people on this globe, but I should stop doing that to set up home with a guy who in all honesty, probably never left? Dean had his faults, a lot of them in all honesty, but he wasn't a kidnapper; he was a man, an exciting man."

"Don't say that, please?"

"Please? Pathetic, just pathetic, you take me hostage, and now you're the one whose begging?"

He stopped talking; Kathy wasn't in the mood to listen.

"I would rather eat a sandwich filled with shit than go out with you, a 'shit' sandwich."

Ronan was really finding it hard to stay calm as Kathy began to move around freely, enjoying every movement thoroughly.

"Actually, if I'm honest, people need shit, it helps plants grow, which we need as a species to survive, but nobody really needs you, Ronan. You are lesser than shit."

Ronan stayed quiet, his tongue slowly checked the crack on his top lip, waiting to speak again.

"You are quite bland, Ronan. Talking about sandwiches, you are like a bland sandwich, absolutely nothing happening in your life whatsoever."

Kathy took a confident step forward.

"You're a blandwich."

Ronan shook his head as if trying to clear it.

"One last thing," she said. "Did you really think I'd be calling a cab to run away with the man who's been holding me captive for a week? I called the police, dipshit, well I sent them a message on the phone, you can text 999 if you can't speak, now, did you not know that? I gave them all the details of what you did and this address. I hope to Christ that you never left home as that's the address I've given them."

Kathy's broad smile seemed grim to Ronan.

"The one person I really feel sorry for is your mum, dementia is a cruel illness, and I wouldn't wish that on anybody. I think that some memories do come back, and recognition does kick in sometimes."

Her smile grew.

"Imagine if she can't remember anything in her life. You spend hours with her talking about being her loving son, the times you spent together, bonding and loving one another and then as soon as you leave, her memories of you come flooding back. Every time you leave, she remembers you, a flicker of who you are makes a slight imprint on her brain; every time you walk out of the door, her mind recalls you and she says…"

Kathy's eyes were filled with delight.

"He's gone. Thank Christ for that."

Ronan didn't speak. There was a loud banging on the front door; the police had arrived and were making their presence known. They both jumped. Ronan recovered first, there was no panic in his voice, and he shrugged his shoulders and nodded.

"Yeah, you are right, you've been right from day one. You were right about me being a nobody, you were right about me being a failure, no friends, no family apart from a mum who doesn't know who I am. I just wanted to be with you, I loved you, Kathy, but that's something people like you won't ever understand."

He ignored the police outside. "You were also spot on about another thing. Yes, I never left home, I never left this house, and neither will you."

Before she could react, Ronan pushed her back on the bed, she tried to get up, but he was on top of her quickly. His hands fit neatly around her throat and began to close. Kathy kicked out wildly, but Ronan held her down. He was choking the life out of her, and there was nothing she could do. She struggled hard, but Ronan's weight was too much for her.

Somehow with a final fight, she swung a hand to Ronan's head, striking him on the temple. His grip released, and Kathy managed to let out a tremendous scream. It was louder than any she had tried in all her time being kept captive. Ronan recovered quickly and continued to squeeze Kathy's throat. The police burst through the front door and then into the bedroom. They hauled Ronan off from Kathy; she had stopped kicking and wasn't moving.

Ronan tried to thrash his arms wildly but was handcuffed as he was escorted out of the property. He implored his innocence about Dean, shouting at every police officer around him. Screaming didn't help him at all, and nobody was listening.

Ronan saw Kathy being carried out on a stretcher. He couldn't tell if she was alive or dead as she was placed into a waiting ambulance. His mum's cat ran out of the house and onto the street. Ignoring him completely after everything he had done for it throughout the years.

The commotion had brought neighbours to the windows again. The fake film cameras were still placed strategically around the front of the house. One couple looked on in awe as the ambulance carried Kathy away. Ronan was still protesting his innocence as he was led away to the waiting police car.

A watching husband turned to his wife behind the twitching next-door curtain. "The acting looks very good."

His wife was completely focused on the police cars and ambulance, holding the curtain aloft and unashamedly watching. "I know. We have to remember this film when it comes out."

The End

Ingram Content Group UK Ltd.
Milton Keynes UK
UKHW011804040723
424524UK00004B/100